"HAVE YOU BEEN KISSED?"

His question seemed to startle her. "I don't know how you mean."

"Tonight. Have you been kissed?" he ground out.

"Henry would never take such liberties. He is a gentleman," she said, lifting her head imperiously.

The relief he felt was staggering, and extremely disconcerting. "I'm very glad to hear it," he said.

With one quick motion, he pulled her to him, giving her perhaps two seconds to scream her protest before pressing his lips against hers.

BOOK YOUR PLACE ON OUR WEBSITE AND MAKE THE READING CONNECTION!

We've created a customized website just for our very special readers, where you can get the inside scoop on everything that's going on with Zebra, Pinnacle and Kensington books.

When you come online, you'll have the exciting opportunity to:

- View covers of upcoming books
- Read sample chapters
- Learn about our future publishing schedule (listed by publication month *and author*)
- Find out when your favorite authors will be visiting a city near you
- Search for and order backlist books from our online catalog
- Check out author bios and background information
- Send e-mail to your favorite authors
- Meet the Kensington staff online
- Join us in weekly chats with authors, readers and other guests
- Get writing guidelines
- AND MUCH MORE!

Visit our website at http://www.kensingtonbooks.com

MARRY CHRISTMAS

JANE GOODGER

ZEBRA BOOKS
Kensington Publishing Corp.
www.kensingtonbooks.com

ZEBRA BOOKS are published by

Kensington Publishing Corp.
850 Third Avenue
New York, NY 10022

All Kensington titles, imprints, and distributed lines are available at special quantity discounts for bulk purchases for sales promotion, premiums, fund-raising, educational, or institutional use.

Special book excerpts or customized printings can also be created to fit specific needs. For details, write or phone the office of the Kensington Special Sales Manager: Attn. Special Sales Department. Kensington Publishing Corp., 850 Third Avenue, New York, NY 10022. Phone: 1-800-221-2647.

Zebra and the Z logo Reg. U.S. Pat. & TM Off.

ISBN-13: 978-1-4201-0378-6
ISBN-10: 1-4201-0378-4

First Printing: October 2008
10 9 8 7 6 5 4 3 2 1

Printed in the United States of America

Chapter 1

Newport, Rhode Island, 1892

"I was thinking of a Christmas wedding," her mother said, as casually as if she were ordering consommé for luncheon from cook.

Elizabeth suppressed a gasp. Her mother detested any show of defiance, but she simply could not allow this. "I haven't even met him, Mother." Remarkable how calm she could be when she wanted to scream.

Alva Cummings pursed her lips and placed her correspondence to the side, a sign of her extreme displeasure. Each morning, Elizabeth had to suffer an audience with her mother, a tedious and cutting recounting of her performance the previous day. And today, it seemed, they were again talking about Elizabeth's marriage to the ninth Duke of Bellingham. "As you know, whether you have met His Grace or not is of little consequence. Instead of arguing with me, you should be thanking me. You will be a duchess. Think of it. A *duchess*."

But all Elizabeth could think of was Henry, the only

man she would ever love. Something in her face must have betrayed her thoughts, for her mother turned her full attention to her nineteen-year-old daughter.

"Sit up straight, Elizabeth. Must you always slouch?"

Elizabeth pulled her body impossibly tighter.

"As a duchess you will be looked upon by everyone as setting the standard for behavior. Despite your average looks," she said cruelly, "the duke has agreed to visit us in Newport where I expect he will propose. And you will agree. I cannot fathom your complete selfishness in this regard. You know your father would benefit immensely and yet you continue to resist this and all other attempts we have made to raise your position in society."

Elizabeth stared at her mother. "*My* position?" she asked, so angry she told herself she didn't care if she raised her mother's ire. But of course she did, and when her mother's eyes hardened to crystal, her entire body was shot with fear.

"You ungrateful little girl. Yes. *Your* position. This match is coveted by every mother—and daughter—here and in England. It is what we have worked on, hoped for, prayed for. And you can sit there and whine to me because your childish heart has been foolishly given to a fortune hunter. It's disgusting and beneath you, Elizabeth."

"He is a good man," she said softly.

"He is a scoundrel. He has had numerous affairs with several married women and it is common knowledge that he has been on the hunt for an heiress for years. And there is rumor of madness in the family. A second cousin or such. And I won't have any mad grandchildren."

Elizabeth shut her mother out, knowing it was all lies.

The best thing for her to do now was pretend to be an obedient daughter, even though her heart sang with a rebellion so strong she could hardly contain it. "I don't wish to talk about this any longer," Elizabeth said.

"Nor do I. Then it is settled." Her mother glared at her as if she could somehow see the secrets in her heart.

"It is," Elizabeth said, knowing she was not lying. For in her heart, her life *was* settled, though it wasn't the life her mother was envisioning. Henry was the only man she would marry, and if the Duke of Bellingham came to Newport and asked to marry her she would simply decline. For now, though, it would be better to appease her mother, to keep her secret safe in her heart. She would marry Henry, for he had asked and she had agreed.

They had been bike riding in New York on Riverside Drive with her two best friends and their mothers, as well as Henry and two other young men. Already her mother had suspected Henry's interest in her and tried to discourage it, but it was far too late. Two weeks before, Elizabeth and Henry rode ahead, hearts racing, faces alight with mischievousness as they left the others behind, ignoring her mother's shrill voice urging them to slow down.

They'd stopped, out of breath and laughing. "Marry me, Elizabeth. We'll elope before your mother can protest. Don't say a word to anyone. We'll manage it somehow. Say yes, my love."

Elizabeth wanted to throw her arms around Henry and dance about with him, but her mother was coming near, her face red with the exertion of trying to catch up with the two. They spoke in hurried whispers, for the

Cummings were leaving for Newport the very next day. "Yes. Yes, I will. Oh, Henry, I'm so happy."

"Nothing could keep me away from you. I'll follow you to Newport in one week," he'd said, his handsome face shining with happiness. He'd cut such a dashing figure that day with his Panama hat and white suit. Elizabeth didn't know a woman, other than her mother, whose heart didn't pick up a beat at the mere sight of him.

When her mother arrived, they tried to stop smiling, but they were both so happy, Elizabeth knew her mother suspected something, if not the whole truth. And that likely explained the painful meeting she'd just had with her.

They'd been in Newport two weeks now. Elizabeth hated it here, had been a virtual prisoner with her mother as the uncompromising warden. She'd not been allowed to accept a single invitation to a ball or picnic, and instead sweltered in her room that didn't even have a view of the Atlantic Ocean. Her windows were so high, they let in light but little else. But despite everything, once she was away from her mother and back in her room, she could smile again, she could think of Henry, remember how he looked, how she could tell he'd wanted to kiss her when they'd made their plans. Everything would be fine. Once the wedding was done, her mother would have to forgive her. And if she didn't that would be fine, too.

Elizabeth wrapped her arms around herself and walked to a small table where she kept her portable rosewood writing desk, and wondered if she could dare write a letter to Henry. The footmen had been instructed not to allow her to leave the house, not even to walk around the beautiful grounds that swept down to the sea.

"Where are you?" she whispered, writing Henry's name over and over before crumpling the paper up. It wouldn't do for a maid to find the revealing paper, then show it to her mother. Henry had said he'd come to visit her. He'd said he'd write. Two weeks had passed since their engagement and she hadn't heard a thing.

A quiet knock she recognized as her governess drew her away from her tortured thoughts. One look at Susan's face and Elizabeth knew immediately that something was horribly wrong. Susan's eyes were red-rimmed and her nose bright red from crying.

"Your mother has dismissed me," Susan said, taking a lace-edged handkerchief and angrily dashing away a tear.

"But why?" Elizabeth asked, feeling the shock of those words pierce her.

"She told me I wasn't needed anymore. That you'd be a married woman soon without need of a governess."

It was probably true that Elizabeth, at nineteen, was far too old for a governess, but Susan was more than that and always had been. Susan was one of her dearest friends, the person she trusted most in the world. She was the only one who knew Elizabeth was engaged, who knew she was deeply and forever in love with Henry. Not even her closest friend, Maggie, knew that.

"I'll tell you something your mother swore me not to tell, but it doesn't make any difference now. Not one bit of difference," Susan said bitterly. "Your young man has been to the house every day for a week and your mother has Swanson send him away."

"He has?" Her deep relief that Henry had not forgotten her was immediately followed by the anguish of knowing he'd been sent callously away. And no one had bothered to tell her. The servants' loyalty to Alva was absolute, for they'd seen too many instances of employees sent to the streets for infractions far smaller than flouting her direct orders. Her maid, the footmen who guarded the doors, even Susan may have given her sad looks, but no one had dared countermand her mother.

"And he's written, too. A stack of letters. All burned. I just don't understand your mother, how she can be so cruel. And now I'm sacked. Just like that." She looked nervously at the door as if Alva would materialize. "She doesn't know I'm up here with you, if she did . . . I have to go, my dear."

"No," Elizabeth said, panic hitting her hard. She could not lose Susan, not now, not when she needed her more than ever. "I'll talk to my mother. I'll tell her she can't fire you. This is impossible."

"I have to go," Susan said, clearly distressed. "You don't know what she's capable of. Don't cross her, Elizabeth."

Elizabeth felt the blood drain from her face and was suddenly afraid she might actually faint. "What are you saying?"

"You cannot marry Henry. She'll do something awful. You didn't hear what she said to me, how much she's against your marrying anyone but that duke."

Elizabeth shook her head. "But he hasn't asked yet."

"He will," Susan said woodenly. "I have to go. I don't want to. You know that."

Elizabeth threw herself against the older woman,

clutching her as if she were her only hope. "Please, Susan," she said. "I'll talk to Mother."

Susan pulled away. "I'll be praying for you." She headed for the door and Elizabeth suppressed a chill that ran down her spine. She'd never known Susan to pray for anything and wondered precisely what she was trying to protect her from.

"Where will you go? How can I reach you?"

"I'll write," she said, but her expression told Elizabeth she was probably unlikely to receive the missive.

"Mark it from my father," Elizabeth said. "She'd never think to cross him."

Susan gave her a small smile, then disappeared through the door.

Elizabeth paced frantically in her room, wondering if she could sneak out of the house during the night to meet with Henry. She didn't know where he was, with whom he was staying, or if he was staying at a hotel. Certainly she couldn't wander about the streets of Newport in the dark calling his name. It was hopeless. Her body throbbed with impotent anger. She had to stop her mother from this madness. She must.

Elizabeth stormed out her door, ready to finally confront her mother. Alva Cummings was still in her drawing room, diligently working on her correspondence, no doubt giving her regrets for dozens of invitations for her daughter. The thought that her mother had most probably read the letters to her from Henry further incensed her.

"Mother, you cannot fire Susan. I will not tolerate it," she said, proud at how forceful she sounded. Her mother didn't even glance up, made not a single motion that she was even aware her daughter was in the room. Elizabeth refused to repeat herself for she knew her mother heard her. The longer she stood facing the silent woman, the more her power drained away, until desperation began seeping past her newfound strength.

"Susan is my friend," she said. "You cannot dismiss her from my life so easily. You cannot."

Alva continued scribbling away, but her face was slightly ruddy, which Elizabeth took as a sign of her anger. Good. She didn't care if she exploded from anger.

"And I'm not marrying the duke. I cannot because I am already promised to another. Henry and I plan to wed—"

"You will not," her mother shouted, standing so abruptly, Elizabeth let out a startled cry. "How dare you make such an agreement without my consent. Or your father's. You have no right."

"We love each other."

Alva's face nearly turned purple. "Have you any idea the sacrifice your father and I have made in order to arrange your marriage to the duke. Do you? Love," she spat. "Marriage has nothing to do with love. And if you think, my dear, that Henry Ellsworth loves anything more than your money, you are very sadly mistaken. I would never allow you to put this family in such a humiliating position. It will not be tolerated. I would have him murdered before I allowed such a man to ruin my daughter's life."

"Mother, I—"

"Get out of my sight. You disgust me," Alva said. Her face was ruddy, but the skin around her lips was stark white. "Get out!"

Elizabeth hurried away from her mother, down a long hall, and to her room where she threw herself onto her bed. Behind her, the door closed, the obvious result of the efficient footman. Two hours later, when she tried to go down for dinner, she was told by the same man that she was not allowed to leave her room and that her meal would be sent up shortly.

Elizabeth whirled around, her eyes frantically going to the high windows that were completely inaccessible. It was almost as if Alva had foreseen the future when she so thoughtfully designed her daughter's oppressive bedroom. It had become her prison.

The next few days were a nightmare for her. Her meals were brought in by servants who dared not say a word to her. The house seemed abnormally quiet, as if someone had died. Indeed, Elizabeth felt as if she were dying inside. How could she go on when her entire life was over? She longed to see Henry, to explain what was happening, to let him know that she loved him still.

On the third day of her isolation, the door opened and her mother's dearest friend, Mrs. William-Smythe walked in. Elizabeth was a mess. She hadn't changed from her nightgown or bothered to brush her auburn hair, even though it was long past noon. What did it matter what happened now? When she saw Mrs. William-Smythe, she felt a glimmer of hope, for she was always such a warm and reasonable woman.

"Elizabeth," she said, her gray eyes taking in her dishabille with slight distaste. "Do you know what you have done to your mother with your callous indifference to her feelings? She has suffered a heart attack, brought on by your ridiculous rebellion. Have you a notion what it means when a daughter literally breaks her mother's heart?"

Despite her anger at her mother, Elizabeth was shocked to hear Alva was ill. She might be angry with her, but despite everything, she loved her and certainly didn't wish her dead. "Is she going to be well?"

"The doctor said it was only a mild attack. This time," the older woman said pointedly. "But if you persist on going against her, she could have another attack, this one fatal. I'm certain you do not want your mother's death on your conscience."

Elizabeth sat down on her bed, her legs no longer able to hold her up. Her life was being sucked from her, her hope drained away by this woman's words. "Of course I don't," she said, looking down at the rich Aubusson carpet at her feet. Then she looked up, her expression tormented. "But is my happiness of so little importance? Should I not have a say in which man I marry?"

"You are far too young to make such an important decision," she said, sounding so much like her mother Elizabeth wondered if Alva had written a script. "If you persist on going against your mother and marrying this man, I have no doubt your mother will be forced into some drastic measure to prevent it. Do you understand what I am saying to you?"

"Yes," Elizabeth said dully, remembering her mother's threat to have Henry murdered. As crazy as it seemed, she was not entirely certain her mother would not have him murdered, so great was her obsession to have her marry a great English title. Mrs. William-Smythe's image blurred in front of her as her eyes filled with tears.

"Then you will agree to marry the duke?"

She blinked the tears away so that she could see the woman clearly when she made her answer.

"Yes. I will marry the duke."

Mrs. William-Smythe smiled as if all were finally right with the world. "I'm so glad you've come to your senses, my dear. I shall go tell your mother the good news. Imagine. A Christmas wedding. She'll be so happy," she gushed.

She left the room, left the girl weeping silently on her bed, and took away any hope Elizabeth had of ever being in love.

Chapter 2

England, Four Months Earlier

Randall Blackmore, ninth Duke of Bellingham, stared in disbelief at the letter before him, a letter that instantly solved his problems. One million pounds, an impossible amount of money, would be at his disposal if only he agreed to travel to America and marry a girl he'd never laid eyes on.

It was so damned tempting. As well as humiliating and insane. But after meeting last week for the third time with the family solicitors it just might be the only thing between salvation and complete ruin. He wanted to ball up the letter and toss it in the fire grate. He wanted to, but he knew he wouldn't. He let out a curse which encouraged a chuckle from Lord Hollings, Earl of Wellesley, his most trusted friend.

"You've been handed a miracle, old boy, and all you can do is take the Lord's name in vain," he said, tsking mockingly. Edward poured his friend a generous splash of fine French brandy. "You can afford this now, Rand," he said, laughing. Edward Hollings had been with Bellingham in the Life Guards, where they'd both enjoyed being part of the most elite military regiment in England. That is until Hollings's uncle had died and he was forced to take on his duties as heir, but that was as far as his commiseration went. His family estate, Meremont, was not nearly as encumbered as Bellewood. Hollings was able to sustain his home and live a life, if not of luxury, then of leisure. Such a life was out of the question for Bellingham. Until now.

"What the hell is wrong with the chit if her parents are in such a hurry to rid themselves of her? I hear she was brought around the continent and dangled out in front of several cash-hungry members of the peerage. No one took the bait, of course," Rand said, his eyes still glued to the words: "one million pounds."

Hollings shrugged. "You met the mother. Did she hint at some strange disease? Or perhaps she's fatally ugly."

Rand gave his friend a withering look. "I'm so glad you are having such a grand time with my misery."

"What did her mother look like, then?"

Rand frowned. He had met her at the opening of an art exhibit in London perhaps one year ago, and noted at the time how grateful he was that her daughter had not been with her and how very disappointed she'd been that he would not get to meet the girl. Ever since inheriting the title, Rand had been beset with mamas, all of whom apparently did not care that he was practically a pauper. He should have known a pauper with a title was still a grand catch.

If he remembered correctly, Alva Cummings was

hardly a pretty woman. At best, one could call her handsome if one was extremely generous. "She must be ugly, then. Hideously so, for this price."

"One million pounds can go a long way to making her beautiful."

The idea of marrying for money was extremely distasteful. Still, he didn't know what he was going to do. Bellewood was in shambles. His tenants, already driven to poverty because of the agricultural depression, were suffering needlessly. Cottages were in disrepair, farming equipment was completely outdated, young men were leaving for London, for America, all because the two former Dukes of Bellingham had dipped so deeply in the well of prosperity, it was now bone-dry. As much as Rand had admired his father and loved his brother, he could not fathom why they had allowed the situation to become as dire as it was. He truly had no other choice but to marry an heiress.

"Don't look so glum, old boy. Get your heir and leave her be. With that money you can buy a little cottage somewhere for her, say in Scotland, and get on with your life."

"One million pounds," Rand said, feeling desperation pull at him. "It would mean everything."

"It's just marriage," Hollings said blandly. "Go see her. You can always change your mind."

Rand looked at his old friend and gave him a grim smile. "I can hardly afford passage." He closed his eyes and let out a long breath. "I really could throttle my father and brother. And would, too, if they weren't six feet under." His words were blasé but the pain inside was anything but. His father and brother had shared a bond that he could never breech. It was as if they were part of a whole and he was simply an extra bit that fell off and was not needed at all. His brother had taken pains to spend time with him when he was very young, and a boy could not have asked for a better big brother. Then, Rand had been shipped off to school when he was nine years old and from then on he never felt a part of anything at Bellewood. All he had were wonderful memories and a sometimes aching desire to go home. Now they were both gone, so he could only speculate why they had behaved the way they had, tossing away a vast fortune on nothing.

Hollings took a long sip of his brandy. "If it makes you feel any better, I don't know a single peer who hasn't had to start looking for money. Some in unusual places. Lord Dumfrey is director of twelve companies. Doesn't do a thing but collect the cash and lend out his good name. And don't even think that you're the only peer who has married an American for her money. Done all the time these days."

Rand tried to take heart in Hollings's speech, but he couldn't help wishing there was another way. If it was just a matter of raising the money to repair Bellewood, he could do that. He wasn't opposed to working for a living; it was becoming common among the more desperate of the peerage. But he could never pay the enormous amount of debt left behind by his brother. Not without a substantial bit of help. He refused to sell Bellewood; he'd only get a fraction of what it was worth. Besides, Bellewood had been in his family for generations and he'd be damned if he'd be the duke to lose it.

God, how he wished he were back in London with his regiment, happily unaware that his brother, the eighth duke, was dying of consumption. By the time he found out, his poor brother was near death and Rand was looking at a future far more grim than the one he'd expected. But not as grim as his brother's, and for that he was somewhat grateful.

He didn't want to be duke. He didn't want to marry some American. He didn't want to produce an heir and a spare. Not yet. Hell, he was only twenty-seven years old. He'd thought he had at least another decade of work in the military before settling down to a calm country life with a pretty English girl. English, being the key word. He would happily have been Lord Blackmore for the rest of his life. Now he would be something else entirely. Good God.

He'd had to sell out his commission with the Life Guards and return home to take up his new duties, only to find out that his first duty as duke would be to find a way to save his beloved Bellewood, one of the grandest estates in England. At least it used to be. Now, thanks to poor investments and outrageous expenses, Bellewood was a shell of what it had been. When he'd been called home to his brother's deathbed, he'd been shocked by what had happened to the great house. The library, filled with nearly forty thousand volumes dating back to the fifteenth century, had been decimated. Paintings, furniture, tapestries, all sold to pay for enormous debt. Indeed, Bellewood resembled a large and quite empty museum. The staff had been nearly all dismissed, which left the house to fall into disrepair, not to mention that vast amounts of dust floated everywhere.

Worst was the stables, the pride of his grandfather, whose love of horses surpassed all else. Bellewood was famous in the British Isles for producing some of the best racers in the world. The stables, the pride of the Blackmores, were an empty shell, the horses long ago sold off to pay for debts or God knew what else. His childhood memories of Bellewood were centered around the stables, hanging about the tolerant stable master and the intolerant grooms. Rand had been happiest in those stables, watching foals being birthed, hefting hay, oiling the tackle. He hadn't realized he shouldn't be in the stables at all, never mind working there. Walking into those stables, hearing nothing but the wind hissing through a hole in the roof, had been heartbreaking.

The grounds were overgrown, the beautiful gardens his mother had taken so much pride in, nearly obliterated by neglect. Strangely, it was the loss of his mother's garden that affected him the most. It might have been his fond memories of his mother doting over her roses, the warm afternoons when he, as a young boy, would escape his tutor and find her there. His mother had been a strict disciplinarian in most things, but she never could bring herself to give him up when he found his way to her. Looking back, he supposed she justified allowing him to stay by giving him a lesson in horticulture. He would pretend interest when all he really wanted was to be near her.

Rand hadn't yet told his mother that to save Bellewood

he would likely have to marry an American heiress. The Dowager Duchess was such a stickler about everything, except little boys who wandered into gardens. She had envisioned for him the daughter of an earl or duke from a family she knew and respected. No doubt, she'd had a list for his brother, one, to her great frustration, Tyler had chosen to ignore. Rand never knew why his brother had not married. Perhaps it was the knowledge that he would die before he was ready. It wasn't as if the dukedom would be lost or go to some unsavory cousin, for he had a younger brother. Rand had never talked about marriage with Tyler. They'd talked of women in general, the need of them, and horses, the joy of them. Now that he was dead, Rand would never know how Tyler had felt about leaving nothing behind, no legacy but unending debt, no children to remember him. Nothing but a brother, who didn't want to be a duke, and a mother who'd been crushed by his death.

His mother was blissfully and almost tragically unaware of his financial difficulties. Shortly after his brother's death she lamented how she wouldn't be able to hold her annual ball. "I talked with your brother about it before he grew so ill and we'd agreed that this year we'd spare no expense. I'm so sick of watching every penny we spend. Of course, now that he's gone . . ." Her voice had trailed off, overwhelmed with the realization that never again would she plan even the smallest event with her oldest son.

Rand had felt his body go completely numb, for he'd just learned from his solicitor that the only way to pay off the astronomical debts accumulated by his father and brother was to sell every bit of property they owned, including the dowager house where his mother had happily lived since his father died three years before.

He found he could not do it. He could not sell his mother's home from beneath her and put her in something far less grand. His mother was a duchess from the diamond-encrusted tiara on her head to the silk stockings on her legs. Those diamonds had long been replaced with paste, to pay for a new breeding mare his brother had to have, but his mother's eyesight was so poor, thankfully she could not tell the difference.

Already the family's London town house and three country estates had been sold to pay for too many years of extravagance and ignorance. It had been a shock, but perhaps it should not have been. If he had spent more time at home, more time paying attention to what was happening around him, he would not have been so blindsided.

And now he would have to pay for two generations of neglect by marrying an heiress, and an American heiress at that.

Chapter 3

August 1892, Newport, Rhode Island

Elizabeth stared in the mirror and tried out a smile. It had been so long since she'd used those particular muscles, smiling felt foreign to her. Her eyes were no longer red-rimmed and swollen, but her face was unusually pale, her eyes missing something. Life, perhaps. Still, she did finally have something to smile at. Her long, tedious imprisonment was about to end. The Duke of Bellingham was set to arrive today to meet the woman who would most likely be his wife.

Elizabeth still could not believe what was happening to her. All her life she'd not been allowed to make even the simplest decision, being reminded again and again that she was incapable of such a task. Now, though, she would be married, in charge of a vast house in England, directing servants, taking care of tenants, planning parties and balls and so many other things she couldn't even fathom. This she was expected to do when even now her mother wouldn't let her pick out the gown she would wear for tonight's dinner with the Duke.

"Ruled with an iron fist, that one is," she'd once overheard a maid say to another. The servants pitied her, even the lowest scullery maid would look at her with sorrow clear in her eyes. As many times as she'd been humiliated by her mother, this by far eclipsed them all.

"You look lovely," Alva said from behind her. "I knew that blue would suit you."

Indeed, the blue of her gown matched the color of her eyes. It might seem a wonderful coincidence unless one was present when her mother was picking out the fabric in France a year ago. It had taken nearly an hour, and Elizabeth had sat there, back straight, hands folded on her lap, as the poor girl held swatch after swatch against her cheek.

"Thank you."

"Your hair," Alva said, narrowing her eyes. "I wonder if that's the best we can do."

Her maid had spent nearly an hour on the intricate style, threading delicate strands of impossibly tiny pearls through it. By the end, her hands had been shaking with the effort and Elizabeth had to tell her to stop, that her hair was beautiful and could not possibly be improved.

"I suppose, given the horrible brown you were born with, it will have to do," Alva said, and Elizabeth wondered if her mother was even aware that Alva's hair, before it had become salted with gray, was exactly the same color as her own. Still, she sent up a silent prayer of thanks that her hair had passed inspection.

"The duke will arrive within the hour. I think we

should be in the Rose Salon," she said, as if she hadn't choreographed the entire evening a dozen times in her head. "You should sit in the cream chair. When His Grace enters the room, stand and curtsy. Let me see it," she commanded.

Elizabeth stood gracefully and gave a small curtsy, looking up at her mother expectantly.

"Perhaps a bit deeper? Oh, I don't know of these English things. Curtsies and the like. Just be polite. And silent unless he or I address you. This is by no means final, and you could still ruin it by saying or doing something foolish."

"Yes, Mother."

"Try to be pleasant. And smile. You do have a pleasant smile at least."

Elizabeth forced a smile that she knew was not the least bit as pleasant as she was capable. Alva gave her daughter a sharp look before turning away. "I expect you in the Rose Salon in five minutes."

Five minutes. And then she would meet the man who would most likely be her husband. She would share her life, her house. Her bed. She closed her eyes in a hopeless attempt to stop the panic in her heart. She was so sick of thinking about the "if onlys" in her life. But she couldn't help but think about how different she would feel if it were Henry she were planning to marry on Christmas Eve instead of a man she didn't know, a man who lived in another country. She wondered if Henry knew the duke was in Newport, if he understood how desperately she longed for him.

It was foolish to think of such things, and completely useless. She could not marry Henry without putting his very life in danger and perhaps her mother's as well. She believed with every fiber in her being that her mother would follow through on her threat to hurt him, perhaps kill him. Her mother's health had made a quick recovery once Elizabeth finally agreed with this marriage, and she'd thrown herself into planning an impressive welcome for the duke. Henry had been put from Alva's mind, for she knew her daughter would never thwart her.

And to Elizabeth's great shame, she knew her mother was right.

"His Grace, the Duke of Bellingham."

Even now, when Rand heard that announcement and realized it pertained to him, he gave a small inward start. But hearing it in the flat accent of an American, it was almost surreal. In fact, this entire journey didn't seem quite real, so he was slightly relieved to find Sea Cliff had an English flair to it and would not have seemed out of place in the countryside back home. He'd found Americans either completely unimpressed by his title, or so in thrall it was disconcerting. Rand entered the so-called Rose Salon bracing himself for the worst. His eyes scanned the room, taking in Alva Cummings, who curtsied when his eyes rested on her, and Jason Cummings, the girl's father, who gave the briefest head-nod bows before coming over to shake his hand. Jason Cummings was a rotund man with thick wavy hair parted precisely in the center. His face was soft, and a fine sheen of sweat shone near his hairline making Rand wonder if the man was nervous about this meeting. He almost felt like laughing aloud, for if anyone should feel nervous and foolish, it was he.

"Welcome to Sea Cliff," Cummings said. "I'd like to show you my yacht if you've the time. Got her four weeks ago. She's sitting at anchor right now, but it's just a small row out to—"

"Jason. Introduce your daughter," Alva Cummings said sweetly. But there was nothing sweet about the expression on her face and Rand had a sudden understanding of why the man before him looked so harried.

Jason smiled tightly. "Of course, dear. Your Grace, my daughter, Elizabeth," he said, giving a little bow toward a bank of windows.

Thank God. That was the first thing that came to his mind when he first laid eyes on the daughter. She was pretty, remarkably so. Her features were small but for her eyes, which seemed far too large for her delicate face. She curtsied nicely and smiled, and again Rand was struck that her smile, like her mother's, didn't reach her eyes.

"Miss Elizabeth," he said, nodding toward her. She immediately darted a look to her mother, as if she was at a loss to know what to do or say. Apparently, the mother must have communicated something silently to the girl, for she curtsied again, and said, "Your Grace."

It was about as warm in the room as an icebox, and Rand was regretting his trip to America with all his being. Humiliation washed over him as he realized that everyone in this room knew why he was here, knew he'd come hat in hand begging for money. "You have a lovely home," he said, even though it was so cluttered with furniture and paintings and flowers he could hardly see the room itself. He was painfully reminded of Bellewood's cavernous emptiness thanks to his brother's attempts to raise money.

"Thank you, Your Grace, although Sea Cliff cannot compare to Bellewood, I'm sure. We heard such wonderful things about your home when we were in England. Didn't we, Elizabeth."

The girl looked startled to be included in the conversation. "Oh. Yes." She wore a blue dress that showed off an incredibly tiny waist, and he wondered at the brutality of her maid to have succeeded in cinching the poor girl so tightly.

"Thank you." He stood there, feeling awkward to be beneath their intense scrutiny. But he supposed it was only natural for them to examine the man who would be part of their family. Their very, very rich family, he reminded himself to make this scene more palatable.

"How was your passage over?" Cummings asked.

"Very pleasant, though not everyone fared as well as I did," Rand said, thinking of another passenger who'd been ill nearly the entire voyage.

"My Elizabeth is a poor sailor, aren't you?" Alva said, almost as if the girl had some control over whether or not she got ill.

Again, the girl gave a startled look, and Rand began to wonder if they'd ever before included her in a conversation. Almost by rote, she responded, "Yes, I am."

Rand couldn't see any strings attached to the girl, but it certainly seemed as if her mother was very apt at pulling them. When Alva nodded to her daughter she said, "Please sit down, Your Grace."

And so he did.

"Have you been to Paris?" Alva asked.

"Many times. It's a beautiful city."

"We bought Elizabeth's dress there."

He looked at her, as he supposed he was meant to, and said, "It's lovely."

The girl's lips tilted slightly into a smile, a forced movement and she didn't meet his eyes. "Thank you."

It struck Rand then that it was possible Elizabeth Cummings did not want to marry him any more than he wanted to marry her. Well, fancy that. All this time he'd been feeling rather put out by this arranged marriage—for he never doubted for a second that he would agree to such a match—and now he was finding out his future bride was rather put out, too. She looked, frankly, miserable.

"I wonder, Your Grace, if you could accompany us tomorrow morning to the Casino," Alva said. "It's quite lovely to see all the fine carriages on Bellevue Avenue. It will be a wonderful opportunity to introduce you to Newport Society."

It was the last thing he wanted to do, to be put on display and forced to be pleasant to a large crowd of gawking Americans. Good God. "It would be my pleasure, Madam," he said, lying very nicely. "For now, though, I wonder if your daughter could show me around your grounds if we have time before dinner." If he left everything up to the mother, he'd likely never get a chance to be alone with the girl until he was forced to propose.

From the corner of his eye, he saw the girl stiffen, and he knew he'd been correct about her. She didn't want to marry him and that made him curious. For didn't every girl dream of marrying a duke?

Chapter 4

Elizabeth wondered idly if she could run away from the duke, run to the sea, jump in and swim away. Perhaps become a mermaid. Perhaps become anything but the Duchess of Bellingham. Elizabeth had become extremely adept at finding something good about everything life handed her. Marrying the duke: bad. Saving Henry's life by marrying the duke: good. Meeting the duke for the first time four months before her planned wedding: bad. Finding he wasn't hideously ugly: good.

No. His grace was anything but ugly. Of course, he wasn't as fine looking as her Henry. Who was? The duke was far too rugged, too big, too . . . everything. Henry was refined, from his straight blond hair to his well-manicured nails. Henry was perfect. All this she'd already determined even though she could admit to herself she'd hardly even looked at the duke.

It was a warm day, the sky nearly cloudless, and the Atlantic Ocean that stretched before them in the distance was almost painfully blue. How perfect this day would have been if she'd been walking with anyone but the duke. Like, perhaps, Henry.

Her mother sat on the veranda, keeping a watchful eye over them. But her mother needn't worry about propriety; she was walking at least five feet apart from him, and still she could feel his looming presence.

Suddenly, the duke stopped walking and stared out to sea. "You don't want this marriage, do you?" he asked, stunning her so completely, Elizabeth let out a strangled sound. All she could think of was that her mother had somehow bribed him into challenging her.

"Of course I do," she said, staring at his hard profile and hoping he couldn't read her lie. Foolish thought.

"You're lying," he said finally, turning to her. "I suppose I could be made to believe you are merely shy, and not completely unhappy with this arrangement."

"I am not shy," Elizabeth said, confirming his suspicions without overtly agreeing with him. He was frowning, and she wondered if she'd just made a terrible mistake. He turned and continued walking along the well-tended lawn, heading for the sharply cut hedge that separated the estate from the rocky shore below.

"I don't particularly want to get married either," he said, surprising her yet again. He shrugged, and for a moment he almost looked boyishly sheepish. "I'm only twenty-seven. I hadn't thought I'd get married for another ten years or so."

"Then why . . ." The money. Oh, God, how could she have forgotten even for a moment about the money. "Oh."

"Yes. Oh." When he reached the hedge he stopped and turned toward her yet again. "These sorts of things go on all the time. In fact, more often than not in England. Still, I suppose it is not what you expected."

"No." Without warning, Elizabeth's throat closed up and she wished vehemently he would stop being so kind. She could feel his somber gray eyes studying her.

"I'm not such a bad sort."

She darted a look up to him, only to see him studying her far too closely. "I'm sure you are a very fine gentleman."

His mouth curved into a smile. "I do try to be." He let out a long breath. "This is how it can be between us. We can marry. I have to have an heir. And we'll get that over with and then we can go on with our lives."

She stared at him, shocked he could be so blunt about what their future would bring. Suddenly the entire idea of a loveless marriage, bearing children for a man she hardly knew, was nearly too much to abide.

Rand took in her stricken face and knew he'd made a mistake. She was only nineteen and no doubt had fantasies about love and romance and all that rot. He didn't want to be cruel, he simply wanted to be honest, to let her know this mockery of a marriage was not something he desired any more than she did. But he was prepared to make the best of the situation. "It's what is done," he said. "I thought that would give you comfort."

"What would give me comfort is for you to go back to England and never return," she said earnestly.

Without thinking, he let out a laugh and quickly tried to sober when he saw she was completely serious. "No, you are not shy, are you?" he asked.

"I told you I was not," she said, and he thought he detected the tiniest smile before she looked back to the house.

So upset was he by this marriage that was being forced upon him, he hadn't given a thought to how the bride would feel. Likely that was because he'd never imagined any girl wouldn't want to marry him. He was a duke, after all. And he knew from the attention women had given him even before he acquired the lofty title that he was somewhat attractive.

"Perhaps I should marry your mother, then. She would be thrilled, I think." He'd hoped to make her laugh aloud, but his jest produced only a smile. "Well, have heart that I haven't asked for your hand yet. You still have time to change my mind about the entire plan."

He'd thought those words would produce another smile, but instead her face took on an expression of such sadness he was taken aback.

"Please don't say such a thing."

She must fear her mother more than he'd thought, he realized. "I assure you, if I do beg off, I will make it completely clear to your mother that I am to blame."

"You speak entirely too lightly of the situation. As if it is a game and not our very lives. As if you do not realize the import of what they have planned for us. As if you do not care at all that we will be stuck together forever."

Despite his great efforts to put the girl at ease, she had the nerve to reprimand him. "I, more than you can know, am completely aware of what I am doing and why I am doing it," he said, feeling anger at his predicament surge through him. "You have no right to lecture me on the seriousness of marriage. If I speak lightly, it was only a failed attempt to put your mind at ease. In the future you can rest assured I will not speak lightly of this. But I will not apologize, ever, for making you my duchess, for allowing you to bear my children, for granting you the privilege of becoming chatelaine of one of the greatest estates in all of England."

During his angry tirade, Elizabeth's eyes widened, her mouth opened slightly as if in shock. "I see I've inadvertently hit a nerve," she said, sounding breathless and the tiniest bit frightened.

"I'm not certain how inadvertent it was," he shot back.

"I suppose you would like an apology," she said, and he couldn't believe how reluctant she sounded.

He was used to women fawning over him, to having them bat their eyes and smile slyly. He folded his arms in front of him and looked down at her, feeling more like a duke than he had in all the previous months combined. Perhaps his blue blood was thicker than he realized, because the idea of this American girl scolding him had rubbed him raw. "I would."

She raised her head, her pert nose high in the air. Then she tilted her head just slightly and narrowed her eyes. "No. I don't think so." And then she turned and began walking back to the house where her mother waited.

For the second time that day, the Duke of Bellingham let out a laugh.

"She doesn't want to marry me," Rand reported to the Earl of Wellesley when he'd returned to the cottage they were renting together for the duration of their visit. The twelve-room house was located just off Bellevue Avenue, one of the lesser homes among the ostentatious ones that lined the road. Edward had rather nicely volunteered to accompany Rand on his journey mostly because he was a bit overwhelmed at home, not yet grown used to being head of a household that included six children. Besides, Rand needed to borrow his valet and Edward wouldn't loan him out for the duration, so Edward and his valet were forced to accompany him. Rand had hinted that Edward might get lucky and nab his own little American heiress, though Edward was almost violently opposed to the idea. Why *would* Edward consider such a notion when there were plenty of pretty English girls? Had there been a single English heiress who could have gotten him out of his financial mess, Rand would have jumped at the chance. Though, he had to admit, they probably wouldn't have been as pretty as Miss Cummings.

Rand couldn't have been more grateful for Edward's company, for he didn't know a soul here and had never been overly comfortable walking into a room full of strangers. A duke and an earl; the mamas would be beside themselves with joy.

Edward sat in the home's rather extensive library examining the collection there. He picked one from a shelf and smiled. "Didn't think to find something this fine here," he said, holding up an ancient book. "*Quadrins historiques de la Bible*. Sixteenth Century here in Newport. Truly remarkable."

"Didn't you hear me?" Rand said, letting a small amount of exasperation come through.

"Yes. She doesn't want to marry you." Edward carefully opened the book. "Remarkable," he muttered again before finally giving his friend his full attention. "Really, Rand, what did you expect? For her to throw herself at your feet in gratitude?"

"Well, perhaps nothing so dramatic. But, yes, I

thought she'd be a bit more happy about marrying a duke. It's one of the privileges of rank, is it not, to have women throw themselves at you?"

"Did she run from you screaming?"

Rand gave his friend a withering look. "I thought I would be up front with her about why I am here. No doubt she knows, so I was not telling her anything she did not already comprehend. We agree on this: She does not want to marry me. I do not want to marry her. And yet we will be married." He shrugged. "I thought it best to confront the issue."

Edward shook his head in sad disbelief. "Have you learned nothing in your twenty-seven years about women?"

"I thought honesty would work well between us," Rand said, sounding defensive. "And I still do. I do realize I have to woo her a bit. It won't do to have her in chains at the altar."

"Or in your bed," Edward said with a grin.

Rand ignored his remark. "I'm not an ogre, after all. It's why I'm here, to get to know her a bit before we marry."

"Yes, I suppose it would be prudent to know your bride a bit before you pledge to love and honor her until death and all that. Is she plain, by the way?"

Rand sat in a nearby leather chair and lifted one ankle onto the other knee. "She wasn't completely . . . unpleasant," he said carefully. In truth, he found himself surprisingly attracted to her physically. He had not expected that at all.

Edward gave him a sharp look. "Not ugly, then?"

"Hardly. She's actually quite pretty. And rich. Which makes me believe her mother was holding out for the loftiest title possible and I was the only duke who took the bait."

"Then a mere earl wouldn't have a chance."

"Sorry, old man, I think not. Once I get the girl away from her mother, she might even be pleasant to talk with as well as to look at. Mrs. Cummings is a termagant. *Miss* Cummings becomes a different person entirely when she is in the presence of her mother."

"Oh?" Edward said, his eyes again drawn to the book he was holding.

"Boring you, am I?"

Edward smiled. "Of course not." He put the book back on the shelf, but it was clear the gesture was reluctant.

"Miss Cummings does not speak in front of her mother unless spoken to. She offers few opinions, and when she does, they are so carefully neutral they are not opinions at all. And yet the brief time I was alone with her, she displayed intelligence and independent thought. It was clear that dinner this evening was torture for the poor girl."

"Then it's just as well you'll be separated from her mother by an ocean."

"Indeed," Rand said thoughtfully. "I've been invited to something called the Casino tomorrow morning. Do you know what it is?"

"Tennis. They are mad about tennis, these people. And apparently society meets there in the mornings to gossip. Sounds tedious to me. But next week there's some sort of tennis tournament that sounds interesting."

"And you'll accompany me there tomorrow, of course. And everywhere."

Edward gave him a tight smile. "Of course."

Chapter 5

Rand stood at the entrance to the Newport Casino's Horse Shoe Piazza and thanked God he'd thought to invite Edward along with him. The lush grassy area, surrounded by the shingle-style building with its dark green trim, was crowded with Newport's elite. Summer whites and pastels were nearly blinding in the morning light, and when Rand stepped into the sun from the shadows, it seemed as if every body in the place turned his way.

"Brace yourself, old man, you are about to be thrust into the midst of the wolves," Edward whispered in his ear.

"You are an unattached earl. Perhaps you should watch out more than I. From what I've learned so far, few people thwart a Cummings and I have been marked with a bright red 'X.' But you, my friend, are fair game."

The two men took bracing breaths before proceeding, pleasant smiles plastered on their faces. "Save me," Edward whispered, causing Rand to laugh aloud.

"Your Grace," Mrs. Cummings gushed, hurrying to be the first to greet him. "Let me introduce you around."

"First I would like to introduce my good friend, Lord Hollings, Earl of Wellesley."

Mrs. Cummings gave a quick, awkward curtsy. "Lord Hollings," she said. "How nice of you to accompany His Grace."

For some reason, Rand got the feeling Mrs. Cummings was not at all pleased that Edward had come along, and he wondered if she wanted her daughter alone to be seen with English nobility.

During the next fifteen minutes, Rand met at least a hundred mamas who fawned over him but fairly beamed at poor Edward. As yet, he had not caught sight of his future bride among the throng of pastel-wearing young women. At some point, Edward managed to escape, the cad, and left him alone to face the adoring throngs. He was called everything from "Your Lordship" to "Your Dukeship" and didn't bother correcting a single person. Americans, after all, were completely ignorant of the peerage. A small orchestra played rather badly in one corner, though no one seemed to notice. Or perhaps they simply did not recognize the bad play for what it was.

Ah, there was Edward, standing by a table laden with pastries. He craned his neck over Mrs. Cummings, whose large and feathered hat blocked most of his view, and wished most ardently that he was with Edward alone in their cottage instead of in this crowded piazza.

"Is Elizabeth here?" he asked, when it appeared Mrs. Cummings had run out of people to introduce him to. The older woman smiled, revealing a mouthful of crooked teeth. He wondered suddenly, if Elizabeth didn't smile because she was so afflicted.

"I believe I just saw her standing in the corner with her cousins. There," she said, nodding her head in the opposite direction of the food. With an inward sigh, he begged to be excused, and headed to where Elizabeth stood looking completely miserable at his approach.

"You could at least pretend to be happy to see me," he said lightly when he reached her side. The two girls next to her giggled.

"My cousins, Miss Julia Cummings and her very much younger sister, Miss Sarah Cummings," Elizabeth said, frowning at the giggling girls.

Rand gave them a sharp bow, eliciting more giggles from the pair.

"Go find your mother," Elizabeth said, and the two girls rushed away. But not before Rand overheard one say to the other, "I thought she said he was horrid. He seemed quite nice to me."

Elizabeth had the good grace to turn violently red.

"Horrid?" he asked, raising one eyebrow.

"I don't believe that was the precise word I used," Elizabeth said with a small groan. "I do apologize. They are very young."

Rand looked longingly toward the table of food. "Would you care to accompany me to the pastries?" Rand wished he could capture the look on her face at that moment, for she looked so ridiculously pleased by his suggestion he wondered if, in addition to everything else, her mother starved her. At least she was smiling and showing a mouth of even, white teeth. She had a lovely smile that transformed her from a pretty girl into a beauty and he was nearly struck dumb by the change in her. "I see you are as famished as I."

Elizabeth gave him a startled look. "Oh. Yes," she said almost absently, for her heart was racing madly as she drank in the sight of Henry standing by the refreshment stand staring at her like, well, like a starving man looks at food. She couldn't believe her mother hadn't noticed his appearance yet, though she didn't know what Alva would do if she did. For now, he was here, Henry was here and looking at her and smiling the way he only smiled for her.

The duke held his arm for her and she placed a gloved hand as lightly as she could without ignoring it completely. He was taking far too long to reach the other side of the lawn where Henry stood in a small circle of people.

"I'd like to introduce you to my friend, the Earl of Wellesley. He's accompanied me here to keep me company. I have asked your mother to include him in any invitations I receive and she graciously has agreed," he said. Elizabeth was hardly listening as he went on about his friend and his estate and for goodness' sake how could she think of anything but her Henry who was standing just a few feet from her?

The duke had finally stopped talking and was looking down expectantly at her. "I'm sorry, it's so noisy here, what were you saying?" she asked. She should at least attempt to pretend interest in him.

He gave her a strange look, then smiled briefly. "My friend, Lord Hollings, the Earl of Wellesley," he said, obviously repeating himself. Elizabeth turned to find herself looking up into the face of a dashing fellow, with bright blond hair and the bluest eyes she'd ever seen. She quickly curtsied. "Pleased to meet you, Lord Hollings."

"I see Rand has dragged you to the pastries. He eats like a fiend and not an ounce of fat on him," Edward said.

Elizabeth forced herself to look at the two Englishmen, though she felt as if her head were being pulled by a magnet in Henry's direction. She could still see him from the corner of her eye and she longed to go over to him, just to let him know she loved him still. How awful it must be for him, she thought, to see her walking arm in arm with the man she was to marry. She dropped her hand then and dared to look his way, being careful to school her features before she did so.

Oh, Henry, Henry. He looked so wonderful, but so very sad. He took a hesitant step toward her and her heart nearly beat from her chest.

"A friend of yours?" said a deep voice by her ear. She started so quickly she nearly knocked heads with the duke.

"An acquaintance," she managed to say, chastising herself for allowing the duke to note her interest in another man.

"Your acquaintance is coming over," he said, then moved to face Henry as he approached.

Elizabeth darted her eyes around, frantically looking for her mother. Please, please don't let her mother see them chatting together as if all were right in the world. She realized that this might be the last time she would ever see Henry if Alva discovered them. No one had more social power than her mother and she would guarantee that Henry would not appear on anyone's guest list for the rest of the Newport season.

"Your Grace, Henry Ellsworth," Elizabeth said, proud that even through her frayed nerves she sounded calm.

"A pleasure to meet you, Your Grace," Henry said smoothly. He nodded to her as if, indeed, she was simply another woman he slightly knew. And then, he grasped her hand and squeezed without looking at her eyes, pressing something into her palm. Elizabeth's heart sang as she closed her hand over a folded piece of paper. No matter what it said, she would cherish it forever, for Henry had written it, had kept it with him on the chance he might pass it to her.

She nodded genteelly, then turned back to the two peers, who were politely waiting for her attention, knowing she had managed to fool them and anyone else who had been looking. Though her heart ached with a terrible combination of joy and pain, no one would know. No one would ever know, she thought, smiling up at the earl.

Rand clenched his jaw, his eyes glancing down at her still-fisted hand and he had the most curious urge to force her fingers open so he could read the missive. Now he knew why his lovely bride-to-be did not want to marry him. It was far worse than not wanting to marry a duke or not wanting to marry at all. She was in love with another man. For some reason, that thought bothered him far more than it ought. After all, hadn't he told her just the day before that their marriage was nothing more than a way for him to get money and an heir? Perhaps it was the thought of her trying to be brave in the light of such a tragedy. While he hadn't expected a wildly enthusiastic bride, he'd hoped for one who was not mourning a lost love.

Rand longed to pull her away so he could speak privately to her. Obviously this Henry fellow was considered part of the New York Four Hundred else he'd not be among this crowd. He wondered why, when the two so obviously loved each other, they had not been allowed to marry. He made a mental note to find out more about the man who moved so easily among those gathered in the piazza.

"Rand, did you know Miss Cummings speaks four languages?" Edward asked, apparently already smitten with his future wife. How she managed to be so charming to every man but him, he couldn't fathom.

"English, of course. French, German, and a bit of Italian."

"Very impressive, Miss Cummings," he said, meaning it. He'd had no idea she was so educated.

"My mother always stressed the value of education for women."

"Ah. So your mother is a student of Emmeline Parkhurst," Rand said, referring to England's most ardent suffragist.

"She's not so radical as your Mrs. Parkhurst, but she does admire her ideals," Elizabeth said.

"And what of you, Miss Cummings?"

"I do believe women deserve the same rights as men. It makes no sense to me that we cannot vote," Elizabeth said. "I'm not quite so enthusiastic as my mother. I am the product of her zeal, which meant for me long hours in the classroom learning tedious lessons while I longed to play outside," she said, smiling.

Rand had a picture in his head of a small girl with an unruly mop of hair sitting in a gloomy classroom being browbeaten by a tutor. "Like you, there were many times I wished to be anywhere but the classroom," he said.

"I think I'll wander to the tennis courts, if you don't mind. I play a bit myself and would like to see your American courts," Edward said, smoothly removing himself from their company.

"Would you care for some pastries?" Rand asked when Edward had left.

Elizabeth looked at the table rather longingly, then seemed to abruptly change her mind. How, indeed, could she hold a plate and eat while clutching an illicit note? Again, Rand had to remind himself he should not be jealous of a girl he wasn't even certain he liked. Strangely, he already felt possessive of her even though nothing had been formally settled between them. In fact, nothing informally had been settled either. Her parents had made the rather gauche offer, which he was, also rather gauchely, considering. Still, the fact she so ardently held a note from her lover while standing next to him was more than disconcerting.

"Perhaps you should put the note in your reticule," he suggested in an overly pleasant tone. She blushed scarlet, as he intended she should. She started to speak with a small shake of her head, as if she was about to deny having a note, but then she stopped.

"That is a good suggestion," she said, looking straight

at him, as if challenging him to take the note away. And damn if he didn't want to. She took the note, not bothering to hide it, and slid the pink-tinted paper carefully inside. Rand couldn't help but wonder what sort of man used pink stationery.

"I would ask that you not make a spectacle of yourself. Or of me," he said, feeling uncharacteristic anger shoot through him. His anger must have come through in his voice, for she shot her chin up.

"I have done nothing of the sort," she said.

"Accepting a note from another man while standing with your intended would qualify as a spectacle had even one other person seen what you did," he said, keeping his voice low. "I am many things, Miss Cummings, but I am not a fool. Nor will I be made to look like one. I have come here in good faith, at the request of your parents, and I will not—"

"Your Grace, if I might interrupt, I would like to introduce you to Mrs. Astor," Mrs. Cummings said.

It was on the tip of his tongue to tell Mrs. Cummings that she may not interrupt, but good breeding prevented him from doing so. "Of course," he said, looking quickly to Elizabeth, whose cheeks were flushed with anger, before bowing toward the acknowledged leader of the New York Four Hundred. But from the corner of his eye, he saw Elizabeth clutch her reticule containing the precious note even harder.

Chapter 6

"I cannot marry the girl," Rand announced to Edward when they were finally back to their rented cottage.

"The note, you mean?" his friend asked.

"You saw it, too, then. Good God, the girl could not be more indiscreet if she tried."

"I'm afraid I would lay blame on the gentleman," Edward said blandly. "He does seem a good deal older than Miss Cummings. In fact, he looks a good deal older than you."

"His name is Henry Ellsworth," Rand said, conveying without saying aloud that he wanted Edward to make some inquiries about the man. Finding out information without letting people realize he was looking for information was one of Edward's greatest skills. "It's clear to me that she's in love with him."

"It is unfortunate," Edward said, walking over to the sideboard and pouring himself a brandy. He lifted the decanter, asking if Rand wanted a bit.

"I suppose I could use a drink, but no. I have a

blasted ball tonight and I think it's best that I be completely alert."

Edward smiled a bit too broadly for Rand's liking. "You think they plan an assignation? Ah, how I love drama."

"As long as it doesn't involve you, you mean."

Edward shrugged. "If she's planning to meet him, it will be far easier for me to trail behind her than you. And I've a feeling you wouldn't handle it very well if you did stumble upon the young lovers."

"I thought we agreed he was not so young," Rand said, feeling slightly put out by the entire thing. "Honestly, I refuse to force the girl to marry me."

"You're not forcing her to marry you. Her mother is," Edward pointed out. "And based on what I saw at the Casino this morning, if this heiress doesn't work out, there are more. And more. And more."

"You are drooling," Rand said dryly. "And you don't have nearly the debt I do."

"Still, it would be rather nice to live the life of leisure our forebearers did. Though I daresay I'm more than glad I'm not in your position."

"I honestly don't want a life of leisure," Rand said. "I don't mind work, as long as it's meaningful. But I could work for the next hundred years and not pay off even the interest of the debt my brother accumulated. How he did so while so sick, I'll never know."

"Perhaps that's why he did it. He knew he would die and so decided to squander it."

"I've thought of that," Rand said quietly. "Many times."

Edward took a small sip. "We've gotten off the subject of your jilting the poor girl."

"I think the 'poor girl' would do a jig if I announced to her mother that I could not marry her." Rand threw himself down onto a large leather chair and stared at the empty fireplace, feeling out of sorts. It wasn't as if he didn't fully realize why he was here. It shouldn't bother him that he had an unwilling bride. She'd get over it or not and he would be able to save Bellewood and finally help his tenants.

"This truly troubles you, doesn't it," Edward said, his tone slightly amazed.

"Of course it does."

"Surely you didn't think to have a love match."

Rand raise one eyebrow. "Hardly. But I didn't expect my bride to hate me."

"Hate is a bit strong, don't you think?"

"Fine then," Rand said, standing and walking over to a bank of windows that overlooked a small rose garden. "Not hate. Resent. And I don't want my bride looking at me and—" He stopped and let out a soft swear.

"And wishing you were someone else," Edward finished for him. It was one of the curses of knowing someone for so long; they almost always knew what the other was thinking.

"I suppose that's it. If she disliked me for me, then I think I could take that. I would still proceed and marry her and get my heir and leave her be."

"You're charming enough. When you want to be. Make her fall in love with you."

Rand looked horrified. "Good God, why would I do that?"

Edward laughed. "No reason, old man. No reason at all."

Caroline Astor made it her business to put on the most elaborate ball of the season, known as the Summer Ball. Knowing that the Cummings were hosting a duke and would no doubt try to usurp her as the unofficial leader of the Four Hundred, she put forth all her effort to throw one of the most lavish balls ever, though she would never have admitted such a thing. The Astors and the Cummings had been having a quiet and unspoken social war for more than two decades.

Elizabeth had never before been allowed to attend the famous Summer Ball, by far the grandest event every summer, but this had nothing to do with the fierce rivalry. She had been too young, and then her mother had dragged her all over Europe and foregone the Newport season. Until now. Now she was supposed to be enthralled and charming when she was truly miserable.

Henry would not be here.

His strange note told her as much and that was all it said, which was cruelly disappointing. He had not even told her he missed her or loved her or any of the other things she was longing to hear from his lips. She knew he was likely being overly cautious, and rightly so. But still . . . one kind word would have gone so far to make her happy this night.

She walked through the gracefully arched Italianate entry to the Astors' Beechwood on her father's arm, grateful that he had decided to attend the ball rather than sail off on his beloved sloop. While her father almost always gave in to her mother's demands, at least he was a strong shoulder to cry on when things were at their worst. He, unfortunately, had been in Bermuda when her mother locked her in her room and so had missed the high drama occurring in Newport. Elizabeth wondered if his presence would even have made a difference. Probably not. But at least he would have given her some comforting words.

Now, it was too late. The duke was here and she imagined it was only a matter of time before he proposed. He hadn't seemed the least deterred by her rather blunt statement he should return to England. At least she would be able to see her friends who had been barred to her all summer while she remained a prisoner in her room.

The thirty-nine-room mansion was not nearly as large as Sea Cliff, but then, Caroline Astor had wanted to convey the feeling of a true summer cottage. Elizabeth liked it immediately, from its beautiful understated exterior to the welcoming interior. Elizabeth couldn't help but smile when they walked through the crush of people into the white and gilt ballroom. Her father pointed to the ceiling where smiling mermaids gazed down at her.

"Supposed to be like we're underwater or some such," her father said.

The ballroom was not overly large, but it was a whimsical place where guests danced beneath sparkling chandeliers. Dangling from the chandeliers were droplike crystals that Elizabeth guessed were meant to evoke a feeling of floating beneath the sea. Three hundred guests, fairly dripping diamonds, gathered in the ballroom and mingled outside on the terrace overlooking the Atlantic Ocean.

"This is your first Summer Ball, is it not Elizabeth?" her father asked. Lately, it seemed as if her father had lost touch with her and found it surprising that he saw a woman coming toward him instead of a little girl. At that moment Elizabeth wished with all her being that she was still the little girl her father doted on so shamelessly.

"It is. And probably shall be my last," Elizabeth said blithely. She looked up to her father and was struck by how very sad he looked for a small moment before he forced a smile. It was almost impossible not to plead to him then and there, amongst all these people, to stop the inevitable wedding. He squeezed her hand as if he knew what she was thinking and needed to give her strength. Elizabeth's heart wrenched, but she smiled and was glad when her father looked relieved.

"Chin up, eh, Elizabeth?" he said.

She almost gave in to tears, but smiled brilliantly instead just knowing he understood.

Once she'd read Henry's note, she'd completely dreaded this ball, for she would have to suffer the company of the duke. Oh, she knew she was being unfair and catty, but she did not care. She could think of him only as "the duke" for that is how she'd thought of him for weeks now. If he did not exist, if her mother had not attended that particular art gallery on that particular day, she would most likely be walking arm in arm with Henry right now.

The orchestra was set up in the Wedgewood room off the ballroom to give more room for dancing, though this early no one was dancing yet. From the corner of her eye, Elizabeth spotted her dearest friend hurrying over to her. Margaret Pierce, fondly called Maggie by her friends, stopped in front of her, beaming her excitement.

"You may make your escape now, Father," Elizabeth said, leaning up to kiss her father's cheek.

"Your mother is somewhere about," he said, pretending to look around for her. Elizabeth knew he wanted more than anything to join the men in the billiard room where whiskey and cigars were not only approved, they were mandatory.

"Where is he?" Maggie gushed when her father had left.

"Who?" Elizabeth truly did not know whether her friend was talking about Henry or the duke.

"The duke, silly. And I hear he brought an earl with him and they were both at the Casino this morning. Mother wouldn't let me go because I was sneezing even though I insisted I wasn't sick and that it was very likely the roses she's placed in every corner of our home was causing me to sneeze. Really, I would have felt much better had she let me attend the Casino instead of being confined with all those roses breathing on me. And then I could have met your duke and his friend the earl." All this said with hardly a breath. It was so good to see Maggie after her absolutely dismal summer. "Well, is he here yet?"

Elizabeth laughed. "I don't know."

Maggie made a quick pout. "Oh." Then her face sprang into a smile. "But they are coming, are they not? My mother insisted they were and that's why I've squeezed into this dress. How do I look, by the way?" Maggie twirled about, causing her beautiful butter-yellow dress to twirl with her. Very few people could successfully wear yellow, and Maggie, with her dark curls and striking brown eyes, was showing off the dress in spades.

"It's beautiful. And you know it," Elizabeth said, feeling rather like an old dog watching a puppy play around it.

"And you look . . ." Maggie paused, her eyes filling with tears. She was like that, laughing one minute, capable of tears the next. "You look like a duchess."

Elizabeth made a face.

"You do," Maggie insisted. "Oh. Don't you want to?"

"Not particularly," she said, looking down at the deep blue satin gown, which showed a disconcerting amount of cleavage. It was not a dress for an unmarried nineteen-year-old girl, but her mother had insisted that a duke would want a duchess, not a girl. She felt incredibly conspicuous standing next to Maggie.

Maggie's eyes swept up to her hair. "How long did that take?" she said in wonder.

Elizabeth laughed. Her mother had found a French woman who could accomplish the most intricate hairstyles imaginable. And her hair, which was wavy and thick and nearly impossible to control, had always been the most difficult aspect of her toilet. A tiara, sparkling with diamonds, perched atop it all. "Two hours," Elizabeth said, groaning.

Maggie brought a hand up to her own simple style and grimaced. "Ten minutes."

"I think you look lovely," Elizabeth said fiercely.

Suddenly, the din in the ballroom quieted as a footman wearing the Astors' blue livery stepped forward and announced the latest arrivals. "His Grace, the Duke of Bellingham and the Earl of Wellesley, Lord Hollings."

"Gracious," Maggie said. Like most Americans, Maggie was completely unused to such lofty titles. "To think, you'll be 'Her Grace, Duchess of Bellingwood,'" she said, comically lowering her voice to footman level.

Elizabeth laughed, glad that her friend was there to make light of everything. "It's Belling*ham*," Elizabeth said. "As in *pig*."

It was such a ridiculous statement that Maggie laughed aloud, causing everyone around them to shush in unison, which only caused the two girls to laugh more.

"You are terrible," Maggie said, when she'd finally sobered enough to speak. "You don't really think him a pig, do you?"

"No," Elizabeth said rather begrudgingly. "He's not so bad."

Maggie touched her friend's arm. "But he's not Henry, is he?"

Elizabeth closed her eyes briefly. "I know I shouldn't pine over him. But I saw him today and I cannot stop my heart from beating madly. I wish I could."

"You saw him today? Will he be here tonight? Oh, this is too delicious," Maggie said, then quickly added when she saw Elizabeth's expression, "and awful for you. Of course having the man you love meet the man you're going to marry would be awful."

"It is. But I have not agreed to anything yet," she said, staring blindly at the swirl of men and women before her.

"Oh. I thought it was all but announced. I'd heard you agreed to the match. It's been pure torture not being able to talk to you these past weeks. Everyone thought you were being a complete snob, cutting us out just because you're to be a duchess. Of course, I knew better because I know your mother better than anyone else and I told them that if you were not attending balls and such it was because your mother wouldn't allow it."

"Thank you for your loyalty," Elizabeth said.

"Well, to be honest, I was a bit upset when your butler turned me away. And you didn't return any of my letters." Maggie stopped, looking at Elizabeth's stricken face. "You didn't get them, did you?"

"No," Elizabeth said, shaking her head in disbelief. She'd assumed it was only Henry's notes she'd been deprived of. But apparently her mother wanted her cut out of life entirely until she agreed to the match.

Suddenly, Maggie clutched Elizabeth's bare arm and looked over her shoulder. "He's coming," she whispered harshly.

Elizabeth didn't dare turn to look. "How close are they? Can we escape?"

"Escape to where?" came his voice, clipped and English and so deep something in her chest rumbled.

"I don't think she meant escape to," said another male British voice. "I think she meant escape from."

Elizabeth nearly rolled her eyes but restrained from

doing anything so ill-mannered. "Lord Hollings, Your Grace, please meet my dearest friend, Margaret Pierce."

"Mademoiselle," Lord Hollings murmured, lifting Maggie's gloved hand for a kiss.

"Pleased to meet you," Maggie said, dipping a quick curtsy and darting a look to Elizabeth to see if she'd done the proper thing.

"I think when meeting peers you are supposed to dip to the floor and remain there until they crook their finger at you," Elizabeth said. And then she demonstrated but rose before anyone crooked their finger.

Apparently, Lord Hollings found her delightful, while the duke did not. He frowned, his eyes so intense on her she wondered what he could possibly be thinking. Certainly that little bit of fun with her deep curtsy could not have made him angry.

Then he leaned toward her and said discreetly, "If I were you, my dear, I wouldn't lean quite so far when wearing that dress."

Elizabeth gasped and immediately felt her face heat almost painfully. She quickly recovered, "If you were *me,* Your Grace, you wouldn't need to marry."

His answer was to raise one haughty brow. His nonreaction was completely disappointing. "I've come over to make certain I obtain at least one dance with you before the evening is out. A waltz, preferably."

"I'll check my dance card," Elizabeth said, knowing full well it was completely empty. Usually by now at least a dozen young men would have come to her and asked for a dance, but no one had yet approached her. She wondered wildly whether her mother had made some edict forbidding men to dance with her. "Yes, I think I do have a dance open. A waltz, too."

Before she could stop him, he'd gently taken her lace-covered card, which was attached to her wrist by a thin silk cord, forcing her to lift her hand.

"I see you have another dance available. The *Blue Danube* by Strauss, a particular favorite of mine. If you would be so kind to save that dance for me as well, Miss Cummings."

"Of course," she said, pulling her wrist ungently away from him. Two of the four waltzes were promised to the duke. But it didn't matter; it wasn't as if Henry would make an appearance and ask her to dance. It no longer was important who she danced with.

"Pencil my brother in for the Virginia Reel," Maggie said quickly. "He always dances with me for that and I can never keep up with him. I end up flailing about the dance floor. I do think he does it on purpose."

"Miss Pierce, I would be honored to dance with you. I fear I'm unfamiliar with the reel, but would enjoy a waltz or polka."

Maggie beamed. "A polka. I just adore dancing the polka, don't you? They are always such happy songs, while I find waltzes rather maudlin and sad. I suppose it depends on the author. Strauss, for example, can be uplifting, but the *Emperor Waltz* nearly brings me to tears every time. Do you think that was his intention?"

Lord Hollings seemed taken aback for a moment, as many people were when they first met Maggie. It was difficult to believe anyone would be as vivacious as she was without pretense. Maggie truly was the happiest person Elizabeth knew. Elizabeth held her breath waiting for Lord Hollings to say or do something; Maggie was, if nothing else, unique.

"You are delightful," he said finally.

"I am, aren't I?" Maggie said, smiling brightly. Then she leaned forward a bit as if imparting a grave secret. "I fear not everyone finds me so. Some people find me a bit tiresome."

Elizabeth let out a laugh, surprised by Maggie's candor and self-awareness. Nearly everyone said that Maggie Pierce was only tolerable in small doses. Elizabeth had never agreed, for she had needed a large dose of Maggie throughout her rather serious life. Frivolity was something other girls could aspire to, but Elizabeth was always expected to act and look proper. From the earliest age Elizabeth could recall unending lessons in deportment, hours spent holding a book properly, not for the content of the book but to practice proper posture when reading. Maggie had been a bit of sunshine in her otherwise dreary childhood. She often wondered had her mother known how much delight Maggie had given her that she would have forbidden their friendship.

"Let us see if I can grow weary of your charm tonight," Lord Hollings said, much to Maggie's delight. "Would you care to dance now?"

Although very few people were dancing, the orchestra was playing a lively *schottische,* a dance very much like a polka.

Maggie smiled, not even trying to hide her pleasure that the earl had asked her to dance. She was unused to attracting the attention of such handsome, well-heeled men, and was a bit taken aback. He probably was simply being a good friend to the duke, entertaining Elizabeth's friend so that the duke could be with her. Lord Hollings was an excellent dancer who, unlike so many men, seemed to truly enjoy dancing. After the rousing dance, he asked her to accompany him to the refreshment table, another unexpected surprise.

"Well, Lord Hollings, I must warn you that if you are here looking for a great American heiress, you will not find it in me," she said, laughing. Perhaps English nobility were under the impression that all American girls were wealthy.

He looked a bit startled, then laughed. "Are all American girls as candid as you are?" he asked.

"Not all. I think I should warn you, there are quite a few mamas who will be more than delighted to find that you have accompanied the duke on this trip." Looking about the room, Maggie noted that many were looking at them at the moment and few were smiling.

"I'm well aware of that fact, Miss Pierce. And what about your mama?"

Maggie wrinkled her nose. "She has her sights set on one of the Wright brothers. There are four of them, and I suppose they are nice enough."

"But?"

"But I truly have no desire to marry at all. I know that many girls dream of the day they will marry. It's all they can talk about. But ever since I was very young, I simply could not picture myself shackled to the same man for the rest of my life. Am I shocking you? I have never told another soul this, and I don't know why I am telling you, but there you have it."

Maggie looked at him, fearing he would be staring at her as if she were slightly crazy. Instead, he was smiling. "It seems we are on the same page, Miss Pierce. I have no intention of marrying for at least another ten years, and certainly not an American."

"Whyever not? Do we have horns? Cloven feet?" She looked down at her own small feet, now nicely encased in a pair of yellow slippers that exactly matched her dress.

He threw back his head and laughed. "I'm fairly certain you don't have horns, but I have yet had the pleasure of seeing any American girl's bare feet. I can accept your word, however. My not wanting to marry an American girl is complete snobbishness on my part, I confess. Given the choice, I'd rather marry a girl from my own country."

"Very well," Maggie said. "I can understand that. However, how can you predict that you will not marry for another ten years? What if you were to fall in love? Madly so. It could happen, you know."

"I have known some of the most beautiful women on this planet and have not succumbed to that irrational state. I feel sorry for the men that do. And what of you? How can you predict the future?"

Maggie tilted her head. "But I've already met everyone there is to meet and I have not fallen in love, so I can safely say that I will remain unmarried. And happily so."

He laughed again, and Maggie realized she was having the most fun she'd ever had with a man. Likely it was because she knew he was so far beyond her, she could be herself.

"I have a proposition," Lord Hollings said, looking around the room with mock horror. "I will save you from the attentions of the Wright brothers, if only for the time we are here in Newport, if you save me from the talons of all those mamas."

Maggie smiled brightly, loving the idea of such an intrigue. "That sounds perfect," she said. They shook hands, beaming smiles at each other, then joined in on another dance, just to shock anyone who had noted them. To share two dances with one girl was serious business, indeed. Spying her mother's beaming face, Maggie hoped she didn't realize this was her second dance with the earl. All she needed was her mother setting her sights on an English earl. Goodness, it was as farfetched as Elizabeth marrying a convict and getting Alva's approval.

Elizabeth watched her friend dance off with a bit of trepidation. Whereas she had been brought 'round Europe and attended many balls there, Maggie had led a far more sheltered life and she feared for her friend. She was so very naive of men, especially peers.

"Lord Hollings seems taken with Maggie," she said, trying to sound as nonchalant as possible, but obviously failing.

"You needn't worry. He is a gentleman and knows how to deport himself with debutantes," the duke said rather testily.

"Have I angered you?"

Rand let out a puff of air. "No. I'm sorry if I am not better company this evening. I find these sorts of entertainments akin to subtle torture. And now it appears the only other person I know here will be duly occupied for most of the evening."

Elizabeth smiled wryly. "Then we are in agreement on that point, at least."

Elizabeth fiddled with the cord of her dance card nervously, until she realized what she was doing and dragged her hands to her sides.

"Do you ride?" the duke asked.

"I adore riding my bicycle," Elizabeth answered without thinking. "Oh, you meant a horse. I have been on two horses in my life and was completely terrified both times." The duke looked slightly disappointed, as she thought he might. "Do many women ride in England?" she asked, feigning ignorance. In her short time in England the year before she had been amazed at the horsemanship nearly all the women displayed.

"Every woman rides in England," he said dryly.

Elizabeth suddenly felt overwhelmed by everything she did not know about living in England and being a duchess. She hadn't gotten past the idea of not marrying Henry, never mind what her day-to-day life would be as a duchess. Would she sit on a throne and look down upon her subjects with a frown, commanding them to do her bidding? Would she sit about planning balls and soirees? Would this be her life? It seemed gloomy and interminably boring to her.

"You've never been on a fox hunt, then."

He might have asked if she'd gone to the moon. "No. Not a one."

"Good," he surprised her by saying. "Not much for the hunt, to be honest, though you'll find many are in England. But you must learn to ride. Absolutely." He said it with a smile, but he sounded so imperious she felt her anger piqued.

"I don't care to learn. I truly don't see the need with motorcars becoming more in vogue. And, of course, bicycles. It's marvelous exercise and when you're done with it, you simply put it away. Without feeding it or fueling it. Have you ever been on a bicycle, Your Grace?"

Rand looked down at the stubborn turn of her face and suppressed a chuckle. She really was trying to thwart him at every turn, and instead of being annoyed with her, he found her charming. It was difficult to believe this was the same girl he'd had an agonizing dinner with, one who sat stiffly and whose addition to the conversation was a sedate nod. "A bicycle? No. I have not had the chance to try."

"Well, riding a bicycle is absolutely imperative," she said, sounding as lofty as he had insisting she learn to ride a horse.

He grinned down at her and she smiled back. "Touché," he said, doffing an imaginary hat. Her eyes sparkled, even though she was trying valiantly not to smile. It was almost as if she'd made a pact with herself not to like him no matter what he did. No woman, at least none he'd ever heard of, had disliked him. Edward would certainly have told him if one had.

"Ah. Our waltz is next," he said as the last strains of the country dance sounded.

Elizabeth gave him a startled look, which she quickly masked. Her face completely expressionless, she put a hand lightly on his arm as he led her out to the floor where they awaited the first strains of the *Blue Danube.* He nearly smiled again when he realized he might as well have been dancing with a phantom, her touch was so light. Suddenly he decided to have none of it, and as the orchestra began to play, he swirled her about, forcing her to either stumble or grab on for her very life.

"There you go," he said grimly. "You have not melted from my touch."

Her cheeks flamed making her look even more beautiful, and it struck Rand that if he had to marry someone, he was damned lucky to be marrying such a beautiful girl. "You should get used to this," he told her.

She looked up at him and for the first time he realized her blue eyes were speckled with green flecks. "Used to dancing? I can assure you, Your Grace, that dancing and its many forms has been drilled into me since childhood."

"No, that is not what I meant. Used to touching me," he said smoothly, and only grinned wider when she stiffened. He knew he should not torture the girl, but acting as if he were the very devil and not a rather nice man who happened to be a duke was beginning to grate. "It is difficult to dance the waltz when you are as pliant as a statue," he went on. "I could kiss you until you relax, but I daresay your mother would not approve."

The nostrils in the small nose flared. "*I* would not approve," she said haughtily.

"Oh," he said, bringing his voice down a bit, "I think you would." And then he laughed because she looked so outraged it was all he could do.

"You enjoy making fun of people."

"Actually, I never make fun of people. Perhaps you bring out the devil in me, Miss Cummings."

"He must be very near the surface if I do," she said, which only brought about another laugh.

Someone watching them from the perimeter of the ballroom would have thought them a delightful couple having a delightful time. They would note Elizabeth's flushed cheeks, her shining eyes, how closely she danced with the duke. And they would also comment on the way the duke kept smiling, how his eyes drifted over her face as if he very much liked what he saw. They would have been wrong, at least halfway.

Elizabeth was not enjoying the dance. The duke was absolutely insufferable. Intolerably so. This must be the longest waltz Johann Strauss had written. It seemed to go on interminably. While all the time the duke laughed at her. She could not wait until the last strains of the waltz sounded and she could escape outside where her cheeks could cool and where she could forget the way just the thought of the duke kissing her made her entire body heat. With embarrassment, of course. How dare he be so forward with her? It was not as if they were already formally engaged. She wondered if he talked to all women so.

Finally, the dance ended and she stepped immediately

from him, dropping her hands to give a brief curtsy. "There's Maggie. If you'll excuse me, Your Grace," she said, and turned away before he had a chance to even thank her for the dance.

When Elizabeth reached her friend, she grabbed her arm and led her toward her mother.

"What's wrong?" Maggie asked. "Did you see us dancing? Isn't he handsome? And an earl, too. I've never danced with royalty. Do you think he's met the queen?"

"He's not royalty, he's a member of the peerage. Whatever that means. And I'm sure I don't know who he's met," Elizabeth said, losing patience with her friend.

"Or care," Maggie said astutely. "What is wrong?"

"I want to get out of this ballroom. Please come with me for a walk outside."

A look of real concern crossed Maggie's face. "Of course."

"Mother, Maggie and I are going to take a turn 'round the garden," Elizabeth said when they'd reached her mother.

"Very well. And, Elizabeth, I thought you and the duke made a fine couple. Many have remarked on it."

Elizabeth said nothing, simply turned away with Maggie on her arm. When they finally reached the terrace and were away from the crush, Maggie gave her arm a squeeze.

"Is he really that awful?" she asked.

"Yes," Elizabeth said, staring determinedly to the Atlantic. And then, "No. He's not completely awful. I've told you that. But he's insufferable and he enjoys making me angry. I think if I knew him simply as an acquaintance

I wouldn't even like him and I certainly wouldn't want to marry him." She felt her eyes begin to burn and squeezed them shut. She would not cry, it solved nothing and only showed weakness of spirit.

"Come on," Elizabeth said, "let's walk to the gazebo. It's so hot in the house, I feel as if I might faint."

"I wish I were as wealthy as you. I wouldn't mind so much marrying the duke."

Elizabeth turned with shock to her friend.

"Oh, don't look at me so. You must admit he's the most handsome man here. By far."

Elizabeth wrinkled her nose. "Do you really think so? I find him so . . . masculine."

Maggie laughed. "My dear, that is the best part of him. He looks like a scoundrel. A pirate, even, with that dark hair and piercing gray eyes. How could you not think so?"

"Pirates are romanticized criminals of the worst ilk," Elizabeth said, setting her jaw stubbornly.

"I didn't say he was a pirate, I said he looks like one. Tall and fierce and . . ."

"Oh, for goodness' sake, Maggie, do be quiet. I don't want to talk about the duke or the earl or anything. I just want to walk about and get cool."

Maggie put on a little pout that lasted, perhaps, ten seconds. "I'll marry the earl, then. He's nearly as handsome as the duke and not nearly as dour. I do find the duke rather dour, but then again, that adds to his charm, doesn't it. The dark, tortured duke."

"Maggie," Elizabeth said, sounding slightly exasperated.

"Oh, you know I am just joking. You are no fun."

"I'm plenty fun with the right people," she said stubbornly.

The lawn was scattered with couples and women strolling about, but was large enough that the two could talk without fear of being overheard. The sky was darkening to night and the first stars were dotting the late summer sky. Servants were hurrying to light lanterns, which had been strung from poles to light the paths crisscrossing the lawn. It was a magical scene and one Elizabeth tried to enjoy as she walked arm in arm with her friend. She let out a sigh and Maggie gave her a searching look.

"I'm trying very hard not to be maudlin, but it's just—" She let out a shriek of pain as Maggie dug her fingers into her arm. "Ow."

"Henry," Maggie said, whispering harshly.

Elizabeth's heart nearly stopped. "Where?"

"By the beech tree. Oh, Lord, Elizabeth, what are you going to do?"

They had stopped still, clutching each other, aware that anyone walking nearby could see Henry as well as they. But at that moment, no one was close enough to recognize anyone as dusk settled onto the lawn.

The beech tree was one imported from Europe, a huge tree whose large, beefy branches drooped down much like a weeping willow. But the canopy of privacy created by such a tree was unsurpassed. The Cummings had such a tree in their garden, one that had delighted Elizabeth when she'd discovered its secret. For once you passed through the branches that dipped into the ground, you could not be seen. The foliage created a thick screen, a cool cavernous place where one could walk about or picnic. Or plan a secret rendezvous.

"I thought you said Henry wasn't coming," Maggie gushed. "I think this is the most romantic thing I've ever seen."

"That's what his note said. Oh, Maggie, what shall I do?"

Maggie gave her friend a little shove. "I'll keep watch," she said, her eyes lit with excitement. "Go."

And so, Elizabeth walked as if on clouds to the man she loved most in the world.

Chapter 7

"Darling." Henry grabbed her hands and brought them to his mouth before pressing his cheek against hers. His cheek was smooth, as if he'd just shaved, and it was so good to touch him. "I'm so glad you understood my note."

Elizabeth's eyes widened. "But I didn't. I was so upset when I thought I wouldn't see you again. I cannot tell you how happy I am to see you. These past weeks have been a nightmare."

"You know I've been trying desperately to see you," he said, pulling her farther into the cave the tree made around them.

"Yes, Susan told me. My mother let her go and she finally got the courage to tell me you'd been calling nearly daily and writing notes. I never got them," she said.

"I thought as much," Henry said fiercely. "I'm afraid your mother is very much opposed to us. And I see she's found someone more favorable."

"The duke," Elizabeth said darkly. "He's come all this way and I expect him to propose any day. And I must say yes, Henry, I must."

"No. You cannot," he said, clutching her hands even tighter. "Run away with me, darling. Your mother will come 'round. And your father. I believe he has a soft spot for you. He surely would not cut you off."

Elizabeth shook her head. "You don't understand at all. I don't care a bit about the money. You are not a pauper after all." She could not see Henry's expression in the darkness of the tree, so she plunged ahead, knowing they had little time together. "My mother has threatened to kill you, Henry, unless I agree to marry the duke."

He stepped back from her in shock. "She what? Surely you don't believe—"

"But I do," she said earnestly. "I never would have agreed to marry the duke had it not been for such a threat. She has been absolutely horrid these past weeks. And when I resisted, she had a heart attack. If I continue to resist, our doctor has reported she may yet have another more serious one, perhaps even fatal."

"That would solve our problems," he said heatedly.

"Henry!"

"I'm sorry, darling, it's just that I'm so very frustrated with all this. Surely your mother cannot persist when she knows how much we love each other."

Elizabeth shook her head, feeling as if it might explode. "She knows and does not care. She only cares about obtaining a title to connect with the family."

"And the duke? Is he simply a pawn in all this?"

Elizabeth gave a bitter laugh. "That is the irony, Henry. He truly is the fortune hunter that my mother claims you to be. It is only his title that puts him in high regard. I fear he has made no pretense of any tender feelings toward me. It is only my father's bank account that has him so enraptured. This is simply more than I can tolerate," she said, putting her gloved fingertips to her temples and pressing hard.

"Do you wish I hadn't come?" Henry said, so stiffly her heart hurt.

"No. Even if this is all we have." Elizabeth felt tears running down her face but didn't care. How had her life turned into such a nightmare? "We could still run away, couldn't we? I don't have to have all this," she said, looking down at her gown. "I don't even want it."

"I had no idea your mother was so set against our marrying," Henry said thoughtfully, almost as if he admired her mother's stance.

"I know she threatened to have you killed. And at the time I believed it completely. But now, I don't know. I just don't know. I think perhaps she knew it was the only way to get me to agree to see the duke. Even if she does mean it, we could go far away. I don't care. Even to California. I hear San Francisco is quite nice now."

"California?" Henry asked, sounding bewildered.

"If it's the only way to be together, then why not?"

"Because this is our home," he said. "We cannot be driven away. I refuse to be."

"But we could be together," Elizabeth said in a small voice.

"Yes, but to what end? How could we possibly live and where? No, it's impossible. We should elope and then go to your father."

"Go to him for what?"

Henry cleared his throat. "For forgiveness, of

course." She could see him smiling even in the gloom beneath the tree. "He would deny you nothing."

"Not if it went against my mother," she said woodenly.

"They would not cut you off completely. No parent would," he persisted. "I will write to you. I need to know you will be there. The Vanderbilt ball next week. I'll see you there and we'll make plans. I need to know you still love me, darling, before I set anything in motion."

Elizabeth's heart sang with renewed hope. "Yes, yes, I do love you." And then in a rush before common sense could take over, "Make your plans."

Rand stood on the terrace next to Edward pretending to enjoy the whimsy of the Japanese lanterns lit so prettily around the lawn, but his eyes were pinned to a single female who stood as still as a statue staring toward a large European beech tree.

"You don't think the girl is stupid enough to plan an assignation," Edward said.

"I do completely."

Edward let out a sigh. "What do you plan to do about it?"

"I'm not certain," Rand said with feigned calm. He wasn't certain because at that moment, the rage coursing through him made all thought incoherent. It was startling and completely unexpected this strange possessiveness he felt toward the girl. He simply could not believe she was having a tryst beneath his very nose. "I would like you to go meet Miss Pierce and lure her away, if you could. It shouldn't be difficult as she seemed to be quite taken with you."

"Rand." Edward said his name with a warning tone.

"Don't worry. I'm not going to kill the girl. Strangle a bit, perhaps." Edward laughed until he realized Rand was not smiling.

"You *are* joking, are you not?"

"I wish I wasn't. I wish I were the sort of person who was capable of violence because right now I feel violent."

Edward stared at his friend. "Don't tell me you're in love with her," he said aghast.

"Good God, no. But she is my intended, or rather she will be. And right about now I feel as if I'm being cuckolded."

Edward nodded, slightly relieved. "I'll see to Miss Pierce."

Rand watched as Edward spun his magic. Though it was clear even from a distance that the girl was hesitant to leave her friend, it was also just as clear she couldn't come up with a valid explanation to be standing in the middle of the lawn alone. When the two reached the stone terrace, she gave him a startled look as he nodded to her politely.

"Your Grace," she said, forcing Edward to stop. "Why don't you come in and have some refreshments with Lord Hollings and I? I absolutely adore the little lemon cakes Mrs. Astor serves each summer. You must try them." Even for someone as cheerful as Maggie, the invitation seemed a bit forced.

"Thank you, but no. I believe I need some more fresh air. It's rather stifling in there, don't you agree? You must, else you would not have spent so much time enjoying the night air. Alone."

Miss Pierce gave him a tight smile, and Edward gave him a look of warning, before the two disappeared into the house. When he turned around, he saw a slight movement near the tree and decided to take a little stroll. One never knew who one might meet, after all.

"Miss Cummings. Is that you?"

She jerked her head up and took an extraordinarily short time to compose herself before walking toward him. From the tree.

"Would you care to stroll with me?" he asked.

"Actually, I'm getting a bit chilled and was going back inside," she said, and continued walking by him toward the house. He grabbed her arm firmly, ignoring her small cry of outrage, and steered her away from the house. Some girls might have screamed, but Elizabeth it seemed had been well-schooled on the art of not creating a scene.

"I'm so glad you've decided to join me." He looked down at her and she stared straight ahead. She was such a stalwart little thing, he nearly smiled.

"We had a beech tree like that in our garden growing up. Much larger, though. It was a wonderful place to hide. I imagine they were imported from Europe."

"I believe so," she said, her voice sounding strange.

"A perfect place for a tryst."

She stiffened next to him. "I wouldn't know."

"Wouldn't you," he said blandly.

"I want to go back inside now."

"That is too bad."

Her arm felt slim beneath his hand and he thought he felt the slightest trembling. Good. He wanted her afraid at this moment, he wanted her to feel as much discomfort as he had when he realized she was beneath that damned tree with Henry Ellsworth.

Finally, they reached the end of the lawn and stopped. She crossed her arms in front of her as if she were the affronted one.

"I do not want you seeing him again," he said, before he even realized what he was going to say.

"I don't know what you mean." Ah, she was getting her fire back. He smiled at her, which only made her frown more fiercely.

"Henry Ellsworth. The man you think you love."

She gasped and his smile widened.

"You are rude," she said. "How dare you imply—" She stopped and let out a breath, and he watched as myriad emotions crossed her features. Then, lifting her chin, the affect of which was ruined by the slight quivering there, she said, "Yes, we love each other. And you are keeping us apart."

"You cannot love him. You cannot love anyone you have not been with for more than ten minutes at a time. I am always amazed how quickly foolish girls fall in love."

"I am not foolish and I am not a girl. You cannot know what is in my heart, or his."

He stepped to her, their bodies only inches apart. They were so close, he could feel her panicked breath, coming out in short puffs, hitting his throat. "Have you been kissed?"

His question seemed to startle her. "I don't know how you mean."

"Tonight. Have you been kissed?" he ground out.

"Henry would never take such liberties. He is a gentleman," she said, lifting her head imperiously.

The relief he felt was staggering, and extremely disconcerting. "I'm very glad to hear it," he said. "Because I daresay I wouldn't want my mouth touching yours if you had."

With one quick motion, he pulled her to him, giving her perhaps two seconds to scream her protest before pressing his lips against hers. She kept her mouth shut tight, her body stiff against his as he moved his mouth gently against hers even as he held her relentlessly in his arms. "It doesn't matter whether you enjoy this or not," he said against her lips, feeling angry and perverse and jealous beyond measure. "Your friend beneath the tree is likely watching and cannot know you hate me. He did not steal a kiss and now he must watch you willingly kiss me." She gasped and he chuckled lightly.

"I do hate you," she said. "I will never willingly touch you. I will never willingly kiss you. You make my skin crawl."

Rand lifted a hand to her face, holding her so loosely she could easily have wrenched free. He moved a thumb along her full bottom lip and felt her tremble beneath him. "You're trembling," he said softly, mesmerized by the way her mouth felt beneath his thumb.

"I'm cold. And frightened."

He smiled, his eyes looking into hers. "Yes, you are," he said. "But not for the reasons you think." He stepped back, releasing her and thought for just a moment she might actually rear back and slap him, but she restrained herself. Frankly, he thought he deserved a good slap.

"You are cruel beyond measure," she said, her eyes darting to the beech tree and for a fleeting moment he actually felt sorry for her. Anger overcame that softer emotion almost immediately.

"You would be well to remember that should you ever think to speak to Mr. Ellsworth again I will make your life a living hell. I will not be made a fool. I will not." Rand forced a smile that wasn't truly a smile at all. "Shall we go back to the ball?"

Rand hated the way she looked at him but didn't know what else he could have done. Certainly he was not going to allow her to continue this fantasy that she could be with Mr. Ellsworth. He'd best secure her as his bride as soon as possible. This entire trip was not going at all like he expected, most surprising being his own reactions to her. He had never in his life threatened a woman and had anyone told him he would, he would have laughed. Even now, his words still ringing in his ears, he was slightly ashamed that he had sounded so cruel for he was not a cruel man. Make her life a living hell, indeed. Other than marry her, he was unsure what he could do to make her more unhappy. He didn't know why the thought of her being kissed by another man drove him nearly mad, but it did. He wanted to force such weak thoughts from his head, he wanted to feel nothing for this girl.

"When we are married, when you give me my heir, you may see whomever you like," he said, his voice hard. "But until that time, you are not to so much as look in another man's direction. I never want there to be a question of whose child you carry. Do you understand me?"

Elizabeth continued walking as if she hadn't heard a word he'd said.

"Do you understand me?" he repeated, this time grasping her arm.

"I understand completely. I am to be a broodmare for you and then you will cast me free. I cannot wait," she said fiercely.

God above but she could make him angry! He'd never in his life met a woman who disliked him as much as this one did. And the joke was that she was the one woman he'd be saddled with the rest of his life. He wondered briefly as he followed her up the stairs, her back stiff with anger, if his big brother was looking down upon him and laughing.

Elizabeth walked into the stifling ballroom, her eyes straight ahead, for she knew if she met a single person she knew, if one person smiled at her, she would break down into copious tears. "Make my life a living hell," she muttered to herself when she found herself alone in the entryway. "Pah."

She chewed on her thumbnail for a moment before realizing what she was doing, then brought her hand down, her mother's voice in her head: "Stop chewing your thumb, Elizabeth, it makes you look like a scullery maid."

She wanted to be a scullery maid. She wanted to be anyone but Elizabeth Cummings, heiress to one of the greatest fortunes in America. She wished a hundred times, a thousand, but God never answered her prayers.

"Elizabeth?" Maggie walked hesitantly toward her. "Are you all right? I thought I would faint when I saw the duke staring at the tree. What happened?"

Elizabeth shook her head, fighting the urge to bring her thumbnail up for a good gnaw. "I don't know what I shall do. I don't know," she said finally, her voice breaking.

"Come with me," Maggie said, her face set. She grabbed Elizabeth's hand and dragged her to a small powder room off the grand entry.

"Did you know those great palaces in Europe hardly have any toilets?" Elizabeth asked dully. "The ladies actually have their maids stay in line for them. And here we are, at a very large ball, and find our own private privy. I think I shall miss that."

"Oh, Elizabeth," Maggie said, her face crumpling. "I cannot stand to see you so sad."

Elizabeth let out a watery laugh. "You are the one who is crying."

"I'm sorry. Truly I am," Maggie said. "Please tell me what happened."

Elizabeth looked at her reflection in the small mirror above the sink, shocked that she saw what she always saw. She'd somehow thought the past few minutes would have marred her in some way. Instead, she saw herself, looking far more confident than she felt inside. "I think you probably know what happened," Elizabeth said, turning away from her reflection. "Henry loves me. And the duke, he still wants to marry me."

"Was he very angry?"

A small furrow appeared between her eyes. "Yes, he was. Very angry."

Maggie smiled. "Perhaps he is jealous."

"I hardly think so. He was more concerned that I would make him look foolish. I suppose it is natural for a duke to worry about appearances. But the things he said . . . I do believe he has no heart, no understanding at all what it is like to be in love."

"What do you mean?"

"Apparently he won't mind if, after I have given him an heir, I seek Henry out and continue on as if nothing happened." Maggie gasped. "He explained it all as if it were nothing, as if he were explaining how it is that one breeds horses. Or dogs. As if there is no emotion, no attachment whatsoever. As if the very thought that we could have anything like a normal marriage is completely absurd. No, not absurd, but inconsequential. Not worth even thinking about."

"Oh," Maggie said, plopping herself down at the small chair set by a vanity. "How very unromantic."

"I think that is how all these peers think. It's horrid."

"He actually told you this?" Poor Maggie, all her romantic visions of dukes and earls were crumbling to dust at her feet.

"Let me try to recall his actual words." Elizabeth put on her best, haughty duke appearance. " 'When we are married and you give me an heir, you may see whomever you like.' Isn't that rather fiendishly cold?"

Maggie nodded, her eyes wide with horror.

"And he claimed it was impossible for me to love Henry or anyone else for that matter, for how could I possibly fall in love with someone I haven't spent more than ten minutes with at a time."

Maggie smiled sheepishly at that. "He actually may have a point there."

"Maggie! Of all people you should believe in love at first sight. Do not tell me you don't believe Henry and I are in love."

"Well . . . I believe it may be more of an infatuation than true love. How much time have you really spent with him?"

Elizabeth set her jaw stubbornly. "It doesn't matter the length of time but rather the quality of the experience."

"I'd say no more than two hours. Altogether."

Elizabeth was about to argue, until she realized that Maggie was in all likelihood correct. They had danced together. Gone to refreshment. Her mother had allowed them to ride bicycles together. Once. And that had lasted at least an hour. And then there were the letters. One could learn a lot about a person through letters. Henry was a wonderful author, she thought, smiling. "They were two wonderful hours," Elizabeth said wistfully. "But you must also count the times we've sat next to each other at a concert, or the balls we've attended. We may not have been spending every moment of those together, but we were aware of the other every minute. And, besides, what do you know of love?"

"Don't get cross with me," Maggie said, smiling. "I'm simply trying to be the voice of reason."

"I hear enough voice of reason, thank you very much. My mother is that voice, and my father. Susan was. And the duke will probably try to be that voice. I don't need any more reasonableness and certainly not from you."

The girls looked at each other and burst out laughing.

"Oh, Maggie, please, please stand by me," Elizabeth said, grasping her friend's hands.

"You know I shall always be your champion," Maggie said with feeling.

"What did the earl say about this all?" Elizabeth asked, overcome with curiosity.

"Only that the duke was likely going to strangle you and I should stand by at the ready should I hear a scream."

"Did he really?"

"Yes. He's quite funny and I knew he didn't mean it. Not entirely, anyway. I suspect he knew the duke was angry. He is a loyal friend."

"I'm sure he didn't spare too many kind words for me," Elizabeth said dryly.

"Not many," Maggie said honestly. "I do wonder what type of man inspires that sort of loyalty."

Elizabeth let out a groan. "Blind loyalty," she scoffed. "It is clear to me the earl does not know the duke's character."

"I don't see how that is possible for they have been friends since school."

Elizabeth gave her friend a level look. "Do not tell me you are allowing the earl to sway you toward liking the duke."

"I do like the duke," Maggie said. At Elizabeth's look of betrayal, Maggie rushed to explain. "Under any other circumstance, you would have to admit he is rather charming as well as handsome. I think he is in a difficult situation himself."

"He has swayed you. You are firmly in the enemy camp."

Maggie laughed. "Don't be silly. I just want you to be happy."

"Then you want me with Henry," Elizabeth said firmly. Her eyes widened as she studied her friend. "You do, don't you?"

Maggie began fidgeting with her handkerchief. "I truly don't know if he's the man for you," she said softly, as if saying it so would make her words less powerful.

"How can you say that?"

Maggie pressed her lips together. "Oh, I don't know. I'm as confused as you are. I'm simply worried because you seem so certain of Henry and I can't help but wonder if he deserves your devotion. How do you really know, after all? It's not as if he's a longtime family friend that you've known for years."

Elizabeth simply would not let her friend talk sense to her when she knew she was right. "I know in here," she said, putting a hand to her heart. "I will marry Henry and we will be happy." She nearly laughed at the look of confusion on Maggie's face, and then the dawning look of horror tinged with excitement.

"You're planning to elope!" she gushed. "When? Where?"

Elizabeth laughed. "We've made no plans yet. But tonight, the way the duke acted, the things he said made me more certain than ever."

"Elope." Maggie said the word with wonder. "Your mother, Elizabeth, what about your mother?"

"That is a real concern," she admitted. "We'll simply have to deal with her later. Once we are married and she sees how happy we are, she'll have to come 'round. Either that or we can always move somewhere. California, perhaps."

"Henry would never go to California," Maggie said with amazing accuracy.

Elizabeth waved her hand as if it was of no consequence. "Henry's convinced my father would never cut us off, and I am sure he's right, so we'll be able to stay in New York."

"Did Henry say 'cut off' or 'cut out'?"

"What's the difference?" Elizabeth said, sounding testy, because she did, indeed, recognize the difference. "Don't you dare imply Henry is a fortune hunter. The duke is the only fortune hunter here. And I shall not marry him."

With that pronouncement, Elizabeth left the powder room feeling immensely better than when she'd entered it. Maggie, however, felt eminently worse.

Chapter 8

Elizabeth's stomach twisted painfully and for a fleeting moment she thought she might actually vomit, something that happened infrequently when she was truly upset. Her father had requested a meeting with her—an extremely rare event—and Elizabeth could only think it meant the duke had approached him for her hand. She told herself over and over that no matter what he said, she and Henry would still run away together. The Vanderbilt ball was in three days and they would see each other again, and make plans for their elopement. In the meantime, though, she would have to suffer this meeting, her mother's joy, and the awful proposal that the duke was sure to give.

A footman opened the door of her father's study for her, another indication of the formality of this meeting. Her father's study was one of her least favorite rooms. It was oppressively dark, with rich paneling and dark leather furniture. Even the paintings that graced the walls were muted and dark, violent hunt scenes in which horses reared away from lions in terror. She supposed it was a very masculine room and that was why she'd always felt so uncomfortable in it. Her father wasn't sitting behind his massive mahogany desk, as she expected him to be, but in one of the oversized leather chairs placed by the fireplace. The heavy drapes had been pulled back and the windows opened, which allowed in not only a fresh breeze and sunshine, but a few pesky flies, as well.

"Father, you wished to see me?"

Jason Cummings steepled his fingers beneath his chin and looked very grave. Far too grave, Elizabeth thought, if he planned to tell her the duke was set to propose. For a wild, wonderful moment she dared hope the duke had begged off, that even now he was heading to New York to find passage back home.

"Sit down, my dear," Jason said.

Elizabeth sat, clutching her hands in her lap almost painfully as the hope surged through her.

"It has come to my attention that you planned an elopement with Henry Ellsworth," he said, and for a moment Elizabeth could only see her father's lips moving, could hear not another word he said as those first syllables clutched at her heart.

"Are you listening?"

Elizabeth could not meet her father's eyes. "Yes," she whispered. Betrayed. The duke had betrayed her, had gone running to her father like a child tattling. She couldn't think at the moment that he would have been completely justified. She could only think that he had thwarted her plans, ruined her life, broken her heart.

"I went to speak with Mr. Ellsworth."

Elizabeth's head shot up in surprise. "You did?"

"Of course I did. I believe I was long overdue in speaking with the man. Your mother told me to interfere months ago but I never believed you would be so irresponsible. As it is, you have forced my hand. You are never to see him or communicate with him again. All his letters shall be burned and should he be foolish enough to plan another assignation, he will be removed from every social list. Do you realize the humiliation you would bring this family, not to mention the shame upon yourself if you were to have followed through on this?"

"What did he say?" Elizabeth asked, feeling hysteria clutch at her throat.

"It's of no consequence," her father said, looking suddenly uncomfortable with this interview. Her father, one of the most ruthless businessmen in the country, was never at ease with emotional scenes from his daughter.

"But it is, Father. You must tell me."

He seemed to sag a bit in his seat. "Elizabeth," he said softly. "Please let it lie. I don't want you any more hurt than you are."

"Tell me," she said through gritted teeth.

"To give Mr. Ellsworth credit, he would not accept money to leave you alone." Jason ignored his daughter's gasp. "He insisted that he loved you." He took in the look in his daughter's eyes and his expression became even more troubled. "But when I told him in no certain terms that you would be financially cut off should the two of you elope . . ." His voice trailed off. "Elizabeth, let it lie."

"What? What did he say?" Elizabeth asked, tears running unchecked down her cheeks.

"He was not amenable to that. He is not destitute, of course, but he would prefer to marry a girl with a sizable dowry. He's a practical man, I suppose, and it took very little convincing for him to give up his suit. Very little. I don't want you to harbor any hope that he will change his mind. As soon as he became convinced he would not receive a dime upon your marriage, he bowed out. Apologized, even. I don't want you to think too badly of the man. After all, he could not be bought outright."

"As the duke was," Elizabeth said bitterly.

"It's entirely different and you know it."

"The duke could not stomach the idea of losing out on all that money, could he, Father. I mean nothing to him. Nothing at all."

"Elizabeth," her father said in a warning tone. "I'm afraid you don't know what you are talking about. The duke has made every attempt to make certain you are not completely unhappy. Indeed, he has been remarkably patient with you." He ignored her rather unladylike snort of disbelief. "I understand your friendship with Mr. Ellsworth. But he and I have come to an understanding. He is leaving for New York today."

"You're lying," Elizabeth said fiercely. "That does not sound like Henry at all. He's never been concerned about money." Then the soft echo of their conversation made her heart wrench. *"How could we possibly live and where? No, it's impossible. We should elope and then go to your father."* Henry had quickly said he would seek forgiveness, but now Elizabeth was filled with doubt, and her father must have seen that doubt in her face.

"I'm so sorry, Elizabeth. Men are practical beings. I suppose it is a good lesson to learn early on. This Mr. Ellsworth may very well love you as he says he does, but clearly that is not enough."

"No. I suppose not."

Jason swatted at a fly. "You'll have no illusions about your marriage to the duke. It is better, I think, to know going in rather than to discover later that what you mistook for love of you was really love of your money. Perhaps you will find some affection for the duke in time."

"You don't really believe that, do you?" Elizabeth asked, dully.

"I'm truly not the person to talk about such romantic things." Jason cleared his throat. "Speaking of the duke, he has asked for a private meeting with you this afternoon."

Elizabeth truly felt her stomach roil. "I hate him," she said, staring at the dark Oriental rug beneath her feet.

"Now, Elizabeth, it is a sin to hate," her father admonished.

She lifted her head. "It is also a sin to promise in a church before God to love, cherish, and obey a man you wish to the very devil."

Jason stood abruptly, but Elizabeth didn't feel a bit of fear, so she stood as well. "The duke has done nothing but promise to make you his wife."

"He betrayed me," Elizabeth nearly shouted, something she had not done in years.

"What the devil are you talking about? He has been

nothing but kindness. Why this morning when he approached me one his greatest concerns was that you would be happy."

Elizabeth shook her head in disgust, knowing the duke had said the words he must know a father would want to hear. "It is of no matter, as you would say. I suppose we are to have a congratulatory supper tonight. And Mother, I am certain, already has the engagement ball completely planned, right down to which shoes I should wear on my feet."

"That is enough," her father shouted.

"It is enough." Elizabeth turned away, her skirts twisted around wildly, and walked as angrily as she could to the door. When she reached it, she was about to grasp the door handle, when the door was opened by the conscientious footman. "I can open my own door," she shouted to no one in particular. She made it all the way to her room before she allowed herself to cry once more.

She had been in her room perhaps thirty seconds before a soft knock sounded and her mother entered. Without a word, Alva went to her daughter and held her and let her cry without uttering a single word. She held her until Elizabeth's tears stopped, until her breathing returned to normal.

"There now," Alva said, smiling gently at her daughter's tear-ravaged face. She lifted her hand to Elizabeth's cheek and patted it twice, softly, before standing and walking from the room, leaving her daughter staring after her.

* * *

Rand had very nearly thrown more than one million pounds out the window, but it was something his damned conscience and cursed kind heart had forced from him. He didn't know he had it in him until he stood before Elizabeth's father and offered to beg off. Even as he did it, he wasn't entirely certain what he wanted to hear from the older man. As much as he needed the money, and God above knew he did, the idea of forcing a girl to marry him had become completely unpalatable.

"Are you aware that your daughter is in love with another man?" he'd asked Mr. Cummings. "If this match would at all be favorable to you, I think I will gracefully bow out and bid you good-bye."

"I have been made aware of the situation," Jason said carefully. "And no, the match would not be at all favorable." Jason Cummings let out a long breath. "You must think me a terrible father for forcing this on my daughter. You will see someday how very powerfully persuasive wives can be." He let out a chuckle.

Rand, if anything, felt worse. He had not pictured all this emotion and pure angst when he accepted the idea of marrying the American heiress. Indeed, he'd thought he'd be met with a shy, willing girl with a lofty dream of becoming a duchess. He'd met enough of them since inheriting the title. It was just his luck to be tied to the only girl who did not. So he found himself in the untenable position of insisting on a marriage he didn't truly want—though he certainly needed—to a girl who wished him to perdition.

"I believe it is time you proposed to my daughter, if,

indeed, that is your ultimate plan. I cannot take the chance she will take flight."

Rand raised his eyebrows. "Do you think she might?"

"I find I am constantly surprised by my daughter," Jason said dryly.

"Mr. Cummings, I am extremely uncomfortable with—"

The older man held up a hand to stop him. "Despite her recent rebellion, she will come 'round. I know my daughter. She is only nineteen and is enjoying being the center of a tragic love affair, when in reality, she has danced with the gentleman a few times and exchanged a few ridiculous letters."

Rand was in complete agreement, and told her father so. "If that is the case, I will propose to your daughter. I do think we suit, even if she does not."

Jason smiled. "I'm glad to hear it." He stood and came around his desk to shake the duke's hand. "You'll need patience, Your Grace."

"I do realize that, Mr. Cummings."

Jason dropped Rand's hand and returned to his desk. "Now on to the business side of things. I've had my attorney draw up some papers detailing the wedding settlement and a yearly stipend of fifty thousand pounds to continue hereafter."

My God, Rand thought. These people are insane to pay that amount simply to give their daughter a title. The amount of the settlement was ludicrous, another fifty thousand pounds per annum was obscene. "Sir," Rand interrupted. "I have no need of a yearly stipend. I intend to take the money from the marriage settlement, save my inheritance, and invest the rest. I would appreciate, however, any advice you can give on that matter."

Jason gave Rand a measuring look, then carefully crossed out a portion of the settlement with his fountain pen. "Done," he said, signing the document with a flourish.

When the older man turned the document to him, sliding it over the gleaming mahogany service of his desk, Rand felt as if his entire future lay before him. Inalterable and daunting. He took Jason's gold-trimmed mother-of-pearl fountain pen, conscious of the richness of the writing instrument, and signed his name without looking over the paper that legally bound him to marry Elizabeth Cummings.

Chapter 9

Elizabeth entered the Gothic Parlor wondering if the duke was aware how appropriate such a gloomy room was for what was about to transpire. It struck her that she was about to accept the proposal of a man she hardly knew and disliked immensely. She knew only that he dressed well, was tall and a duke. He could be overbearing and direct, but she'd rarely seen him smile, and the only time she'd heard him laugh was when she was being completely rude to him. She didn't know his favorite food or color or whether he enjoyed sweets as she did. She didn't know anything of this man who she would spend the rest of her life with. And she was the only person in the world who seemed to think that mattered.

She found him staring out onto their garden, watching a gray squirrel chase another around a large oak tree. For some reason, the fact that he smiled gently as he watched them play put her slightly at ease. *A cruel man would not smile at squirrels playing.*

"Your Grace," she said, dipping a curtsy.

He turned, smiling still, and for just an instant she

saw what other women saw: a spectacularly handsome man. She pushed that thought firmly from her mind.

"Miss Cummings," he said, giving her the smallest bow. "Thank you for joining me." His hands were by his sides, then he thrust them into his pants pockets, withdrawing them instantly only to shove them behind his back. *He's nervous,* she realized, and that made her feel slightly better as well. Elizabeth managed a small smile, and it was shaky at best. Her nerves were a jangled mess, and were not helped in the least by her father's interview that morning and her bout of tears after. She realized, of course, that she did not hate the duke nor truly dislike him personally, if she were completely honest. She loathed that she was being forced to marry him, but probably not the man himself. See? She was being enormously munificent. She could admit she didn't know him well enough to have even formed any opinion of him. She only knew she hated what he represented: an end to her dreams, her childhood, her life in America. An end to everything she'd known or ever hoped for, and he stood before her smiling as if he were bestowing upon her the greatest gift.

"Please, sit," he said, indicating a heavily carved chair with gold embroidered cushions and lion claw feet.

The phrase "throw her to the lions" spun through her head and she had to stifle a bit of hysterical laughter. Still fighting a grin, Elizabeth dutifully sat, all her training being brought to the fore for this momentous occasion. She would not embarrass herself or her mother by showing one iota of emotion. She would act with the deportment of a future duchess—or at least a well-brought-up American girl.

With a sense of inevitability, she watched as the duke got down on one knee and brought out a ring, and felt her stomach clench almost painfully.

"I will try to be a good husband to you," he said, his eyes on the ring. "We shall make the best of this."

Ah, the romance.

He let out a small laugh. "I rehearsed what I was going to say. Something to put you at ease, perhaps make you smile. But I see I had better just get this over with." He took her hand and opened her fingers gently, placing the ring in her hand. Elizabeth stared down at the ring, a pretty thing with a pink stone surrounded by diamonds. It wasn't grand or gaudy or even very impressive. It was simply a very pretty ring. She slipped it on finding it only a tiny bit too large.

"Will you do me the great honor of being my wife, my duchess," he asked formally.

Elizabeth swallowed past a growing lump in her throat. "Yes," she said. She lifted her hand and couldn't quite believe she had just agreed to become the Duchess of Bellingham. "What is this stone?"

She looked down at him and found him studying her intensely, almost as if he were waiting for her to change her mind. "It's a tourmaline."

"It's very pretty," she said, feeling she ought to say something nice to him. She wasn't a completely horrid person, after all.

He stood and dragged a matching chair next to hers and sat in it. He was so close the skirt of her pale blue day dress covered his shoes and she had to stay the urge to pull away.

"I am not such an awful man, am I?" he asked, tilting his head and smiling.

At that moment, she felt she was the awful one. For what, really, had the duke done to her except show up and offer to make her a duchess. She knew other girls would have been thrilled, other girls who had never fallen in love or made silly dreams in their heads of marrying their true love. "I have acted horribly, not you," she said, looking down at her hands.

"I daresay you had your reasons."

She looked up to him, surprised that he was attempting to understand her reluctance to marry him. His eyes were gray, a dark, smoky gray that could have been mistaken for almost any color from a distance. He had obviously shaved before their meeting, for his jaw was smooth with only the hint of a beard and she wondered, just for a moment, whether it felt smooth as Henry's face always had.

"In two weeks I shall be departing Newport. Lord Hollings and I plan to see a bit of America before the wedding. Your father has told me your mother is planning a Christmas affair, so that gives us a good amount of time to see the sights."

"Yes, it should," she said, trying to hide her relief that he'd be leaving shortly. She had no illusions that Henry would reappear in her life, but she was so sick of pretending to be happy in public when she was not.

"I think we should take those two weeks and try to get to know one another. I understand there are many more balls. And your father would love to get me out on that yacht of his."

Elizabeth felt beyond guilty that he should be trying so hard to act as if they were any other couple. She simply could not bring herself to do the same, not when that very morning when she awoke she'd believed with all her heart she'd be marrying another man. But she had to say something to him.

"I will try," she said softly, and saw something flicker in his eyes, as if he were disappointed with her answer. Or angry.

"Well, then," he said, standing. "Why don't you go tell your mother you are about to become the newest duchess in England."

He seemed so pleased with that statement when all it did was make her feel slightly ill. "I will." Elizabeth rushed from the room feeling his eyes burning into her back.

"She acts as if I am sentencing her to death. Or at least torture. I do not know how long I can remain patient with her," Rand said, pushing back his second brandy. He was not a drinking man, so already he was beginning to feel the effects of the alcohol, a warm soothing relaxing sensation. Perhaps he would become a drinking man, at least until this wretched wedding was over.

"Apparently you'll have to be patient with her until at least Christmas," Edward said, eyeing his friend carefully.

Rand scowled, staring at his brandy as if it were offensive. "Have you noticed that all these American cities are named for cities in England? New London, Bristol, Boston, York. Oh, they'll put a 'new' in front of it as if it's delightfully original, but it's all the same. I'll bet not one of these people has even been to York. And I'll further bet their *new* York is nothing like the original." He paced back and forth in their small library, a place where, to Rand's great irritation, Edward enjoyed holing up.

"Providence."

"What the deuce does providence have to do with anything?"

"The city of Providence. We don't have a Providence back home," Edward said in that distracted way he had when he didn't really care what Rand was spouting off about.

"There's one, then."

"Newport."

"We have a Newport," Rand pointed out triumphantly. "On the Isle of Wight. I've been there, actually, for a wedding. Blasted dreary affair it was, too. A sixteen-year-old girl marrying a fifty-five-year-old earl. Now that's something to be upset about. That's something to cry about."

Edward lifted his head from his book. "Miss Cummings was crying?"

"No. But it was quite apparent she had been. I'm surprised she didn't cry when I gave her that ridiculous ring. I couldn't bring myself to explain it, but I could see she was confused by its inferior quality. Everything's been sold. Everything. Hell, it was the best I could do given the circumstances. I haven't gotten a check yet from her father," he said bitterly. Apparently, the brandy was making him feel sorry for himself, something he

completely abhorred even though he found himself
of late falling into that trap. He put the glass down in
disgust.

"What does it really matter how she feels?" Edward
asked, marking his page, then closing the book and setting it aside. "You didn't agree to this marriage for any
reason other than you needed money. I'm beginning to
think you have illusions of turning this into some sort of
love match."

Rand shook his head. "It's not that. Believe me. It's
that she seems to be so opposed to the marriage."

"And you wanted her to fall at your feet in gratitude
for bestowing upon her such a lofty title."

"Yes," Rand said, brightening a bit. "I think that's it
exactly. It's as if she doesn't have the least notion how
rare it is for someone who is not wellborn to marry a
title. One of her ancestors was an indentured servant.
It's as if she is doing *me* the grand favor and it is *I* who
should be grateful."

Edward chuckled.

"If not for the fact that I needed the funds, I would
never consider such a low marriage. And neither would
you," Rand accused, immediately wiping the smile off
Edward's face.

"True enough."

"For generations we have carefully guarded our titles,
our inheritances, being careful who we marry, who bears
our children. And now, based only on dire financial
need, I am being forced to lower my standards. And I am
the one who should be grateful and apologetic. Bah."

Edward raised one brow. "Were you?"

"Was I what?"

"Apologetic. Good God, I hope not."

Rand felt his cheeks tinge slightly and hoped his friend thought the alcohol to blame. "Not in so many words, but I expressed my sympathy that she cannot marry the man she wants. I should have told her to beg for *my* hand in marriage." The moment the words were out of his mouth, he realized how absurd a statement it was and burst out laughing. "I really can be such an arrogant ass."

"I will not argue that point," Edward said.

"I rather wish you would," Rand said glumly.

"It is one of your finer attributes."

Rand smiled grimly. "I cannot wait until the next two weeks are over and we are on our own. Can you think of anything more tiresome than attending these American entertainments?"

"Now there's a positive attitude."

Rand walked over to the bank of windows and wished he were anywhere on earth but where he was. How he longed for the days when he was in London wearing his uniform, doing his duty for the queen and believing that all was well in his world, when he was responsible only for himself and his men. "I miss the guards, don't you?"

"Fiercely."

Rand let out a sigh, thinking about the girls who batted their eyes at him, the married women who threw themselves at him. He didn't want to think of those days of near debauchery because it made him want to pick up his drink again. Or find a woman.

"I am getting maudlin, Edward. And I don't like the feeling at all."

"Women will do that to you."

Rand threw himself down at the large couch, putting his hands behind his head and gazing up at the ceiling. "They never have done that to me in the past. I rather enjoy their company."

Edward chuckled. "Try seducing your fiancée."

For a moment, Rand was shocked to hear that he had a fiancée, and then intrigued by the notion of seducing her. "It would be wrong of me, not to mention nearly impossible with her mother hovering about."

Edward let out a small grunt of agreement.

"It would be very wrong," he repeated.

"Oh, no, Rand, I was only joking. You cannot think to seduce her. It is still too far from the wedding."

Rand agreed completely and said so. But now that the idea was planted in his head—and other parts of his body—he knew he would not be easily rid of it. Seduce her. Get her to fall in love with him. Or at least not loathe him. He could think of nothing worse than standing at the altar with a woman crying silently beside him as if facing a death squad. If she loved him, marrying her would be far more palatable. It might even take the bitter taste from his mouth when he lied before God and promised to love her 'til death.

Chapter 10

The American Beauty roses began arriving the morning after the announcement of her engagement appeared in the *Newport Daily News*. Elizabeth let out a bubble of laughter when she saw the massive amount of roses. The smell was so intense, the maids had opened all the windows and doors to dilute the sweet scent.

She read each card, smiling at the happy sentiments they contained. Everyone was so thrilled at her news, so happy, so congratulatory, it was difficult to remain completely morose.

And then she saw it and knew and her heart stopped for an instant.

A single rose lay upon a side table between other, much grander bouquets. There was no card, just the rose, stripped of its thorns. Henry. It could only have been from him. She picked it up, smiling softly, and held the bloom to her nose inhaling deeply, as if she could somehow breathe him into her. He still loved her, still loved her. Still loved her.

She heard a familiar laugh behind her and turned to see Maggie. "My goodness," she said, still laughing. "I thought Mother was being original sending you these roses. Have you even found our arrangement yet? I swear I haven't seen so many roses in all my life."

Maggie walked over to her and Elizabeth fought the urge to push the single rose behind her back. It was too late, for her friend's gaze drifted to her rose and her smile slowly disappeared. "It's from him, isn't it."

Elizabeth calmly placed the rose back onto the side table. "There was no card," she said.

"Oh, Elizabeth, why must you torture yourself this way?"

"I haven't the slightest idea what you can be talking about."

Maggie gave her a sly look. "Well, then, since you have so many roses, may I have just that one? I do so love American Beauties. They smell so wonderful." Maggie walked over to the table and reached out her hand only to be blocked, rather forcefully, by Elizabeth.

"Don't you dare," Elizabeth said, laughing. "You know very well who it is from. And it is of no consequence whatsoever. I am marrying the duke, Henry has returned to New York. And that is that."

Maggie frowned. "Then why is he torturing you by sending you a flower right after your engagement is announced?"

Elizabeth shrugged, trying to look nonplussed. "I suppose he wanted me to know he wishes me well."

Maggie rolled her eyes.

"It's true," Elizabeth said, sagging a bit. "I've realized that no matter what I do or say, short of killing myself or my mother, I am going to marry the duke. But I can tell you, I will not be happy."

Maggie let out a burst of laughter. "You sound like a little girl who won't eat her creamed spinach. I say you should make the best of things."

"Easy for you to say. You're not being forced to marry someone you don't know. Or like."

"I daresay if I was forced to marry someone like the duke, I wouldn't make such a grand fuss of it all," Maggie said, leaning toward one of the larger bouquets and taking a deep breath.

"Then you marry him," Elizabeth shot back good-naturedly. "Better yet, marry that friend of his. The earl." Elizabeth's eyes widened when she detected the smallest blush on Maggie's cheeks, and she pounced on the idea of happily torturing her best friend. "You like him," she declared.

"Of course I do," Maggie returned, slightly indignant. "Who would not? He's charming and handsome and supremely wealthy. And an earl. I am not, if you will remember, shopping for a husband. I know for certain that he is not shopping for a wife. He told me so himself."

Elizabeth screwed up her face. "He did? You hardly had a conversation with him and the topic of marriage came up?"

"You know how I talk when I'm nervous."

"Or excited or happy or sad or angry or . . ."

Maggie gave her a face. "I asked him if he were here looking for a bride like his friend the duke. He was actually quite rude about it, now that I recall. He said the last thing on earth he wanted to do was marry, and particularly

not an American girl." She turned thoughtful. "At the
time, I didn't really think about it, but that was rather rude
of him to say, wasn't it?"

"It certainly was. Perhaps he wanted you to get the word
out to all the mamas that he's not in the marriage market."

"Or perhaps he just wanted to get the word out to
me," she said, sounding remarkably glum for Maggie.

Elizabeth gave Maggie's arm a gentle squeeze. "Come
on, help me pick out a gown for the Vanderbilt ball
tonight. Mother wants me to wear that awful green gown
and I want your opinion."

Maggie Pierce wanted to throttle her best friend within
an inch of her life, but restrained herself from doing so
because that would have been contrary to everything
everyone thought of her. She did not get outwardly angry,
she rarely cried, she hardly ever raised her voice or even
acted as if anything in the world was of great concern to
her. But inside, good Lord, inside she was a seething stew
of emotions that she never, ever allowed out.

And so, when Maggie rushed over to Elizabeth and
told her how beautiful she looked in her gown purchased in Paris and designed by Charles Worth himself
and Elizabeth wrinkled her nose in distaste while looking down at said gown, Maggie did, indeed, want to
throttle her. The gown was magnificent, with a broad
collar that left much of her chest and shoulders bared.
Instead, she said: "I would adore a dark green gown to
wear instead of these tedious pastels that Mama makes
me wear. I'm older than you and she still dresses me as

if I were sixteen and at my very first ball. But I do love this gown," she said, twirling a bit and watching her pale, pink gown move about her.

"I do love that you're here," Elizabeth gushed, making Maggie feel slightly guilty for wanting to strangle her friend just moments ago. "I don't know what I would have done if your family had foregone Newport this year."

"Mama is still holding out hope that I will attract a husband. Speaking of which, is the duke here?" Maggie asked, really wanting to know if the earl was there. She enjoyed his company and felt completely at ease with him since he had told her in no uncertain terms that he was not looking for a wife. Because of that, he was the safest man to be with, for Maggie's mother was pushing her toward one of the Wright boys and she disliked every one of them—or at least disliked the idea of any one of them as a husband. If they thought an earl had captured her attention, they were sure to give up on her. Mama was ecstatic that she'd danced with the earl twice at the Astors' ball and had walked out with her as well. She didn't have the heart to tell her that the earl was only a ploy to help her escape those boisterous Wright boys.

"He's here," Elizabeth said, scowling, looking across the vast ballroom at the duke. Unlike the Astors' Beechwood, the Vanderbilts' summer cottage, The Breakers, was ostentatious, opulent, and vast. The ballroom was massive and would have looked completely at home in any grand European manor house. The ceiling was painted to look like a summer sky at sunset, puffy white clouds tinged with yellow. Massive chandeliers dropped from the ceiling lighting a brown marble checkerboard floor that gleamed beneath the lights.

"Really, Elizabeth, you should at least attempt to pretend you are happy with the engagement. I do wish Henry had simply left without sending you that rose, then you would be in a much finer mood tonight."

"But that rose is the only thing that is making me happy," she said, which further made Maggie want to growl at her friend. She'd never told Elizabeth what she knew about Henry Ellsworth and she was fairly certain she never would. Being the bearer of bad news never worked out for the bearer, her mother always told her. Mama was a stickler for what could and could not be said in public, the greatest of these was that, upon threat of death, one should never, no matter how tempted, remark that a son did not look like a father. It had never occurred to Maggie until very recently why this was such an important rule. When she'd shared her mother's wisdom with Elizabeth, they'd spent the entire afternoon trying to figure out just who really was Roger Taft's real father because he didn't look anything like the man claiming to be his sire.

"Look, they're by the fountain," Maggie said, hooking her arm in Elizabeth's reluctant one. "And they've seen us see them and are heading this way. Smile, dear."

Elizabeth plastered on a beautiful smile that only someone who was completely oblivious would not know was completely false. Alas, Maggie thought, Elizabeth did not share her talent.

"I see you are playing the happy fiancée tonight.

Thank you," the duke said sardonically as soon as they reached the two girls.

Maggie burst out laughing, stopping only when she noted that Elizabeth's smile had disappeared.

"I've come to claim my dances, Miss Cummings," he said, and Maggie found herself liking the duke far more than Elizabeth did. How she could not fall head over heels with someone as handsome and charming as the duke, she just didn't know. And that was just another reason for her wanting to strangle her friend. Honestly, any woman of even the smallest intelligence would choose the duke over Henry Ellsworth, the conniving cad, and Maggie knew Elizabeth as having far more intelligence than the average person.

Henry, long before he'd begun his ardent pursuit of Elizabeth, had pursued her. It wasn't until she'd discovered he'd made some rather indiscreet inquiries into her lack of fortune that he smoothly backed away. That had been the year before when Elizabeth was on her European tour and had missed the summer season in Newport. She would have warned Elizabeth outright, had her friend not been completely in love by the time she discovered they were secretly courting. And then, to Maggie's dismay, it did actually appear as if Henry was as smitten with Elizabeth as she with him and she didn't have the heart to say anything against him. It became obvious to her that Henry had never felt for her as he felt for Elizabeth, so she kept her doubts to herself, something she now deeply regretted. Maggie could have prevented her friend so much pain had she simply gotten the courage to break the bad news to her friend that Henry was the fortune hunter everyone feared he was. She'd heard it directly from her own brother the day after Elizabeth's secret meeting beneath the beech tree. Samuel was always right about such things.

"The first waltz, of course," Elizabeth said demurely, and Maggie almost laughed again for Elizabeth was not demure in the least.

"All the waltzes," the duke said, causing Elizabeth to jerk her head up in surprise.

That is when the earl pulled Maggie aside on the pretense he wanted to secure his dances with her. He was looking very fine in his formal attire, which emphasized his athletic build. He was nearly as tall as the duke, but slightly slimmer, and Maggie couldn't help but think how fine he must have looked in his military uniform. His sandy hair, usually a tad disheveled with a tendency to curl up a bit in Newport's humidity, had been brutally combed back revealing a rather nice forehead. Unlike Papa, the earl was not losing his hair and did not look as if he ever would.

"Thank goodness you're here, sir, for the Wright brothers have just arrived en masse," Maggie said, smiling up at the earl.

"I shall save you from their pursuit," Lord Hollings said gallantly.

"I do have to warn you, though, that your mission is fraught with danger," she said with an air of secrecy. "My mama is, even as we now speak, gossiping furiously with her friends and is planning an English wedding."

"Do you think we can carry out our mission, given its perils?"

"Failure is not an option," she said, sounding brave even though her eyes twinkled with laughter.

The earl grinned in that easy way of his. "You would make a wonderful spy," he said. "Though I daresay you should better school your features. You appear to be having far too much fun thwarting your mother. What shall she do when I leave in two weeks never to return?"

"Why, she will have to buy me a new gown to help mend my poor broken heart," Maggie said with drama.

"You are very devious for such a pretty little thing."

Maggie felt her heart swell just the tiniest bit and silently called out a warning to herself. This was simply a game. It would be pure disaster if she actually allowed herself to develop any real feelings for the earl. Then she truly would be left with a broken heart that a trunk load of new gowns couldn't cure. "Spies and the like must be devious to survive," she said pertly. *And they must not ever begin to believe that their secret life is real.*

"I'm afraid our companions are not having as grand a time as we," Lord Hollings said, turning grim.

"Well, how would you feel if you were being forced to marry?"

"She would do better to get used to the idea," Edward said rather curtly.

"I was speaking of the duke," Maggie said with bemusement. "You may unbare your teeth, sir."

Lord Hollings let out a chuckle. "I'm afraid I am loyal to a fault."

"How could loyalty ever be a fault?" Maggie asked, even though her loyalty nearly sent her friend off with a fortune hunter.

"Blind loyalty is certainly not an attribute I would wish to possess," he said pointedly.

Maggie looked away, sensing he was berating her for her loyalty to Elizabeth only because he did not know she had been the one to betray her best friend. She prayed Elizabeth would never know that she was the one who warned her father. She simply couldn't bear to know Elizabeth was headed for disaster. Still, she felt anger surge through her at his subtle criticism that she was blindly loyal and she felt her face heat slightly.

"My dance card," she said suddenly, smiling brightly and pulling it out for his inspection. "Which dances would you like? Or am I being presumptuous?"

"You're angry. Why?"

She looked at him with shock. No one could read her. No one, not even Elizabeth, who thought her endlessly cheerful or as transparent as she herself was. Nothing could be further from the truth. "Why would you say such a thing? Of course I'm not angry." She smiled brilliantly at him to prove it.

"You are. You are even a bit angry that I noticed you are angry."

Maggie laughed, no longer attempting to mask her emotions. "I suppose I took exception to your censure."

The earl looked taken aback.

"You hinted that I was blindly loyal to Elizabeth when that is not true."

"Ah," he said as realization hit.

"And how did you know I was angry?" she demanded.

"Your eyes," he said simply. "They turn to fire when you are angry. There's a tiny spark right there even now," he said, pointing to one eye.

Maggie laughed aloud.

"Doused with mirth."

Across the room, Maggie's mother beamed, already trying to decide whether a spring or late winter wedding would be better. And how would they ever get a trousseau together in time. They would have to travel to Paris, of course, and be back in time for Miss Cummings's wedding, for they certainly could not miss the social event of the year. And how ever would they get the funds for such a trip? Her mind was in a happy whirl watching her daughter laughing with the handsome earl. What a wonderful, wonderful summer season this had turned out to be.

Rand couldn't fathom why he had demanded Miss Cummings dance each waltz with him. It could be construed as either excessively romantic or irritatingly domineering, and he didn't have to try very hard to determine which she thought the gesture was.

Raising one delicate brow, she said, "Do you get your gift of command from your years of military service or your months as duke?"

"From my hours as a fiancé," he said blandly. There, he'd made her smile. Her face fairly transformed when she was not scowling, or worse, forcing herself to smile. Her eyes, wide and far too large for her face, turned to half-moons and the effect was quite charming.

"If you smiled like that all the time, I daresay your dance card would be filled in mere seconds." To his surprise, her smile widened; he would have thought such a remark guaranteed to produce a frown.

"I don't really care about filling my dance card," she

said, as if sharing a great secret. "When my mother and I were in Europe, I would pray with all my being that no one would approach me. But because I was an American and in possession of a great fortune, it was always full."

"Do you truly dislike dancing then?" he asked, surprised that any young girl would.

"No," she said thoughtfully. "I actually adore dancing and parties. I disliked the idea that they didn't truly want to dance with me. They much rather would have preferred to dance with my father's bank account."

He would have laughed if she hadn't looked so very serious. "So, you felt sorry for yourself. And I imagine you told yourself that you should not, because a hundred girls, a thousand, would have taken your place in a second."

She looked at him as if surprised he would have even the smallest understanding of how she felt.

"It is the curse of the privileged," he explained. "Don't you think that everyone in this room has met eyes with some poor beggar on the street and felt guilty that we thanked God we were not that beggar?"

"That is exactly how I feel. But I think you are far too charitable with the others. I don't think they give a single thought to anyone outside their small circle. And if they do, it's to throw money at it to make themselves advance only in the eyes of their peers. Or to say it is the beggars' own fault that they are in such a situation."

Rand examined her solemn face as she watched the others in the ballroom and couldn't help wondering if anyone else knew how very intelligent she was. "You are quite cynical for one so young," he said.

"I do try not to be," she said, laughing a bit. "I wish

I were more like Maggie. She's never morose about anything. Or angry or bitter. I must be growing quite tiresome to you."

"I cannot take another minute of your company," he said, and laughed when she looked as if she believed him. "I see that hope springs eternal in your soul."

"You can be quite awful," she said with mock sternness. The orchestra began playing the first waltz and he gallantly held out his arm.

"I believe this is our dance, Miss Cummings," he said formally.

"And all the other waltzes?"

"I don't think I could bear to see you in another man's arms," he said lightly, and an uneasy feeling hit him that what he said was all too true.

Edward decided after the first dance with Miss Pierce, that he would make it his mission to crack through her happy facade before he left with Rand on their travels. For some reason, he found provoking the girl remarkably amusing. She chattered incessantly about nothing, something that normally would have bored him into a coma. But she had a way of observing others' idiosyncrasies that had him laughing more than he had in years.

"There's Mr. Belmont," she said, tilting her head in the direction of a handsome man talking to Elizabeth's mother. "He's terribly infatuated with Elizabeth's mother and doesn't leave much secret about it. He lives alone above his stables and treats his horses better than most humans. I sometimes skip over there when I'm hungry and gnaw on some of the fresh vegetables he stores there for his mounts."

Edward raised a skeptical eyebrow.

"I can see you think I'm lying, but the tastiest carrot I've ever had was pilfered from his horse's bin."

Edward looked down at her as if she were quite mad. "If you are that desperate for food, I can arrange to have carrots delivered to your door."

She smiled impishly up at him. "I was five and being punished for not eating my lunch. I can't remember what it was, but I'm certain it was something very objectionable. We went to visit Mr. Belmont and his horses that afternoon and I was quite starving. I was a plump little thing, you see."

"Yes, I can see that," he said, just to watch her reaction. She did not disappoint him. She laughed.

"You are overly fond of trying to antagonize me, are you not? Well, I can say for a fact that I will not allow it."

He got the most wicked idea then, one he knew he would follow through on because if there was one thing about him, it was that he was often unable to stop his wicked impulses. "These balls are unbearably warm. I'm afraid I long for the cool English countryside. Shall we walk about the garden?"

"Let me ask my mother, first," she said primly.

When she returned, clearly holding in a bubble of laughter, he placed her hand in the crook of his arm. "What has you so giddy?"

"Oh, my poor, poor mother. I'm afraid we have her nearly in a swoon of happy delirium. She practically pushed me toward you. I think she is the one who will need a new gown to mend a broken heart when you leave, not me!"

"We have her fooled well, have we?"

"Completely, poor girl. I suppose I'll have to make it up to her by marrying one of those onerous Wright brothers," she said, laughing.

Edward didn't think her jest was funny. Certainly Maggie could do better than those rowdy boys, whose admittance into society was dictated only by their stepmother's great social status. He simply did not understand these Americans and their strange rules of status. England had a wonderful order. One knew where one belonged, which was an extremely comforting thing. Members of the peerage married members of the peerage. At least that is how it used to be until things became disastrously tied to economics. He had a sudden recognition of how Rand must feel, throwing away generations of tradition in an ironic mission to save his legacy.

"Surely you can do better," he said, feeling anger for her.

"I don't know if I care to," she said lightly.

He couldn't see her eyes so could not determine whether she was jesting or not. He couldn't tell from her tone, from her body, from the way she held her head. It was damned irritating not to be able to read her. As an officer, he'd made a study of men—and women—to see if they were being completely honest in their words. He'd gotten quite adept at ferreting out transgressors simply by asking a few simple questions. "So you truly don't care who you marry?"

"It seems to end the same way no matter if it's a love match or a business arrangement. Which is why, as I've told you, I haven't any interest in marriage at all."

"And how is it that all marriages end?"

"Badly. I suppose there are a few old couples out there still holding hands and enjoying one another's company. If they are out there, they certainly aren't members of the Four Hundred."

"What, precisely, is your 'Four Hundred'?" Edward asked, steering Maggie down a shadowed path lined with sweet-smelling beach roses, whose incessant blooms perfumed the air from May to October.

"It's a made-up list of names of prominent people," she said. "As far as I can tell, it's a list of people with a lot of money or great connections. It is only my friendship with Miss Cummings that has our family skating on the fringes of society, for we are definitely not on that list."

"What do you think of the list?" he asked, trying to provoke her.

"I really don't think of it at all," she said, turning to smile at him.

It struck him that the more she smiled, the more she was lying, and he thought he'd test his theory. "I'm going to kiss you as soon as we are alone," he said matter-of-factly.

Maggie stumbled the tiniest bit before recovering, clinging to his arm to stop herself from tumbling to the ground. "What?"

He almost laughed at her expression, which she hadn't managed at all to school into a smile. "I said, I'm going to kiss you." He looked casually around, then, before she could utter a single word or bring her panicked facade into a false smile, he kissed her, and God above knew the moment his lips touched her soft, pliant ones, that he wouldn't be able to stop with just one. She let out a small sound that might have been a protest or might have been surrender, but he didn't care. He found he liked Maggie just as much when she was talking as when she was not. And not talking at the moment seemed infinitely better.

Slowly, he drew back and gazed down at her upturned face. "There," he said softly. "There is an honest expression." She immediately scowled before she could catch herself.

He watched as she carefully schooled her features. "Is your experiment over?" she asked politely.

"For now."

"That was not part of our game's rules," she said. "I am afraid if you continue on in this amorous way, you will be in danger of falling in love with me. I do not wish to be a party to breaking your heart when you leave for England. I must ask, then, for the sake of us both, for you to never kiss me again."

He smiled, trying with all his might not to laugh aloud. She was, quite simply, the most delightful girl he'd ever met. "I see I'm a far better kisser than I believed," he said, and was rewarded by the faintest flare of her nostrils.

"I've experienced far better," Maggie said, smiling brightly. "And far more sincerity. If you would please escort me to the ballroom, I believe Arthur Wright has reserved one of my waltzes. Arthur is the least onerous and least boisterous of the Wrights. He fancies himself an expert on Egypt, a subject that fascinates me entirely." Not waiting for him, she turned and walked back to the Vanderbilt mansion, with the dignity of a queen. He found himself smiling at her back as he followed her.

* * *

Elizabeth was leading the poor duke on a merry chase. Or not so merry, she thought happily. Since that first waltz, two more had sounded in the Vanderbilt's grand ballroom, but Elizabeth had mysteriously been unavailable. Now that they were engaged, no one seemed to think it at all odd that they were not spending any time together.

"Where is the duke?" Alva asked, turning away from Oliver Belmont. The two had been talking incessantly about a home Mr. Belmont was planning to build in New York. Nothing was of more interest to Alva than construction. In fact, she had already made plans to visit the newlyweds within the first year so that she might supervise improvements to the duke's Bellewood.

"I haven't the slightest idea where the duke is," Elizabeth said, stifling a yawn. "I believe I saw him going off in the direction of the billiard room." In fact, she knew precisely where he was because she'd asked one of the Wright brothers, Albert, to show the duke the room. It was a manly haven of cigar smoke, fine brandy, and gambling. Once there, she knew it would be near impossible to get him away. The only men left in the ballroom were either too young to enter the billiard room or too old to care where they were. Or those who were completely smitten by someone, as was the case with Mr. Belmont, who continued to hover near her mother.

"I do wish Father were here," Elizabeth said pointedly.

"Whatever for?" Alva asked, clearly understanding her daughter's question and just as clearly pretending ignorance.

Elizabeth had no notion how her mother and father had ever gotten married. It had not been an "arrangement" as so many marriages had been, and yet it also had not been a love match. Her parents, who were so completely different, rarely agreed on anything—except, perhaps, that she should marry the Duke of Bellingham. In her memory, it truly was the only thing upon which she could remember her parents presenting a united force.

Elizabeth watched the dancers in a polka, spying Maggie dancing with Arthur Wright. She seemed to be having an uncommonly good time, she thought, feeling just a bit sorry for herself. How she wished she could be carefree and happy as Maggie always was. It seemed her friend never had a care in the world, which is what made it so easy for her to unburden herself on her friend, Elizabeth thought with a twinge of guilt. She looked around and found Maggie's mother frowning heavily at the pair who seemed to be having such a grand time, and Elizabeth let out a giggle.

"What is so amusing?" Alva asked.

"I believe Mrs. Pierce has her heart set on the earl for Maggie and is none too happy with her at the moment," Elizabeth said lightly.

"She's daft if she thinks to elevate herself to that degree," Alva said acerbically. "I will have to speak to her before Maggie makes a complete fool of herself over Lord Hollings."

Elizabeth felt her entire body heat with anger, but she held it in check as she so often had to with her mother. "I don't think she's doing anything of the sort," she said with a calm she did not feel.

"You are not to *think* at all. Leave the thinking to your mother and father. Maggie would be wise to do the same."

Cheeks tinged red, Elizabeth stared unseeingly at the dancers. She would never understand her mother and she wondered when she would stop trying.

"I'm going to the powder room," she said, because she was so used to telling her mother every move she made.

"I see His Grace. I believe he is looking for you," she heard her mother say as she continued walking away. "Elizabeth! The duke!"

She kept walking, her fists unknowingly clenched, her teeth set, her mind raging. She walked past the powder room, down a long hallway with its gleaming marble floor, past a library, a sitting room, her eyes on a set of French doors at the very end of the dim corridor. She walked until she reached them, then stopped, hanging her head down as if walking that short distance was almost too much for her. Then, lifting her head, she pushed open the doors, letting them fly and bounce against the wall, letting them fall closed with a bang as the cool night air touched her heated cheeks.

"I can't even relieve myself without permission," she whispered. She found herself on a small terrace on the side of the house. It was empty of everything but a single chair set in one corner. Perfect. She sat down in it, brought her knees up and hugged them against her, not caring at the moment that she wrinkled her gown terribly. She sat there for a few minutes before setting her feet flat on the stone surface, letting out a long sigh as she smoothed her skirts. Before long, the duke would be gone on his sightseeing trip and she would shop for her trousseau and then Christmas would come and her wedding. Her wedding. A baby. A boy. Please let the first child be a boy so she could be free. Elizabeth wasn't even certain what she would do with such freedom. She knew only that should she have a girl she would never force her to marry or even sit up straight or wash or eat with utensils. She would raise her to be wholly wild. Despite herself, Elizabeth laughed at her own thoughts.

The muted sound of a waltz came to her through the night air, as well as the closer sounds of a mosquito. She waved her hand in front of her face, grimacing. The bugs would force her inside where she would find the disapproving look of her mother and perhaps the disappointed look of the duke. She stood and gave a deep curtsy. "Her Grace, the Duchess of Bellingham," she said, trying to match the lofty tones of a footman. It simply felt silly and wrong. She cleared her throat. "Mrs. Henry Ellsworth."

A small furrow formed between her brows, because that didn't sound quite right either.

"Miss Elizabeth Cummings." She gave a wistful smile, because finally she found a title she felt comfortable with.

Chapter 11

His fiancée was avoiding him. She obviously did not care if she knew him when they married. They had spent only a small amount of time together before he'd proposed, and that had only been because her parents were sick with worry that she'd elope with a fortune hunter. He wondered if Miss Cummings were foolish enough to try to elope anyway. God help her if she did.

Rand found this entire thing humiliating enough, he refused to chase after a woman who clearly did not want to be found. For the past week, he'd attended balls, picnics, concerts, and lavish dinners and exchanged no more than a few polite sentences with the girl. It was damned irritating. What was more irritating was that he could not get her out of his mind. It was almost as if he were infatuated with her, something that had not happened in years. When he was in the Guards, women were so easily obtained it had been more sport than romance. Married women, he supposed, knew better than to fall in love with a young officer and a second son at that. He kept remembering that kiss, brief though it had been. He'd kissed a hundred women, why couldn't he get that one less-than-satisfying one from his mind? Perhaps that was it. He'd never in his life kissed a woman who hadn't wanted him to. It bothered him, wondering whether or not she found him lacking.

Rand dragged a hand through his thick hair in frustration. He did not want to marry a stranger, but it appeared he was going to. He had but one week left before he and Edward left on their small tour of America and would return to New York just days before the planned wedding. And she knew it, damn her.

Rand decided that in order for his future bride to stop avoiding him, he would have to confine her to a very small space. They were going for a ride and it was not going to be down Bellevue Avenue where everyone would be spying on them. He would drive her to Portsmouth, to the pretty New England farms that stretched out along the Atlantic. He and Edward had ridden out there not two days ago, finding it pastoral with gently rolling hills and sturdy stone walls, and reminding him very much of the Yorkshire countryside. Riding out among green fields he understood for the first time why the first settlers had dubbed the area *New* England.

He drove up to Sea Cliff with a rented horse and phaeton to find Elizabeth waiting for him near one of the grand classical pillars that adorned the front of the grand house. With her was a maid, for her mother was a stickler for propriety.

"A beautiful day for a ride," Rand said, looking up to a sky filled only with puffy white clouds, the kind one could see shapes in.

"Indeed," Elizabeth said, stepping forward and taking his hand to be put up into the phaeton. She smiled, but it was only polite, not welcoming and certainly not joyful. The poor maid struggled with a basket, so Rand took it from her, raising his eyebrows at its weight. He placed it on the boot, then helped the maid onto the narrow cushion seat there.

"Are we expecting company?" he asked Elizabeth lightly and stared in disbelief when he saw her cheeks blush.

"I thought that instead of riding to Portsmouth, we could go to Bailey Beach. It's so much cooler there and I do belief Miss Pierce and Lord Hollings were planning an outing—"

"No."

She put her jaw out mulishly, then smiled. "Wouldn't it be more fun with people about?"

"I am ecstatic to be only in your company."

"But Bailey is something you really should not miss. It's quite nice there when the seaweed is thin," she said, wrinkling her nose at some remembered stench.

"We can go tomorrow. Today we are riding out to Portsmouth."

He could almost hear her teeth grinding together and had to stop himself from losing his temper with her. Was an afternoon alone with him so distasteful that she would go to such lengths to avoid it? He swallowed down a sharp retort, told himself to be patient with her, and swung himself up onto the phaeton.

"Would you care to drive?" he asked. She looked at

him with shock, then finally showed the delighted smile he'd been hoping to see.

"Are you certain?" she asked, taking hold of the reins and looking around her as if she were doing something naughty. "I haven't done this in years so you must be ready to take over at the slightest notice." She turned back to her maid with a laugh. "You'd better hang on well, Millie, there's no telling what can happen now."

And with a nice little flick of the reins, she got the pretty bay moving forward. Grinning happily, she looked over to Rand, her face glowing with excitement. He realized that it would probably take very little to make her happy, just a bit of freedom, allowing her to do things her mother had probably forbidden her to do.

"All right then, you're doing fine," he said as they approached the entrance to Bellevue Avenue. "Pull gently, now."

"I have done this," she said, sounding slightly indignant. Then she gave him another grin. "It was a pony cart, but it's the same basic principle, is it not?"

"Oh, Lord," he heard Millie mutter from behind them.

Elizabeth seemed nervous, but also exhilarated as she held the horse waiting for a small amount of traffic to clear. "If you see a motorcar coming toward us, take over," she said, then flicked the reins and pulled onto Bellevue going, Rand noted happily, in the direction of Portsmouth.

"Do you have many in Newport?" Rand asked, surprised.

"No," she said a bit sheepishly. "But I wanted you to be prepared for anything. I did see one in France last year."

Rand began to relax now that he could see she was doing fine with the phaeton. "Did you? I have not had the opportunity as yet. Edward has. Lord Hollings, that is. He said it was magnificent."

Elizabeth let out another delighted laugh, her blue eyes glued to the road ahead. A tricky intersection was coming up and she deftly slowed the phaeton down. "I would not call that contraption magnificent. It seemed rather loud and smelly to me."

"More smelly than a horse?"

"Perhaps not," she agreed. "Whoa."

She pulled on the reins a bit too harshly, the over-reaction of a novice driver. Rand immediately put his hands over her gloved ones and adjusted the tension. "There. Don't overreact or your horse will, too."

"I know," she said, angry with herself.

"It takes practice," he said, letting go of her hands that had held the reins so tightly, he clearly felt her rigid knuckles through her silk gloves.

Before long they were out in the countryside, Elizabeth still at the reins, seemingly enjoying herself more than he'd ever witnessed before. Newport, and the traffic, was left far behind and they drove along the smooth, hard-packed sandy roads lined by farms and small forests, glimpsing Narragansett Bay in the distance. Rand directed Elizabeth down a narrow road that led in the direction of the bay, leading her to a private little spot overlooking the blue waters and the mainland beyond.

"It's lovely," Elizabeth said, handing the reins over to

Rand and dusting off her gloves. "Thank you for letting me drive. It's the most fun I've had in months."

Rand hopped down, then went around to help her down, and would have helped Millie, but she was already on the ground trying to heave the basket out of the phaeton. "Here," he said, rushing around and grasping the basket. He let out an exaggerated groan at its weight.

"What do you say we take what we need and leave the rest for Millie to sort out," he said, opening the basket. He laid out a blanket and started tossing food into it while Millie fluttered nearby making small sounds of protest. He gathered the blanket up and hefted it over one shoulder. "There we go. That should be enough to feed us twice over. Millie, you may sit beneath that tree and eat to your heart's content. Take a nap, if you like. Miss Cummings and I will be right down that small path, just a few yards away. I assure you, you will hear Miss Cummings scream if I decide to push her off the cliff and into the bay." Millie giggled. "Enjoy your free time," he said, and began walking down the narrow path fully expecting Elizabeth to follow behind.

He heard her whisper something fiercely to Millie before she lifted the skirts of her white and green-striped dress and hurried after him. "I don't believe Mother intended for us to abandon Millie," she said when she reached him.

"I don't care what your mother intended," he said, then turned toward her. "Do you?" It was a challenge and he could see she knew it.

A smile formed on her lips so slowly that at first Rand didn't recognize it as such. Then it bloomed, lighting her face, and he grinned back at her. "You know," he said, turning back to the path. "You really are quite pretty when you smile. I wasn't certain I could stand looking at you for a lifetime until I saw it."

He heard a snort that could have been a stifled laugh or a sound of outrage. He didn't know and didn't care. It was a beautiful day and he was on a picnic—alone— with a beautiful girl who would in just a few short months be his wife. For the first time in a long time, the future seemed a little bit brighter.

"Here we are," Rand said, after they'd walked a short way through some tall reeds. It wasn't much of a cliff, more of a gentle drop-off that probably wouldn't kill a kitten should it stumble from the edge. But it was a pretty spot and secluded with nary another soul in sight but for some fishermen down the bay on a small skiff. Rand dropped the blanket and spread it out to examine what he'd so hastily dropped into it.

Elizabeth eyed him with some uncertainty, then fell to her knees to see what he'd managed to pilfer from the basket. "Oh," she said, a note of dismay. Her gloves, which were not made for anything more strenuous than holding a parasol, were quite ruined. With a small frown, she peeled them off and tugged loose the broad green ribbon that kept her straw hat from flying off, placing it by her gloves.

"Do continue," the duke said, a devilish gleam in his eyes.

Elizabeth pursed her lips and considered putting her gloves and hat back on just to spite him. But it was warm here, despite the shaded area and the bay below them.

"I'm perfectly fine," she said, trying to sound haughty and failing miserably. She didn't feel haughty at the moment and didn't want to expend the energy to be so. The duke was being very charming and she found herself having far more fun than she would have expected.

"I believe I owe you an apology," she said, placing a large piece of fried chicken onto a napkin and handing it to him.

"Oh?"

There was nothing to do but plunge ahead, so she did. "I have been avoiding you for the past week and for that I am sorry."

"I know you have."

She grimaced. "I expected you would," she said, keeping her eyes on the business of dividing up the food. He clearly had put no thought to what he'd thrown on the blanket, for it appeared he'd put three different desserts and very little actual food. She sat back on her heels and finally looked at him, fearing he'd be angry. Instead, he was looking at her steadily as if trying to see what her thoughts were. His dark gray eyes were disconcerting in their intensity and she quickly pretended to be interested in her piece of chicken.

"What other things do you enjoy, other than tearing down the streets on a phaeton?"

"I'd hardly call what I was doing as 'tearing,'" she said. "I like riding bicycles."

"So you've said."

Elizabeth was momentarily confused, until she remembered that during one of their very few conversations she had mentioned riding bicycles. She shrugged.

"I think it would be better to tell you what I dislike. I dislike hunting, swimming, and boats. My father, as you well know, has a yacht, which he insists we must use for long trips. My seasickness is truly a curse. I cannot even sit on a rowboat in a placid lake without feeling ill. I adore Paris, but the thought of getting on a boat and sailing there is enough to stop me from going. I truly thought I would die when we went to England last year. And then my mother, who has a stomach made of iron, insisted we go to Paris. I have to tell you, I have never been so frightened in my life. On a map, the channel doesn't seem particularly large or daunting. It was purely dreadful."

The duke laughed aloud.

"So glad that you find my misery amusing," she said dryly, producing another chuckle.

"You will be happy to know that once we reach England we will be there for a fair number of years. I've too much work to do to leave anytime soon."

"Oh?"

He looked down, as if regretting saying anything about his plans. Tossing the well-picked bone onto a napkin, he said, "My ancestral home is in need of work, as well as the tenants' homes. I fear it will take years before I can return it to its former glory."

Years and my father's money. Neither said such a crass thing, but Elizabeth knew what he was thinking. She wouldn't have thought it should bother him. After all, it was well-known between the two of them why he was here. "What will be my duchessily duties?" she asked, having fun with him.

"Duchessily?" He raised an eyebrow and one corner of his mouth tilted up. "I imagine you'll have plenty to do," he said, dismissively.

"You don't know, do you?" she asked, stunned.

"I hardly do. I was not home very much growing up and even when I was I didn't pay attention to what my mother did. She liked to garden."

She felt her stomach sinking slightly. "Oh," she said, a bit bewildered. "Do you think your mother could help me?"

She might as well have asked if the devil could help her, so horrified was his expression. "Does your mother not want to help me?"

"My mother."

"Yes, she is alive, is she not?"

His brows furrowed and the sinking feeling got worse. "She's not, that is to say, she's unaware that I will be returning to Bellewood with a bride."

She stared at him, her mouth slightly agape. "I don't understand."

Suddenly he grabbed her hand, holding firmly even when she would pull away.

"Brace yourself, Miss Cummings," he said, making her trepidation grow in bounds. "My mother is a terrible snob. She makes your mother seem like a socialist. I did mean to tell you about her." He made a sick face. "Some day. Before you actually met her. She is not going to be happy about this marriage."

"Because I am an American?"

He nodded, still holding her hand, and suddenly she

was glad he had. "And because you are not a member of the peerage. She had a list, you see."

"A list?"

"A list very much like the one your mother had. A list of titled gentlemen. But my mother's is an extensive list of the daughters of peers. It was for my brother, of course. She hasn't had time to start browbeating me with it."

Elizabeth swallowed heavily. The only thing that was good about her marriage was her escape from her mother. But, if what the duke was saying was true, she was simply going from the pot into the fire. She started to laugh. For her entire life, her mother's primary goal was to get her a fantastic match, a match that would make every mama green with jealousy, the highest title could only be what her daughter would deserve. Never had either of them thought that Elizabeth would be considered unworthy of anyone. The Cummings were second to none in American aristocracy, but they were commoners, rich upstarts, to anyone else.

"Why are you laughing?" he asking, pulling a bit on her hand. "I've just told you the most disturbing thing."

Elizabeth waved her free hand at him, begging him to stop talking so that she might stop laughing. "Oh, it is too, too funny," she gasped. "You are marrying a peasant. And I am marrying a pauper," she said, nearly losing her breath she was laughing so. Tears of mirth streamed down her face. "Don't you think that is ridiculous? All this maneuvering and machinations and crying and look at us."

The duke put a hand on either side of her head.

"That's what I've been trying to tell you," he said, smiling at her. "But we can get through this. All of this."

She sobered suddenly and gazed at him, feeling as if real tears were only a heartbeat away. "Do you think so, Your Grace?"

"Please call me Randall," he said, his eyes drifting to her mouth so that she knew he was going to kiss her. He moved closer, until his mouth was so close, she could feel his breath against her lips. "Please."

"Rand—" He stopped her with his mouth on hers and she found herself leaning toward him, still on her knees, her hands clenched by her sides. He moved his mouth gently, but his body was taut against hers, as if he were straining against a terrible weight. Henry had never kissed her. Never. And this man was kissing her for the second time, making her feel liquid and hot and confused. She didn't like it, and yet something stopped her from pulling away, something animal and base and full of need that had nothing to do with whether she liked him or not. She put her hands, still clenched tightly, upon his shoulders, not knowing whether to pull him closer or push him away, so she let out a little sound.

He pulled back, his eyes holding a strange light. "Miss Cummings," he said with a bemused smile. "I am not going to murder you, I promise." He glanced at each shoulder where her fists were still clenched. She looked up at him uncertainly, then slowly unfurled her hands. "Much better. Now, your mouth."

"My mouth?"

"It is much more pleasant to kiss when it is not hard as stone," he said.

He was making fun of her. How should she know how
to kiss when no one had ever taught her? Was there a
right and wrong way to kiss? From what she'd seen, it
was a mere pressing of the lips, and that's exactly what
she was doing. She wished that Henry had not been such
a gentleman, for then she would be able to show His
Grace she knew something about kissing. She felt her
face grow hot with anger and a bit of embarrassment.
"I am so sorry my lips are not to your liking," she said.

"Oh, no, Elizabeth," he said softly. "Your lips are
very, very much to my liking." He touched them with
the pad of his thumb and she pressed them closed.
"Relax, love. Relax." He kept moving his thumb over
her lower lip, creating such a dizzying sensation she
didn't stiffen when he brought his head closer. "Relax,"
he said, his mouth against his own thumb, which continued to move in such a seductive way against her. For
once, he didn't sound imperious or even like a duke, for
he was asking, beseeching her, really, and that seemed
to make all the difference. He dropped his thumb away
and his mouth, warm and soft and hard, pulled at her
lower lip and she let out a sigh. "There," he breathed.
Elizabeth clutched at his shoulders only because if she
had let go, she surely would have melted to the blanket. She could not have imagined that a man's lips
against hers would feel so completely . . . intoxicating.

And then, his tongue, touching her mouth, moving
inside, and she felt as if something were taking hold
of her, something wild and free and desperate. How did
he know such things? His mouth moved against hers,
and with a groan, he deepened the kiss and she let him,

welcomed him, suddenly forgetting she was nervous, forgetting she did not want to be with him. Forgetting to wish he was Henry. Oh, Lord, his kisses made her forget even who she was.

Finally, he drew back, his forehead against hers. "That was much better," he said, laughing a bit. "You are a very good student, my dear."

She smiled, ridiculously proud that he seemed so flushed, that she had somehow made him feel the same breathless way he made her feel.

"Do you know how to swim?" he asked suddenly, jarring her senses yet again. She still knelt, still held her hands against his shoulders, still felt his hands in her hair, strong and sure and oddly wonderful.

"No."

"Then why did you want to go to the beach?"

They found themselves grinning at each other.

"To avoid just this situation," she said, trying to sound affronted but failing miserably.

"I like this situation," he said. He gave her a quick kiss, then pulled back to grab one of the small lemon tarts cook had packed.

She slumped back onto her heels and stared at him through narrowed eyes. Then, without a word, she took one of the tarts and bit into it, almost as if daring him to stop her. It was a small bit of rebellion and one he would never know. Her mother had forbidden her from eating sweets, so she ate this one with relish. And when she was done, she took up another, wondering what it was about this man that made her act and do things she had never done before.

Chapter 12

Alva Cummings was in her glory. No one, other than perhaps Caroline Astor, could come close to organizing a grand ball the way she could. It was all a matter of spending more money, making everything more lavish, inviting more important people than anyone else could. And for her daughter's engagement ball, the last of the summer season, Alva had outdone herself.

Elizabeth suspected that all those weeks where she had been confined to her room and the weeks that followed, her mother had been planning this event, for there was no way she could have affected such a ball if she had not spent weeks and even months planning it.

Elizabeth's suspicions were confirmed when she realized the favors for the cotillion were antique French etchings, fans, and gilded ribbon that her mother had brought back last year from Paris. The beautifully intricate Chinese lanterns were little duplicates of Sea Cliff that had come directly from China. It made Elizabeth realize that, as much as she'd longed to have some control over her life, she never really had any. Her mother had never sought her opinion on anything, not even the wedding dress that was secreted in the New York home, which Alva had ordered from Charles Worth. Every detail, from the ornate dance cards to the gold-trimmed, silver napkin rings, had been chosen by her mother months ago.

Despite a tinge of resentment, Elizabeth couldn't help but marvel at what her mother had accomplished. At the end of the grand hallway, a brass fountain, filled with blooming flowers, had been erected. Hyacinths, lilacs, and a tower of pale pink hollyhocks surrounded the fountain, and tiny hummingbirds seemed to float above the miniature garden. Forty small tables, covered in fine Irish linen, were set up in the dining hall and spilled out onto the veranda. The terrace was filled with exotic plants, including ferns and palms trees. And, as if Alva had control over the heavens, it was a spectacularly beautiful night.

Alva didn't stop with simply decorating the house, the lawn was turned into a fairy land, with palm trees lit by butterfly fairy lamps. As dusk fell, the mansion became more beautiful, an enchanted palace. Elizabeth wandered about the house and grounds before the guests arrived amazed at what she saw, and realized with a bit of panic that she would be expected to produce this kind of grandeur for the duke. She had never seen anything quite so beautiful as Sea Cliff on the night of her ball.

"There you are, Elizabeth. It's time for us to get dressed," Alva said, looking about the gilt ballroom one last time.

"Everything is wonderful, Mother," Elizabeth said, feeling a sudden overwhelming tenderness for her mother.

Alva let out a quick breath, as if she didn't have time for more, and said, "Let us hope everything goes as planned."

"I don't see how it cannot for you have planned so well."

Alva gave her daughter a quick smile. "Up to dress. And do please stop by my rooms before you venture downstairs. I want us all to go down together just in case some early guests have arrived. Then we'll greet everyone in the pink room," she reminded her for the third time.

Elizabeth followed her mother's brisk steps up the stairs at a bit more leisurely pace. Even though she was getting on well with the duke, her heart still ached for Henry. She'd kept his rose, now blackened and dried, in a small drawer by her bed and took it out each night before trying to sleep. Everyone would think her quite foolish for still loving him, but she simply could not turn her heart off as much as she wished she could. Henry had been so fervent, so completely enraptured by her, and that was a heady thing, indeed.

The duke . . . he was still such a stranger to her. Though he'd been in Newport for several weeks and everyone knew of the engagement, the ball was to be the formal announcement. Elizabeth hadn't been alone with the duke in three days, and had only exchanged polite words well in the earshot of her mother. He was formal and stiff and not at all like the man who taught her how to kiss, who let her hold the reins and dared her to race to town. He hardly even held her eyes, and she wondered why she even wanted him to. It was maddening to think that she would not be able to know any more about him before their wedding. She had so many questions, about his childhood, about Bellewood, about what he expected from her. It was all a swirl of unknown.

Her gown was laid out on her bed, and finally her

mother had allowed her to dress the part of a debutante. It was white satin, trimmed with rich white lace, a dress that had been remade from one her grandmother had worn for her engagement. That, as everything else, was dictated by her mother. Her gown, the heavy, diamond-studded tiara that sat so regally in her hair, even her shoes, which her mother had ordered small, because she refused to acknowledge that her daughter's feet were larger than they should be, were all ordered by Alva. Elizabeth had stopped resenting it, and rode upon her mother's plan like a piece of flotsam on an endless wave. Straighten your back. She straightened. Lift your chin. She lifted. Smile dear, smile. She smiled. And then, when the first guests started to arrive, when she stood next to the duke, she was let free and expected to act properly on her own, with only her mother's words in her head.

"You are beautiful tonight," the duke said, when there was a brief break in the line. She could not think of him as Randall. Not here in this formal setting.

Elizabeth thought she looked silly, like a little girl playing dress-up wearing a faux crown. Her mother had insisted on the lavish tiara, but Elizabeth was slightly embarrassed by it, as if she were trying to be something she was not. But she took the duke's compliment nicely and thanked him and told him he looked very fine in his formal outfit. He seemed stiffer, if possible, than she'd ever seen him and she remembered that he disliked such events. He bowed and shook hands and nodded when appropriate, but he rarely smiled. Then again, neither did she. By the time the Cummings were done greeting guests, Mullally's Orchestra had begun to play for the informal dance before the light dinner. Already she was exhausted and the evening wouldn't end until at least four in the morning.

"Would you care to dance?" the duke asked, coming to stand in front of her and bowing.

She looked up at him in surprise. He was a different man, this evening, far more formal than he'd ever been before. He held out a stiff arm, his gloved hand curled in a loose fist.

He leaned toward her slightly. "Your mother wants us to begin the ball," he said.

And so for the first few strains of a Strauss waltz, they danced alone on the gleaming marble floor, unsmiling and self-conscious beneath the gaze of everyone in attendance. The women sighed aloud and Elizabeth heard a smattering of manly chuckles. How she hated being the center of such attention, and her cheeks flushed knowing even as they did that everyone would take note and wonder why. They would suppose, she thought, that she was blushing for the duke, that it was the bloom of love or some such silliness. And to spite them, she refused to smile, refused even to look at the duke to see how he was faring. They didn't talk, even when the others joined them on the dance floor. When the waltz ended, the duke bowed before her, held out his arm, and escorted her to her father.

"Sir," he said, before handing her off and giving her a small bow. She curtsied, feeling silly and had to stop herself from putting her hand on his arm to stop him. He had kissed her, he had brushed his mouth against hers, and this night he hardly looked at her. Elizabeth danced with her father, with Maggie's brother, with Mr. Belmont and Major Gibbs. It was her duty to dance every dance, to never falter, to never yawn or beg to sit. By the time dinner was announced, Elizabeth thought she would faint from thirst and hunger. But she sat with her mother and father and the duke even though she longed to sit with Maggie and the earl. They looked like they were having so much fun, while she felt as if she even dared smile her mother would give her a *look*.

"I hope you're finding everything in Newport to your satisfaction, Your Grace," Alva said pleasantly.

"I am, indeed, Mrs. Cummings. Yesterday I took in a bit of tennis at your Casino. Quite nice," the duke said.

"I heard you play well," Jason Cummings said. "Never was one much for running about whacking a ball. Too old, I suppose. It's a young man's sport."

"Or young woman's, Father," Elizabeth said, and got a severe look from her mother.

The look did not escape Rand. Every time the poor girl opened her mouth she got some sort of reaction from her mother and usually it was not favorable. He continued to be amazed that the girl she was in front of her mother was not at all the woman he saw when they were alone. He was trying his best to act formal at this ball in particular, for every word he uttered, every look he gave her would be noted by someone. He'd even seen some sort of reporter wandering about the place and been told the gent was from the *New York Times*.

"I suppose you're right," Jason said. "I hear the Canfield girls are quite good."

Alva let out a light laugh, that was somehow cutting. "The Canfield girls are so exuberant on the court," she said in her sweet southern drawl that Rand noticed she affected when she was particularly offended by something. He was still getting used to all these American

accents, surprisingly as varied as England, though more
difficult to discern. Unlike Britain, where the educated
aristocracy sounded much alike, the Americans did not.
Bostonians sounded nothing like the southerners, though
they could be equally held in esteem. Elizabeth sounded
nothing like her mother, whose southern drawl could be
so pronounced.

A footman came to whisper something in Alva's ear and
she instantly lost her pleasant look. "If you'll excuse me,"
she said, and got up from the table to handle whatever disaster had befallen the Cummings' ball. Once she was gone,
Elizabeth visibly relaxed, and Rand was self-deprecatingly
aware that he did, too.

"Your mother and my mother would either be best of
friends or mortal enemies," Rand said near Elizabeth's
ear. She stiffened, and he thought at first that he'd insulted her mother. But he looked at her mouth and could
tell she was, rather desperately, trying not to laugh
aloud. Then she shushed him.

"You are not allowed to shush a duke," he said softly,
if not imperiously.

"And you are not allowed to make sport of your
duchess's mother," she shot back.

He lowered his head and laughed. "You are not my
duchess yet."

She looked at him askance, as if she feared she may have
insulted him somehow, but looked decidedly unrepentant.

Impulsively, he put his hand around her left wrist, which
lay on her lap. "I have missed you," he said, and she looked
at him with such shock, he nearly laughed again.

"You saw me two days ago."

He withdrew his hand and tried not to be disappointed

in her response, but he did feel rather idiotic to have blurted such a thing. "Quite so," he said. "But I should have liked to have gone on another picnic." She immediately stared at her Cornish hen with heightened intensity. Rand, who never felt foolish with women, found himself acting like a moonstruck youth. He rather felt like one at the moment. Of course she'd be thinking of their kiss. It wasn't as if he didn't want to kiss her again, and far more, but he'd only meant that he wanted to be alone with her in a setting far less formal than this. So they could talk. And kiss.

Just like that, he grew hard, just from *thinking* about kissing her, just from sitting by her, from touching her wrist.

And she was carefully sawing through her Cornish hen probably wishing he was still in England. His humiliation was complete.

Then she turned to him, her blue eyes wide, staring at him as if willing him to know what was in her head. His eyes drifted downward to her mouth, her plump lower lip, the freckle, my God, the freckle at one corner that he'd not noticed before, and he saw that she was smiling a Mona Lisa smile, like she shared a secret.

He grinned at her, feeling relief rush through him just as fast and hard as lust had.

"I do enjoy picnics," she said, her gaze direct and unwavering and Rand had a difficult time not leaning forward and kissing her, giving these pseudo-peers something really interesting to talk about.

I do believe I'm falling in love with you. "Then we shall picnic every day when we are married," he said, and watched her smile broaden just a bit.

Chapter 13

"You have gone too far, Mother," Elizabeth said, holding up a copy of the society gossip magazine, *Town Topics*.

"I have no idea what you are talking about," Alva said, but she gave the magazine a quick look before schooling her features.

Elizabeth held the magazine up to the fading light to read for her mother: "'We have discovered that Miss Cummings will wear a corset cover and chemise embroidered with rosebuds and that her clasps are made of gold.' My underclothes are no one's business but my own."

Alva waved a hand at her distraught daughter. "Oh, they just wanted a little tidbit. I think it's delightful how many people are curious about your wedding. It's already being called the wedding of the century."

"Better the farce of the century," Elizabeth said bitterly. The past months had been a long nightmare of wedding plans. Her mother did not bother consulting her on a single detail, including whom would be selected as her bridesmaids. She'd confronted her mother tearfully when she realized Maggie wasn't standing up by her simply because her pedigree didn't match some of the other girls. Worse, she'd included Charlotte Grayson, a girl she actually disliked. Her mother wouldn't budge on the issue.

She hadn't seen the duke at all, though about a month after his departure he'd sent her a pair of lovely silk-lined kidskin gloves. He'd sent no note, but she knew immediately they were from the duke. It was such a thoughtful gift that she'd held them in her hands for several minutes before putting them aside. And then, a week later came a box full of lemon tarts, which her mother immediately confiscated. "Why ever would the duke send this?" she said, before giving the tarts to their housekeeper to disperse among the servants.

In addition to the small gifts, he wrote several polite letters that read more like travelogues than letters from a fiancé. It bothered her more than a little that he signed the letters "Yours Truly, the Duke of Bellingham." She would take out those gloves and put them on and wonder if he truly could know how much those gloves could mean to her. She could hardly remember what he looked like, and her trepidation about marrying a stranger increased daily. That picnic they'd shared seemed very long ago.

Her appearances in New York had been carefully staged by her mother, who gloried each time *Town Topics* or the *New York Times* put her name in the paper. The *Times* had printed exhaustive details of the wedding, including the type of floral arrangements, the order of songs, the people attending, the food to be served at the reception. The reporters knew more about her wedding than she did. People were beginning to hang about the front of their Fifth Avenue mansion on the hope that they would get a glimpse of a future duchess.

"My life has become a circus," she said dramatically. And even that statement couldn't ruffle Alva's feathers. "Don't you care that I'm suffering?"

"Not in the least," Alva said sharply. "I only care that you are an ungrateful girl."

Elizabeth let out a huff of frustration and threw herself down upon a settee. Before her mother could utter a word about sitting up straight, she did so, with great flourish.

"I know these past weeks have been difficult for you," Alva said nonchalantly. "That is why I have arranged for you and Margaret to go out shopping. Quite anonymously, of course."

"Truly, Mother?" Elizabeth said, so happy she couldn't stop herself from throwing her arms around her mother. Alva suffered her daughter's spontaneous affection for the space of perhaps three seconds before she gently pushed Elizabeth away.

"If you leave before nine o'clock I doubt anyone will spy you leaving in the plain carriage. Wear a shirtwaist and skirt and your dark cloak. No muff, of course, and that little velvet hat, you know, the one with the small white feather? You should probably remove the feather," she said thoughtfully. "You may take this time to purchase your Christmas gifts. I suggest something nice for the duke would be appropriate. He will be your husband, after all."

With a sinking feeling, Elizabeth suspected her mother already had picked the item out. Still, she asked, "What would you suggest?"

Alva smiled. "I took the liberty of buying something for him."

"Quelle surprise," Elizabeth muttered.

Alva's smile disappeared, but she continued undaunted. "I knew how busy you were going to be and likely would not have the time for such a frivolous thing. If you stop by Tiffany's, they have the most wonderful fountain pens. Your father said the duke admired his, so I ordered one for him. It's beautifully engraved."

"I'm certain it is. Thank you, Mother." Elizabeth could forgive her mother's presumptuousness if she was going to be allowed a day of freedom and shopping with her dearest friend. That night she went to bed with a smile on her face for the first time in months.

Maggie and Elizabeth were beside themselves with excitement. They felt like spies, peeking out the windows of their simple carriage to see if anyone were following them. Elizabeth hadn't had such fun in ages, and she prayed no one recognized her. The drive to Broadway took nearly thirty minutes, for traffic was heavy with Christmas shoppers. The city was decorated with trees and garland, and everywhere people were bundled up against the frigid winter air. There was a wonderful festive air about the city, and the girls, filled with cheer and heady with freedom, giggled like schoolgirls. A snowfall a week ago left the streets wet and muddy, and the small piles that remained along the walkways were dirty. Along Barclay Street, a man was selling Christmas trees from a great pile stacked in the middle of the road.

"I do hope it snows before your wedding so all this dirty stuff is covered," Maggie said, wrinkling her nose at the mud-covered slush. She looked up to the gray sky. "It might snow a bit today. It feels like snow, doesn't it?"

"What does snow feel like?" Elizabeth asked, smiling.

"Like it feels today. Like snow. Oh, I just love the Christmas season. It just does something to me. It's magical. And with you getting married, it's going to be even more magical."

Maggie's good cheer was contagious, and Elizabeth wouldn't even let talk of her wedding bring her down. "It is rather all exciting, I suppose."

"What's wrong?"

"I haven't seen the duke since August. *August*. It's almost as if he doesn't exist at all, that some stranger could be standing at the end of the altar and I wouldn't know the difference. I'm just nervous, I suppose."

"I'd be a fright," Maggie gushed. "Imagine all those people. They'll be throngs outside St. Thomas's. I heard they'll be putting extra police out just for that. Can you imagine? I don't expect anyone to be hanging about when I get married. *If* I get married." Maggie gave a rare frown but nearly instantly recovered. "Have you heard from the duke lately? The last you told he was in Washington."

Elizabeth examined her gloves. "He's in New York now. Staying at the Waldorf, of course. He's written fairly regularly and sent some lovely postcards. He's been very thoughtful." She let out a sigh. "Have you heard from Lord Hollings?"

Maggie smiled. "Why ever would I?"

"It seemed to me you spent quite a bit of time

together in Newport. I thought perhaps you had found yourself an earl and we could be neighbors. Two Americans taking those English by storm. I was hoping, secretly."

"Lord Hollings and I had an agreement," Maggie said laughing. "He would stay by my side to dissuade those Wright boys from hounding me, and I would stay by his side to get those marriage-minded mothers away from him. My mother is beside herself, of course. I think she was already trying to think of ways to get me to Europe to buy my trousseau. It was fabulous fun at the time, but poor Mama. I think she truly is heartbroken and I feel a bit guilty. More than a bit, really."

Elizabeth gave her friend a friendly smack on her arm. "I cannot believe you didn't tell me about this. It would have been such fun."

"You were a bit preoccupied this summer, if you remember."

"Just a bit," Elizabeth said, as the carriage pulled over to the side of Broadway. "We're here. It shouldn't take long to fetch the pen, and then we're on our own." The footman helped the women down from the carriage and into the throng of Christmas shoppers. "Look, Maggie, it's begun to snow. How wonderful if it keeps up."

"Enough to cover St. Thomas's and close down the city?" Maggie suggested.

"Mother would find a way to clear every speck of snow from the streets, so such a wish would be futile," she grumbled. "Look," Elizabeth said, pointing to the famous clock above Tiffany's entrance. "It's only half past nine. We have hours and hours before I have to be home.

We're having a small dinner tonight. Only fifty people or so," Elizabeth said, laughing. "And His Grace will be there as well. I am quite nervous about the entire thing."

Maggie linked arms with Elizabeth as they crossed the street. "You shall be fine. This snow is a good omen, you'll see."

The two girls entered Tiffany's smiling widely at the scene before them. It seemed every New York male was in the store buying some trinket for their wives and daughters. They all had similar looks of desperation on their faces, for Christmas was only two days away.

Elizabeth found a clerk and asked him to find her mother's order.

"Oh, Miss Cummings," the clerk gushed.

Maggie held a finger to her mouth and shushed the blushing young man. "We're here incognito," she whispered, smiling mischievously. "No one is to know. No one. It certainly wouldn't do for the duke to know his Christmas present ahead of time, would it."

The clerk straightened. "No, miss. I'll be right back," he said furtively.

"Thank you, Maggie. I can't tell you how weary I am of all this attention. You can go look at those rings, I'll wait here. The fewer people who see me, the better."

Maggie wandered off, attracted by the beautiful necklaces on display for the Christmas season, and Elizabeth examined the case of fine fountain pens in front of her. Her mother's gift was a good idea, she thought as she took in the intricate designs on the pens, though she wished she knew the duke well enough to have come up with something a bit more personal.

"Elizabeth."

Elizabeth stiffened, her heart felt as if it stopped, and the blood seemed to drain from her head in a rush. She'd know that voice anywhere, that smooth, cultured wonderful voice. Henry.

"My God, it is you. My God," he said, and Elizabeth tried desperately to school her features into something less joyful.

She swallowed and turned, afraid she might faint. "Henry." She hadn't thought to ever see him again, but there he was, standing in front of her, looking so dear, so sad and disheveled, with a bit of melting snow still clinging to the shoulders of his overcoat. She'd forgotten how simply seeing him could affect her, how her heart would race. She'd truly thought she would never see him again, and yet here he was in Tiffany's staring at her as if she were the most precious thing on earth.

"Oh, my dear, I've been looking for you forever it seems," he said in a happy rush. "I didn't dare try to visit you. Every time I've been out in town, it seemed you had just left or hadn't yet arrived. The Oelrich affair. I was there, but you had gone. I've been going quite insane."

"Henry," Elizabeth said, ending on a bit of hysterical laughter. "I got your rose. It was you, wasn't it?"

"Yes. I couldn't bear to leave without sending you a token of my love. You have no idea how difficult it was to leave you. But your father was quite adamant, you see. Oh, here." He reached into his overcoat and pulled out a small envelope. "I've been carrying this around with me for weeks, hoping I would see you. Oh, Elizabeth, I've been going mad without you."

It was on the tip of Elizabeth's tongue to ask why he'd so easily been persuaded by her father, but she stopped herself, for he looked so incredibly distraught. "You shouldn't be here. You shouldn't be talking with me," she said instead. An unexpected surge of anger hit her, shocking her a bit, for as long as she'd known Henry she'd never been even a little bit angry with him. But how dare he come to her the day before her wedding and tear her apart this way. She'd thought she'd finally gotten over him, but seeing Henry again left her feeling raw and wounded and terribly confused.

"Here," he said, putting the envelope into her numb hand. Her entire body felt numb.

"What . . ."

He looked around as if fearful they would be caught. "Just take it, my dear." Elizabeth curled her hand around the paper, searching his eyes for some clue as to what the envelope contained.

"Elizabeth?" Maggie asked, coming up beside her, her voice brittle. Maggie did not bother hiding her displeasure at seeing Henry. "Are you all right?"

"Merry Christmas, Miss Cummings," Henry said, ignoring Maggie and giving the hand that held the small package a shake, silently beseeching her to remain silent about the gift.

"Yes," Elizabeth muttered. "Good-bye."

And then he was gone, melting away into the crowd, leaving Elizabeth standing in Tiffany's among a throng of men and women, swaying on her feet. Maggie grasped her arm.

"Elizabeth, what did he say to you?"

She hadn't seen. Maggie hadn't seen Henry give her

the package. She didn't know. For some reason, Elizabeth secreted the envelope in her reticule, and forcefully brought herself out of the shock Henry left her in.

"He wanted to wish me well," she said, staring blindly at the crush of people around them. If even one of them recognized her or Henry, her mother was certain to hear of it.

"He should have left you alone," Maggie said fiercely. "The very last thing you need right before your wedding is Henry coming to talk to you."

No, Elizabeth thought, the very last thing she needed was to marry a stranger, a man she didn't love. "You're right," she said instead. "He shouldn't have. But I'm fine. Really I am," Elizabeth insisted when Maggie gave her a frown.

"Miss Cummings, your purchase," the clerk said, handing her a beautiful rosewood box with intricate inlay that contained her future husband's wedding gift. Oh, God, she felt as if she were going to explode from all the feelings coursing through her. "Would you care to examine it before we wrap it for you?"

"That's not necessary," Elizabeth said absently. "Please just wrap it."

She should take the letter and throw it in the trash without reading it. She should ignore it, push it from her mind, pretend she'd never seen Henry, never seen the anguish in his eyes, never heard the despair in his voice. *Damn him,* she thought. *I was over him. I'd accepted what I was to do. I like the duke. I'm fairly certain I do.*

"Come on," Elizabeth said cheerfully after she'd tucked the duke's gift into her reticule beside Henry's package. "We've all kinds of time. Where do we go next?"

Maggie gave her a long look, but she smiled at Elizabeth. They walked from Tiffany's arm in arm, both pretending to be far happier than they were, and both thinking they were fooling each other. And themselves.

It was not only a letter, though that would have been more than enough to crush her. Inside the sturdy little envelope, well-worn and a bit tattered from staying inside Henry's overcoat all those weeks, was a small diamond heart centered by a tiny pearl dangling from a long, delicate chain. Elizabeth had waited in near agony for the privacy to open the letter. She'd arrived home and gone directly up to her room only to find her maid busily preparing the gown she was supposed to wear that very evening when the duke arrived for dinner. It seemed a lifetime before she bobbed a curtsy and left. Elizabeth carefully opened the envelope, as if even that were a precious thing, knowing even as she did so how foolish she was being.

My Dearest Beloved,

I cannot tell you how my heart aches at the thought of you being forced into a loveless match. I want you to know that you are loved, even if from afar. Wear this heart against you, keep it with you forever, as I will keep your heart with me. If I only see you from afar, I will know that you hold my heart. It is only a token, a promise that some day we will be together. Even if it is a sin, isn't it more of a sin that we have been torn from each other? Do what you must to deceive and be safe, pretend anything to get you

*through the months ahead and know that I will
always know the truth: that you love me alone.*

*Until we can be together, my darling,
H*

Elizabeth felt as if she were being torn in two. She
was angry with Henry to write such words, to suggest
such a sordid thing as adultery. And yet . . . when she had
seen him, she'd been so happy for that small instant
before she remembered her life had been inalterably
changed. She stared at her reflection in her vanity mirror,
asking the frightened, confused girl staring back at her
what she should do. She *knew* what she should do with
the letter, with the necklace. She knew, she knew. Even
as she placed the delicate chain around her neck, she
knew. Even as she put the letter between the pages of her
address book. She knew.

But she didn't.

Because this was one thing she could do that was her
own. All her life she'd been told what to eat, wear, say.
She'd been told who her friends ought to be, who she
could like, love. Marry. She told herself she didn't put
that chain around her neck for any other reason than that
she could, that no one would know about this small rebellion, that no one but her could know its significance,
could know that somewhere inside her, another Elizabeth lived, a far braver girl who could thwart her mother
and marry the man she loved. The girl in the mirror
could do all that. But the real one, the one sitting in her
darkened room was getting married tomorrow to a man
she hardly knew and certainly did not love.

Chapter 14

If Elizabeth had been nervous before her outing with Maggie, now she was completely unhinged. She couldn't bear to see the duke, she couldn't bear to do anything but sleep. And that is where her mother found her not twenty minutes before the guests began arriving.

"Elizabeth, are you ill? Please tell me you are not. It doesn't matter, we'll carry on, even if I have to wheel you into the church. Get up," she shouted when her tirade produced nothing but a groan from the sleeping lump on her daughter's bed. Nothing could get her out of this bed and dressed and ready to see fifty guests. Nothing could make her smile and pretend she was the giddy, happy bride-to-be.

She felt her bed dip as her mother sat down beside her. "Are you ill?" she asked again, this time with real concern in her voice.

"I think I am," Elizabeth muttered.

"Have you a fever? I'm certain it is just nerves. You should have seen me the night of my wedding. I couldn't sleep a wink. I was scared to death at what I had started. But, see, it's all worked out."

"I can't go down, Mother. Please understand."

"Elizabeth. There will be many, many times in your life when you do not feel like carrying on. But you must carry on. You must. This is one of those times. You cannot leave our guests waiting for you. They won't believe it if I tell them you are ill. And what of His Grace? He hasn't seen you in months. What is he to think?"

"I don't care."

"Elizabeth," her mother said sternly. "Sit up."

Groaning, she did. And then her mother slapped her face. "You silly, stupid girl. Get dressed immediately. And smile. And see that Millie fixes your face."

Her mother marched from the room fully expecting her daughter to comply. With one hand on her burning cheek, the other drifted to the chain around her neck and her small bit of rebellion. If this was all she had, it would have to be enough. At that moment wearing it had less to do with Henry than it did as a sign of her independence, as pathetic as that was.

Within moments, Millie appeared in her room and began pulling her things from her wardrobe she needed for the evening. "We haven't much time," she said. "I'll do your hair in a simple topknot this evening. That will make tomorrow seem so much better, don't you think, Miss?"

"That's fine, Millie," Elizabeth said, heaving herself out of bed. Despite her mother's slap, she still felt groggy and not quite herself. She looked in the mirror dreading seeing a handprint on her cheek, but was relieved to see it was simply a livid pink. If Millie made the other side as red, she'd end up looking like a clown. After donning her gown, Millie got a pot of rouge out but Elizabeth stopped her. "It's not so noticeable now," she said.

"But your mother—" Millie stopped abruptly, apparently seeing something in Elizabeth's gaze that halted her argument. "Perhaps if you just give the right cheek a bit of a pinch," she suggested as she picked up a brush. Millie made short work of her hair and Elizabeth found herself ready to greet guests a full five minutes before she was needed. She looked at her reflection quickly, checking only to see if the thin chain could be seen beneath the thick rope of pearls she wore.

Rand had been dreading this night for weeks. Soon after he'd left with Edward on his extended tour of the states, he realized it had been a mistake. At the time they'd planned it, the trip seemed like the perfect thing to do: see the girl, determine if she suited, propose, leave, marry, and go home. Now, he found himself a besotted idiot looking forward to seeing a girl he knew was probably not looking forward to seeing him. At least not to this degree. About one month into their tour, he suggested to Edward they could go to New York early, get to know the great city before they returned home. It was unlikely he would ever return to America, he explained. Edward's reaction was predictable. He accused Rand of being a lovesick calf, which Rand immediately denied, even though, damn it all, that was exactly what he'd become.

He'd been gone too long. The fledgling bond he had

shared with Elizabeth was sure to be diminished, if not erased all together, and they would face each other at the altar as the complete strangers he'd thought he wanted them to be. He tried to tell himself not to stare when he first saw her, but when he saw her come into the Grand Salon on her father's arm it was as if someone took a hammer to his stomach.

How had she become so beautiful? Her color was unusually high, her hair swept up in a simple style, piles and piles of it that he found he couldn't wait to take down and drown in.

Beside him, Edward nudged him and gave a soft "moo." It took him perhaps three seconds to realize his friend was calling him a lovesick calf. He gave him a sardonic grin, before turning back to Elizabeth, his heart full with the knowledge that in a mere twenty-four hours they would be alone, and very probably not nearly as fully clothed as they were at the moment.

"Your Grace," she said, dipping a curtsy. She didn't meet his eyes and instead rested her gaze on his tie.

"Miss Cummings."

Another curtsy. "Lord Hollings."

"Miss Cummings."

And then she moved on, greeting the other guests with the same warmth—or lack thereof—she'd shown him. He'd been standing there in near rapture at the sight of her and she'd greeted him as if he were one of her father's friends—and one she didn't know very well.

He looked over to Edward and shrugged when his friend raised a telling eyebrow.

"Is that your heart she just stepped on?" Edward asked lightly.

"No. My dignity."

Edward laughed. "What did you expect, her to rush into your arms in greeting? Never in my life have I seen a more proper girl. I daresay she wouldn't sneeze unless given permission."

"She has far more gumption than that," Rand said, looking at Elizabeth and missing the telling look Edward gave him.

"I wonder if her friend will be here tonight," Edward said.

"The talkative one? I haven't seen her."

"I shall be bored, then," he said, already sounding exceedingly bored. "I wonder what you shall do without me when you go on your honeymoon. Must you drag me about with you every time you go somewhere? These dinners are interminable."

Rand smiled at his friend's common complaint. "It is nearly over. You may take the first steamer to England after the wedding. Besides, what would you have done these past months? This was a grand adventure and you know it. Far better than being at home with your stepaunt and her overly large brood. You very well may benefit from all we learned."

"If I have to sit through one more lecture about agricultural advances, I shall become a drunkard. Our situations are far different, thank God." Rand would forever be grateful to his friend for tolerating his newfound passion for learning everything about farming. If he was going to make a success out of Bellewood, he would have to compete with the Americans and grow produce as cheaply and efficiently as they did.

"No more lectures and only one more dinner. You should feel sorry for me. I have to stay here until at least March when the seas calm down enough for Miss Cummings to travel. I wish I were home now."

Edward looked over to his friend. "This all weighs heavily, doesn't it?"

"You've no idea. I wouldn't be here, would I, if it didn't." He looked for his fiancée and found her chatting with a small group of people, smiling as if delighted in the conversation. They were all elderly, all women, and yet he felt a twinge of jealousy that they could hold her attention. He wondered what would happen if he wandered over to her and put his hand on her back, just high enough to touch the skin that was exposed so enticingly. If he leaned toward her and pressed his mouth against her exquisite neck, if he tasted her.

"I wish to hell this was all over," he said shortly.

A footman walked by at that moment carrying a tray of champagne. Edward grabbed two, handing one to Rand. "To getting the hell out of here," he said, lifting his glass.

Rand smiled and took a sip and wondered what the hell he was going to do in bed with a bride who wouldn't even look at him.

Dinner *was* interminable, despite Alva's efforts to keep the conversation lively and interesting. Elizabeth simply would not look at him, as if doing so would so unhinge her and she'd have to run from the room. Perhaps worse was that he was beginning to suspect that others at the dinner party had noted the bride's rather chilly reception for the groom. What had happened since he'd been gone? Certainly he had not expected her to hang on his arm and gaze at him with adoration, but when he spoke at the dinner party she did not even lift her head to acknowledge him. Rand had thought the gifts, the letters would have been enough to keep him in her thoughts. While he had no illusions she loved him, he at least hoped she liked him and missed him a bit while he was gone. Because he damn well missed her.

It struck him then, like a blow to the gut, that she had seen Henry Ellsworth. And perhaps not only just seen him, but had an assignation. She didn't only look exceedingly unhappy, she looked guilty. And why wouldn't she look at him? Rand was well aware his thoughts were drifting the way a jealous husband's would, but at the moment he did not care. The thought of her gazing into that man's eyes, all doe-eyed and love-soaked, filled with the tragedy that the big mean duke was keeping them apart—it was far too much to bear.

After dinner, the party moved to the music room where a string quartet was set to entertain. Rand, with the determination of a soldier on a vital mission, headed directly to his fiancée.

"You have been avoiding me," he said softly when he reached her side.

She looked at him with surprise that was so contrived, he nearly laughed.

"You are a poor actress," he said.

"I must admit it is a bit awkward, seeing you again after so long. And on the eve of our wedding," she said.

"Something that could easily be remedied by some conversation."

She took a bracing breath as if about to face a task that was not entirely pleasant. "Your letters were quite interesting," she said, dutifully. "It was almost as if I have been to all those places myself. Your descriptions were quite . . . thorough."

"I'm afraid writing is not my forte. I would have waxed poetic for you had I been capable of putting such sentiments on paper. Lord Hollings did offer to write the notes for me, but I thought that rather disingenuous. I suppose you are quite used to flowery letters of adoration from your great many admirers."

Her cheeks heated profusely, serving to fuel his suspicions that she had been in some sort of contact with Ellsworth. "I'm certain my letters weren't the stuff of poets, either," she said dryly, ignoring his comment.

No, Rand had to admit, they were not. They were, however, a catalogue of wedding events, stuff he could have gleaned from the *New York Times,* which seemed to be covering every detail of the wedding in amazing detail. Her letters were brief and held nothing personal in them. They could have been from a business associate for all the warmth they contained.

"And I noticed you did not include the fascinating information about your garters. Diamond clasps and all that."

Elizabeth grimaced. "I want you to know I had nothing to do with that article. My mother has been delighting in handing out tidbits about the wedding. I gave her a firm talking to about the matter."

"I would think that diamond clasps on garters was more of a tidbit about the wedding *night* rather than the actual wedding," he said in an effort to get some sort of reaction from her. She gave him a reaction, but it was not the one he expected: alarm, turning to fear. Or was it revulsion? He thought she would blush or perhaps gently chastise him for bringing up such an indelicate topic, but she had done neither of those things.

"Is thinking about our wedding night so objectionable to you, then?"

Alva saved her daughter by announcing that everyone should take their seats, forcing their brief talk to a close. He held up his arm and she placed her hand in the crook of his elbow, a light touch, the touch of a woman who doesn't feel comfortable, who doesn't wish to touch at all.

Chapter 15

Fifth Avenue outside St. Thomas's church was beset by an enormous throng of onlookers. It seemed as if every young woman in New York City was craning their necks to catch a glimpse of Elizabeth, likely wishing they were walking down the aisle to marry a handsome duke. Police officers, looking decidedly unhappy with their duty, held the crowd back from the cathedral's broad entranceway. Sitting in her coach waiting for the crowd to clear, Elizabeth peeked at the crowd waiting outside the church, with its two-hundred-sixty-foot tower looming over them. The tower seemed almost sinister to her, and she hoped God would forgive such a dark thought about His house.

"Why are they all here?" she said to herself. "Why do they care?"

"Because you are a Cummings. Because you are becoming a duchess. It is every girl's dream. They come to see American royalty," her mother said. It was as if her mother, having planned this day all her life, was more than pleased with the turnout. It made Elizabeth feel slightly ill, knowing she had to step out of the carriage and be in view of hundreds of strangers. The press of faces along the street made Elizabeth feel more like a curiosity, a sideshow attraction. They were all smiling, as if it was a grand and happy day, as if they were somehow a part of what was happening. No one could call what Elizabeth was feeling simple nerves—she was terrified.

"My goodness, Elizabeth, you are not going to your execution," her mother said, laughing.

"I'd gladly trade places with any one of them," she said softly. Her mother pressed her mouth tightly, likely restraining herself from saying anything that would further upset her.

"There she is!" someone shouted from the crowd, forcing Elizabeth to pull back from the curtained window. She wondered if Henry were in the crowd waiting for a glimpse of her. She prayed he would do nothing foolish, like storm into the church and drag her away. And perhaps in a small part of her heart she prayed he would, if only to escape this madness. If he did, she wondered whether she would go with him or not? Or would she stand by the duke, dutiful and calm, and say her lying vows. She wasn't certain if she still loved Henry or if she loved the idea of the freedom he represented. She was still so angry with him for tormenting her heart. And yet, she wore the necklace beneath her wedding dress. Oh, just imagine what her mother would do if she knew she wore a gift from Henry beneath her gown. That thought, at least, made her smile.

Though Elizabeth longed to run into the church like a woman being chased by an angry mob, her mother put a restraining hand on her arm and hissed, "Turn and smile at them."

So she turned. And smiled.

It wasn't until she stepped into the church to walk to the room where she would make the final preparations that her fear hit her full force. Until that moment, she'd simply been dragged along, surrounded by a swirl of activity and smiling faces and everyone telling her how lucky she was. The church was decorated magnificently, as only her mother could have planned it. St. Thomas's clergy was most likely thrilled to have had their entire church decorated for Christmas at no expense.

Huge garlands of holly draped from the church's great dome. The aisles were lined with hundreds of red and white poinsettias, and her own bouquet, large and unwieldy, was of poinsettias and holly. Elizabeth had always loved Christmas, and now she would always remember it as the day she was forced to marry a man she did not love. Every Christmas, until the day she died, the holiday would be tainted with this farce.

Suddenly, it all became too much for her, too much red, too much lace, too many pearls strung around her slim neck. Her corset, pulled so tightly she looked slightly distorted, made it nearly impossible to breathe when all she wanted to do was take deep, deep breaths and try to get through the day. She left her mother in the vestibule and went to a small room where her father waited for her to walk her down the aisle. For some reason, the sight of him in his dark gray pinstripe trousers and black frock cloak made what had seemed like a dream a striking reality. This was her wedding day. Her father was giving her away, and then she was going to be a duchess. Her life would never be the same, would never be her own.

She felt the blood drain from her face. "I . . . Father. I can't do it." A sharp stab of nausea hit her at that moment and she bent over and vomited into a small trash can.

"Elizabeth," her father shouted, coming immediately to her side.

Her empty stomach heaved and protested against her brutally tight corset.

"I can't, Father," she repeated, still hanging over the can. Her bouquet lay beside the trash, her diamond tiara tilted forward and threatened to fall into the can. "I can't. I can't. How can you make me do this? How?"

She looked into her father's face, seeing empathy and love. And guilt—but perhaps that was just her imagination. "You'll be fine, my girl. You'll see. The duke is not a cruel man. He seems intelligent. You could have done much worse, you know. You could have ended up with someone like me." He laughed, clearly hoping to gain a smile from his daughter. "Now, don't you cry. What will the duke think to see tears?"

"I don't care. And he doesn't, either. He cares only about the money," she said, even though she knew that wasn't true. "This is not what marriage is supposed to be like. My Christmases are ruined forever," she said, knowing she sounded like a little girl. At the moment, her most fervent wish was that she could be a little girl and it was Christmas and she would wake up to find presents beneath the tree brought by St. Nicholas. Instead, she would become a man's wife, wake up a duchess, and she would never, ever capture the wonderful magic of her childhood Christmases.

Her father chuckled and patted her back awkwardly, letting her cry. "All your Christmases are not ruined," he said. "You're not a little girl anymore, Elizabeth. You are a beautiful young woman." This last was said a bit gruffly.

"He doesn't love me. And I don't love him. We shall be miserable," she said, ending with a soft hiccup.

"I think he may be halfway in love with you already. Who wouldn't be, with my little Beth?"

"Oh, Father," she said, breaking down further upon hearing him use her pet name. He gave her his handkerchief and she dutifully blew her nose. "I'm sorry. I know I'm being silly. It's just hit me all at once, what I am doing. I shouldn't feel sorry for myself. I know that," she said a bit fiercely. "Half the women in New York are outside wishing they were in here. The poor duke would feel horrible if he knew I was in here crying." She took a bracing, shaking breath, at least as much as her corset would allow.

"Feeling better?"

Elizabeth nodded, giving a little sniff. "Perhaps we should wait just a bit for my eyes to clear."

Jason nodded. "I'll go tell everyone you're repairing your gown. Here," he said, straightening out her veil and tiara. "Now it can be true."

"Thank you, Father."

Jason cleared his throat, then left the small room to inform her groom that his bride would be out directly. Already she was twenty minutes late. He was probably imagining that she was running away. In truth, she suspected her mother feared something awful would happen to stop the wedding. She'd been hovering over her for a week, and she was quite certain that the footman positioned down the hall from her room was there solely to make certain she did not escape.

Her father was right, of course. The duke was not a cruel man and he was very handsome. And if they never loved each other the way she and Henry had loved, perhaps they could become friends. How many married couples were in love, anyway? Certainly not her mother and father. Still, she wondered what her mother would have done, her strong, ferocious mother, if she'd been forced to marry someone while loving another.

Rand nearly smashed the glass he held after Jason left him alone with Edward. Repairing her dress. What balderdash. Already he could hear the titters from the congregation, the speculation that she was about to leave him at the altar. No doubt she was hoping Ellsworth would rush into the church and save her from the horror of marrying him.

"Calm down, old man. You look about to explode."

"Her dress better have a tear the size of New York in it to make me wait here like an errand boy," he said. Already, she was thirty minutes late coming down the aisle, thirty minutes of pacing, feeling anger and humiliation spread through his veins like poison.

"Just think of all those beautiful pounds," Edward said.

Rand let out a shaky laugh. At the moment, money was the last thing on his mind. Again and again he found himself *hurt* by her coldness, and that could only mean one thing. He was most definitely falling in love, if not already there. Never in his life had love entered into his idea of marriage. Finding someone beautiful, compatible, wellborn—those were the things that he thought of, if he thought of marriage at all. Now he was finding himself in the untenable position of loving a woman who did not love him, of wanting things he had no business wanting. "I just didn't think it would be so damned humiliating."

Something in his tone, something desperate and unsettling, must have alarmed Edward, for he straightened in his seat where he'd been comfortably sprawled.

"Not having second thoughts, are you?"

He let out a humorless laugh. "How about fifth or sixth thoughts." He rubbed his forehead and let out a long, shaking breath. "I think she has seen that Ellsworth fellow."

"Oh, God, Rand."

He looked up, confused by Edward's bleak tone.

"I don't think she's *been* with him if that's what you're thinking."

"No. It's not bloody likely with her mother chaining her in her bedroom." At Rand's startled expression Edward explained that Maggie had told him Elizabeth had been held on an extremely short leash the past few months.

"Then what was the 'Oh, God, Rand' thing. I've got enough on my mind, thank you, without you upsetting me further."

"You let yourself fall in love. That's what the 'Oh, God, Rand' was about. Not well done, old man."

Rand let out a curse he hadn't uttered since his Light Guard days . . . and on Christmas Eve and in a church. "There are worse things," he muttered.

Edward raised his eyebrows. "Such as?"

"Such as marrying someone you don't love," he said bleakly. "And being in love with someone else."

Edward was about to respond when a young priest signaled that the ceremony was about to begin, and he took his place at the head of the aisle, arms behind his back, Edward standing beside him apparently thinking his emotional state was extremely amusing.

He tried to stop his jaw from dropping when Elizabeth began gliding down the aisle. She held her head high, her arm linked with her father, her waist impossibly tiny. The veil hid her features, even when her father handed her over to him he could not see if she were smiling. He, certainly, was not. Her eyes were on the priest, the altar, her multitude of bridesmaids, most of whom he'd never seen. And then, her father lifted the veil and his heart plunged. She had, indeed, been crying.

Rand was angry, and at the moment, he didn't care if his bride knew it. Certainly everyone in the church would note her pale face, her red-rimmed eyes, and they would know she stood before God and lied her little heart out. He stood there feeling foolish for thinking he might be falling in love, for thinking they might actually make each other happy. For thinking she might someday love him. He'd thought the tears, the resistance, the hope that somehow Ellsworth would rush down the aisle and save her from him were long over. Certainly he had not expected her to look up to him with adoration, but to find her looking at him as if she were marrying the devil himself was more than difficult to bear. And so he was torn between feeling rage and feeling sorry for her, and rage at the moment was the overriding emotion.

Still, she said her lines clearly enough for even the guests in the back of the cathedral to understand. Her hand shook only slightly when she held her finger out for the diamond-encrusted wedding ring that bound her to him forever. When the ceremony was over, the priest wished them all a Merry Christmas, and they turned, Duke and Duchess of Bellingham, to the loud cheers from the congregation. Outside, he could hear more cheers as the hundreds of onlookers who waited for the sight of the new duchess must have realized the wedding was over. Rand looked down at his new wife, but she kept her eyes straight ahead. She'd yet to look at him and he fought the urge to make a crazy face at her simply to obtain some sort of reaction.

"It was a lovely ceremony, was it not?" she asked, after he'd settled down next to her in the carriage that would bring them to her parents' home for the wedding breakfast.

"Lovely," he said dryly. "Perhaps it would have been far more effective had you dragged a cross along behind you."

Her cheeks turned pink and her jaw moved the tiniest fraction into a mulish expression. "You needn't be blasphemous," she said, completely ignoring the meaning behind his words.

"And you needn't act as if you've just been married to the devil."

She took a breath as if she were about to give an angry retort, but instead she deflated a bit. "I am sorry for the delay. Please don't take it personally. It had nothing to do with you."

Her little speech was particularly disheartening, because how could she possibly think that her clear reluctance to marry him was something he should not take personally? What on earth could be more personal than getting married? "You have no understanding of me at all, do you?" he said, angrily. "Do you have a single thought that doesn't concern how you feel? Do you know how humiliating it was for me to wait for you, knowing that everyone in the church knew you were being forced to this? You, my dear wife, are perhaps the most self-centered thing God has created."

She looked at him, finally, in complete shock. "It seems to me that you are getting all the benefit of this union. And that is patently unfair."

"I have just made you my duchess," he said, flabbergasted at her remark.

She actually let out a snort, leaving him so completely baffled he could hardly speak. Before he could deliver a tirade, the carriage came to a stop in front of the Fifth Avenue house, making a path through yet another throng of onlookers. "Do you think they are here to see Elizabeth Cummings?" he asked, his voice hard and uncompromising. "They are here to see the Duchess of Bellingham. Perhaps you should remember that."

With that, Rand stepped from the carriage, trying to keep the grim look from his face as he handed his new bride down. Despite everything, he was still very much aware that appearances were paramount and even if he wanted to throttle his bride, no one would ever know such errant thoughts had crossed his mind.

A wedding breakfast followed, with the bride and groom congratulated a dozen times by the dignitaries who'd attended the ceremony. She stood by him in the receiving line giving all the proper replies, even smiling and looking up to him on occasion. All very proper. But they hadn't kissed and no one had demanded that they do so. This was no ribald celebration but a dignified acknowledgment that America's royalty had tied itself to British royalty.

He wanted to shout at her for being so damned proper, even though he knew she was doing what she had been trained from birth to do. She carried herself with the dignity of a duchess and for the life of him he didn't know why he found it so irritating.

Maggie told herself, perhaps a dozen times, that the earl would be returning to England and she would never see him again so she certainly shouldn't look forward to seeing him now. At least not to the degree that had her heart racing and her entire body heating to the point of discomfort. But the sight of him in the church with his fine coat and tails, his blond hair slicked brutally back, his face freshly shaven, it was enough to make any girl's heart flutter. Her heart, which had been fighting her growing attraction, was beating madly.

"I do feel sorry for them," he said as he sipped champagne.

"Because they are not in love?"

"Because they are *married*," he replied, making Maggie frown.

"I'd forgotten how against the institution you are. I daresay if I was forced to marry, I wouldn't find the duke all that objectionable. And if I were a man, I would count my blessings to be married to someone as lovely as Elizabeth."

Lord Hollings raised an eyebrow, the way he always did when he disagreed with her. Maggie couldn't help think that if they were ever to get married—which they certainly would never—they would have several one-sided conversations. Lord Hollings could say more with that raised eyebrow than she could in a three-minute monologue.

"You carry a tendre for our duke?"

Maggie narrowed her eyes, knowing he was simply being contrary. "You know I do not. I'm madly in love with you," she said, clearly letting him know she wasn't anything of the sort. "It was your letters. So romantic. So filled with promise and adoration."

"Perhaps I shouldn't have written at all," he said, a bit shortly.

"Perhaps not," Maggie said, meaning it. Because every time one of his letters arrived, her silly heart would beat faster and her hands would tear open the letter, only to be treated to a line or two. "Seeing the sights of your capital. What a muddy, bug-infested place it is." "The heat here is unbearable. I do believe I am cooking. Though Charleston is rather pretty." And so on.

"Do you mean that? I only wrote to you because you

are the only other person I know here," he said, far more seriously than she'd heard from him before.

"I liked your letters," Maggie said honestly. "They made me laugh. With Elizabeth under lock and key, they truly were the only thing I had to look forward to. There. Have I redeemed myself?"

"I think you gushed a bit much for sincerity."

Maggie smiled. "If someone apologizes, you really should be more gracious, sir."

He grinned down at her. "I shall try to be."

It was on the tip of her tongue to tell him that she missed him, but she froze there, suddenly finding it impossible to speak at all. She did not want to like him more than was convenient. But it was too late, she realized. She liked him far too well and knew for a long time after, every man who danced with her, who tried to entertain her with their wit, would pale in comparison to the earl. He was, by far, the most fascinating man she'd ever met. And he was leaving, and she would never see him again, so it would do no good to throw caution to the wind and make a fool of herself over him.

Lord Hollings sneezed at that moment, sloshing a bit of his champagne onto Maggie's gown. She let out a little cry of dismay, then laughed.

"My mother told me in no uncertain tones that I was not to have champagne this morning. She told me it was far too early for alcohol, and now I shall smell as if I've been imbibing all morning. You, sir, will have to explain," she grinned up at him, her smile faltering a bit at his serious, almost angry, look. "What is wrong?"

"Do you always have to be so *bloody* charming?" he

asked, sounding angry. "I just spilled my drink on you and you're laughing like some simpleton."

Maggie could feel the blood drain from her face. His anger was as unexpected as it was irrational. "I'm sure I don't like to get upset over something so small," she said, feeling her eyes prick slightly. Then she smiled, a full-blown, full-of-joy and completely false smile. "If you want a better reaction, next time you should spill the entire glass, not just a few drops."

Her smile seemed to make him even angrier, so she kept it plastered on her face.

"If I was ever to spend any length of time with you, I am quite certain you would drive me batty."

"Then it's good that you are leaving soon," Maggie managed to say cheerfully, even as she felt her throat begin to close. She would not cry. She would not let him know how hurtful his words were. "There is my mother talking with Mrs. Wright. She insisted I be particularly nice to her, because Arthur has been so attentive lately, so I think I shall go over to say hello. If we don't get an opportunity to speak again, I hope you have a wonderful trip home. Good-bye, Lord Hollings."

Edward watched her walk toward her mother feeling completely out of sorts. He had been an utter cad and he didn't know why. No. He did know. He knew all too well what was happening to him and he didn't like it at all. Damn the girl for getting to him, for making him think of things he did not want to think about for another ten years. At least. Thank God he was leaving within days. He could ill afford to become a love-besotted idiot, which could happen if he remained in Maggie's company.

He'd missed her on their tour. Desperately. Which was why he insisted they extend it until right before the wedding. It was selfish of him, but Rand hadn't seemed to mind all that much as he was already dreading the social whirl that surrounded his visit. Those letters, God, those ridiculous letters he'd written. He didn't know why he bothered, but he hadn't quite been able to stop himself. Because he knew if he wrote, even a line or two, he'd get pages back from her. Pages and pages of nonsense and wit that was distinctly Maggie. They were well-read now, secreted in his baggage where they would remain until he returned home. And then he would likely burn them. Or not.

Bloody hell.

As if against his will, he watched as she did, indeed, say hello to Mrs. Wright, then continue toward the back of the house. She looked, even from the back, upset. She should be.

He stalked after her, not knowing why, not knowing what he intended to say, but when he caught up with her, she was waiting her turn for the loo.

"Come with me," he said, and walked down the palm tree–lined hall. He hadn't seen so many bloody palm trees since he'd done a tour in India. Thankfully, she followed, because he would have dragged her down the hall if she hadn't. When he was quite certain they were alone, he put his hands on her shoulders, crushing the puffy sleeves there.

"I don't love you," he said, giving her the tiniest shake.

She lifted her chin. "I don't love you, either."

"And I shan't get married. Not for years and years."

"Good luck finding someone who will put up with your overbearing attitude."

"Even if I did get married, I wouldn't marry you," he said, rather desperately. "Because I . . . I . . ."

Her eyes glittered, but he wasn't certain it was from anger or tears. "Because you?"

"Because I couldn't bear it," he said, somehow losing a bit of his voice.

"Am I that awful?"

He closed his eyes briefly. "You must know you are not. Not in the least," he said softly. "Leaving you will not be quite as easy as I thought."

She gave him the smallest of smiles. "But you will leave."

He swallowed, feeling miserable. "I will."

"We've one here from the Duke of Manchester," Rand said, handing the telegram over to her. She took it dutifully, as she did everything, which made him fairly dread what was coming this night. The last thing on earth he wanted in his bed was a dutiful wife. If he could only recapture what they'd had during their picnic. Then again, the months may have distorted that memory, turned it into something it wasn't. Perhaps he hadn't seen the passion in her eyes, perhaps she was giving him the dutiful reaction she thought she ought to.

"Queen Victoria," he said as he handed over to her yet another telegram. They'd gotten a stack of them, all arriving at Elizabeth's home just hours after the ceremony.

"Oh," she said, taking the paper from him and reading over the words. "Have you ever met the queen?"

"I have, but not in my capacity as duke. I was a member of the Life Guards and we were often assigned to guard the queen and her entourage. You will be presented to court sometime after our arrival home."

Her eyes grew wide. "I will? I don't . . ."

"I will have someone come to tutor you. By the time you are presented, you will feel comfortable with the ceremony. My cousin, Sandra, can help you. Countess Dalton. She's married to Lord Dalton, Earl of Sharing."

"I'll never get all this straight."

He smiled as he looked through the stack. "Before you know it, it will be second nature to you. Sandra can assist with that, too. Her children are grown and she has nothing to do but meddle in other people's business."

"Oh." She sounded very uncertain and very young, and he reminded himself that she was just nineteen and without her mother or father for the first time.

"Why did you cry?" he blurted out, even though he knew the answer. "No. Don't answer. Please."

"May I answer?"

He didn't like this meek girl. She may have acted meek in front of her mother, but he knew for a fact she was not meek. He would not have her acting so in front of him.

"Of course."

"I did not want to marry you."

So, she was not meek after all. He really should have prevented her from answering.

"But we are married. No one rescued you. You said

all the proper lines, as did I. I'd like a better reason. An honest one."

A line formed between her brows. "There is nothing more to it than that."

"Do you still fancy yourself in love with Ellsworth?" he asked, steeling himself for her answer, unsure whether he would believe her no matter what she said.

She let out a small gasp. "No."

"Have you seen him since he left Newport?"

"I don't know why it matters, but no." She acted as if he were offering her the greatest insult.

"It matters, my dear, because one of our primary duties is to produce an heir. I would like that heir to have Blackmore blood."

It took perhaps three seconds for her to realize what he was hinting at.

"You are fully horrid."

"No. I am cautious. A man in my position must be cautious. I want the truth. Have you seen him?"

Her cheeks were full of color, but he could not be certain whether it was from anger or shame. "I have given you my answer."

She pulled up a hand to her throat, no doubt imagining that the massive pearl necklace wrapped around her neck was becoming restrictive under his questioning. He stared at her until she finally relented and looked him in the eye.

"We will find out tonight, won't we," he said, feeling surly and out of sorts.

She jerked her gaze away, no doubt terrified at the thought of what was going to transpire that evening.

Perhaps she would never love him, perhaps she would never even like him, but he would show her pleasure. If they had only that, it would have to be enough.

Rosebrier, her family's country retreat in Long Island, had always been Elizabeth's sanctuary. It was the one place she could go as a child and not be constantly supervised. She could slouch, climb trees, skip rocks in the pond with her cousins, and fish with her father. Those idles ended when she reached the age of fourteen, the age her mother had decided she was more young lady than girl. Instead, she had to stay indoors and read, or walk sedately around the grounds under the sharp eye of Susan, who was at all times under the sharp eye of her mother. Their holidays thereafter became all the more dismal because she had such lovely memories of being there as a child. Even with those restrictions, Elizabeth felt more at ease, more like her true self.

And now, Rosebrier had become something else entirely. It had become the place where she would become a woman, where she would spend the first days of her marriage, where she would lose her virginity. It had become a place to dread, for if there was one thing Elizabeth dreaded more than the wedding itself, it was the wedding night.

Her mother's talk had, perhaps, bothered her more than anything. "Do what he wants you to and it won't be entirely unpleasant. And a child could come of it." She wished she had an older sister or cousin, someone to give her a bit more information than that. What, exactly, did "do what he wants" mean. Was she to do anything? Jump off the roof, perhaps?

It was the "do what he wants" that bothered her so. She was so sick of doing what everyone wanted of her. Marriage was to be just another long string of "do what he wants." Would she ever get to do what she wanted?

Still, when they reached Rosebrier late that afternoon, she smiled. It was the most informal of the Cummings' homes, a sprawling shingle-style home tucked in the woods, but within walking distance of the sea. Some day, the duke promised, they would have a more elaborate wedding trip. But for now, they would stay at Rosebrier for a week, then live in the Waldorf Hotel until it was spring and the seas were more calm. She dreaded the sea voyage to England nearly as much as her wedding night.

Rosebrier's lights were ablaze in anticipation of the arrival of the Duke and Duchess of Bellingham, bringing yet another smile. How pretty the house looked, lit up and decorated for the holiday. There would be a large Christmas tree in the main parlor and no doubt her mother had ordered the entire house strung with holly and garland. Elizabeth was grateful that darkness had fallen and the residents of the small town surrounding Rosebrier were at home. She was so tired of smiling and waving to crowds of curious people. When they pulled up in front of the house, a light snow was falling.

"It's snowing," she said, delighted. It was Christmas Eve and it was snowing. She should be like Maggie, who dwelled only on life's happiness. She ignored the sharp pang of homesickness—it was ridiculous, really, as she had only been away from home for mere hours. But she knew from this day forward, she would have no more days of shopping with Maggie, no more nights of operas or dinner parties. It suddenly didn't matter that she'd sometimes disliked formal nights out when all she had to look forward to was living in a foreign country with a man who seemed to dislike her as much as she disliked him. Imagine hinting that she'd had relations with Henry! She conveniently and firmly refused to think about their meeting, or the necklace that still dangled from her neck.

"Is there a local church we might attend for Christmas mass tomorrow?" he asked, as the door of their carriage opened.

"Mother said it would be too disruptive for us to attend mass in town. And I shall be so tired."

For some reason that made him smile. "I should hope so," he said. She blushed, of course, just as he had intended. "Besides, no doubt God will forgive us. We did attend church today."

A footman handed her down, welcoming "Her Grace" to Rosebrier and Elizabeth had to stop herself from laughing out loud. It sounded so very strange to be called anything but Miss Cummings. They walked up the wide porch together, strangers heading for their wedding night. Newport seemed so far away, Elizabeth truly felt she did not know this man beside her. She didn't know his favorite color, the foods he loved, how he liked his tea. Would he send their children away to boarding school? Did he even like children?

They stepped inside to find a line of beaming servants

waiting. Her mother's insistence that they marry on Christmas Eve did not take into account that the servants would have to work themselves weary to accommodate the newly wedded couple. Elizabeth's heart swelled at the sight of so many familiar faces, all standing there with bright smiles, probably thinking their little one had just come from a fairy-tale wedding.

"Your Grace," Mr. Rushton, their butler said, bowing deeply. Elizabeth was quite certain Rushton had never in his life bowed before anyone.

"Merry Christmas everyone," Elizabeth said, her eyes shining with happy tears. It was so good to be here, despite the reason why. When her eyes came to rest on Mrs. Crowley, she was nearly overcome. It had been more than a year since she'd seen her, the only woman she'd known who gave her hugs when she'd needed them most. She could not recall more than a handful of times her mother had touched her kindly, never mind give her the body-jarring embraces Mrs. Crowley had. She'd known, even as a little girl, that the housekeeper had felt sorry for her. Without thinking, she ran into her arms and was slightly shocked that she was now taller than her.

"It's so good to see you, Mrs. Crowley," she said, laughing because she'd starting crying.

Mrs. Crowley smiled up at her, her own eyes shining brightly. "Look at you. A duchess. I don't expect too many duchesses go around hugging their housekeepers," she said, clearly glad that this one did.

"I may hug anyone I wish now," Elizabeth said imperiously, making Mrs. Crowley laugh. She stepped back and looked at the other servants fondly. "As soon as His Grace and I have eaten, you are all dismissed to enjoy your holiday."

"Oh, no, Miss," Mrs. Crowley said, rushing forward. "I mean, Your Grace. Your mother gave strict orders that we work through the holiday, given the special circumstances." She darted a quick look to the duke, her cheeks turning ruddy.

"I believe my wife is in charge here now," he said. "Enjoy your Christmas day. I'm quite certain we can fend for ourselves without too much trouble. I'll sound an alarm should we burn the house down."

Every other person in the room, including Elizabeth, stared at the duke open-mouthed, not quite believing what they were hearing. Because Rosebrier was a seasonal home, the servants did not live there, but in the nearby town. If they gave them the day off, they would be left completely alone, and Elizabeth wondered if a duke could manage such a thing. He didn't even have his own valet, as he'd been sharing Lord Hollings's. Elizabeth had inwardly prepared for a battle, already forming her arguments that no one should have to work on the Lord's birthday, even for a duke. And duchess.

Finally, the small group smiled, delighted that they would have their Christmas, after all, which only made Elizabeth angrier at her mother for being so completely thoughtless. She returned to the duke's side because he looked so out of place standing alone by the door, and really, it was her duty to make him feel comfortable in her home. Then, the strangest thing happened. As if pulled by a puppeteer's string, each servant looked upward, their smiles rather mischievous. Elizabeth looked up, a feeling of foreboding drifting over her like a cool mist. Mistletoe. Perhaps the duke . . .

"I believe they are expecting a kiss," he said, close to her ear. Someone in the room tittered expectantly. "I believe I am expecting a kiss as well."

Elizabeth darted a look at him, then pressed her lips together, slightly irritated that once again duty was calling. Even something as small as a dutiful mistletoe kiss was annoying. The duke must have seen something in her expression, for his eyes, which had been filled with good humor, immediately hardened.

"Let's get this over with," he said, then pressed a quick kiss to her lips. Ridiculously, Elizabeth was disappointed. For that kiss was quite unlike the ones she remembered from Newport. It was businesslike, dutiful, perhaps. The servants clapped as if they'd just witnessed something marvelous, as Elizabeth stood there embarrassed and slightly angry—with herself and with the duke.

"I simply don't like being told what to do," she said in way of an apology, though her tone was far from apologetic.

"And yet you always do as you're told, don't you," he said softly.

She lifted her chin. "Not always."

He smiled down at her and something like relief crossed his features. She would never, ever understand the man standing next to her, she decided.

"We've prepared a light supper in the dining hall," Mrs. Crowley said. "Once you're all settled in, we'll serve you right up. Are you sure you won't be needing us tonight or tomorrow? I could—"

"No. As His Grace said, we'll be fine. You know I can find my way about the kitchen." Mrs. Crowley and the cook laughed, likely remembering as she did all the times she sneaked into the kitchen to raid the pantry. They let her, too, for they knew how very strict her mother was about what she was allowed to eat.

"Well, then, Merry Christmas to you both." She looked uncertainly at Elizabeth. "Will you be needing anything else from me? Do you have any questions? I mean about the house, of course."

Elizabeth knew that dear Mrs. Crowley was asking as kindly as possible if she had any questions about her wedding night.

"No. I'm fine," she said, not daring to look at the duke for fear he'd see her lie.

Chapter 16

"Do what he wants. Do what he wants. Do what he wants." She said the words until they had no meaning as she paced in her bedchamber waiting for his knock. He would knock and she would run to the bed and pull up the covers and call him in. And then, and then . . .

Do what he wants.

Elizabeth wasn't completely naive. But she supposed she was about as naive as any nineteen-year-old of her acquaintance. Certainly the fundamentals of what was about to happen were obvious, she supposed. Suddenly the vision of dogs rutting came to her and she squeezed her eyes shut. It was not like that.

Was it?

No. Of course not. She must remember those wonderful kisses on their picnic, the way they made her feel, well, wonderful. That marvelous liquid heat that surged through her, which had become such a distant memory she wasn't certain it was real.

She gnawed on her thumb, then jerked her hand down. Really, it couldn't be that difficult. After all, every human since the beginning of time had managed to do it, and apparently do it well, given all the children running about. She took a deep breath and let it out. Then nearly jumped out of her skin when she heard a noise next door in his room. The duke. Like a flash, she was in her bed, her bedcovers pulled up to her chin, her body so tense it began to ache. And then . . . nothing. Slowly she began to relax, but her eyes were still pinned to the adjoining door where he could step through at any moment.

In a small bout of rebellion, Elizabeth had not donned the nightgown her mother had purchased for her, the lacey, silky thing that clung far too tightly to her and wasn't at all warm. She'd tried it on, saw her reflection in the mirror, and noticed her nipples, erect from the cold, were clearly visible through the clingy fabric. That would never do. So, stepping firmly to her wardrobe, she pulled out her voluminous winter gown, all soft and warm and comforting, and hugged herself when it was on.

She could not know that she was a vision in either gown, that a man who had not been with a woman in months would take one look at her, with her dark, wavy hair flowing down her back, her small breasts pushing against the thin white fabric, and want to fall to his knees in gratitude. All her life, Elizabeth was made unaware of her beauty by a mother who was convinced vanity was one of the greatest sins. So when Elizabeth looked at herself in the mirror, she saw only a frightened girl with her hair down, not the desirable woman that she truly was.

Now, waiting in bed, she felt about ten years old waiting for a whipping from her mother. She dreaded it, but simply wanted it over.

"Do want he wants," she whispered, feeling her panic grow. "Oh, for goodness' sake," she said softly, but harshly. "Come in and get on with it."

"Elizabeth." He called out to her and for a crazy minute she thought he might have heard her. "Would you come here, please."

"Do want he wants. Do what he wants." She walked to the adjoining door and opened it and gasped. For there, sitting on his bed waiting for her, was her half-naked husband looking far more beautiful than any man had a right to, like a painting by Michelangelo. And he was smiling.

Rand felt for the girl. He truly did. He could still remember his first time, the anticipation, the utter embarrassment, the ultimate pleasure. Only for Elizabeth, he was quite certain she felt no anticipation. This wasn't what he had planned—and planned and planned—in his head. He'd pictured coming into her room and making love, making her come, making her scream with pleasure. But he'd realized somewhere between the wedding and this moment that he was going to have to tread a bit more carefully with her. He was nervous as hell that he'd scare her or ruin this for her—or him. What did he know about bedding a virgin? He'd heard they cried, that there was blood. God, blood? How much and just how difficult *was* it to get to where he wanted to go? He'd reminded himself that he'd never heard of anyone bleeding to death over such a wound, but the whole idea that he'd have to hurt her was damned disconcerting.

And if he was nervous about the whole thing, she was likely in a panic.

"Come here," he said, patting the bed beside him. She hesitated, then steeled herself and walked to his bed, her eyes forcibly anywhere but below his chin. He didn't want to frighten her, but he saw no purpose in drawing things out and undressing awkwardly in the middle of things. Besides, he always slept in the nude except for the coldest of nights. The bed dipped slightly when she perched on the very edge of the bed. He likely could have laid his pinky finger on her and she would have fallen to the floor.

"What did your mother say about tonight?" he asked. Her cheeks heated and she looked down to her lap.

"She said to do what you want."

He chuckled and she darted a look at him, irritated that he laughed, no doubt. "I don't think that likely went over well with you." She shook her head, all meek, waiting for his commands. "What do you want?" he asked.

She looked at him with surprise. "To run from the room?"

He full out laughed then, and she actually smiled. "That is not an option. Not yet." She immediately frowned and he realized if he wanted to do this right, he was going to have to be very careful. "I'm going to hand you the reins."

"I beg pardon?"

"You are in charge of this."

She looked at him as if he'd sprung a second head. "You are not a virgin," she said, but there was a question there.

He made a strange sound in his throat.

"Do not laugh at me."

"I'm not," he said rather solemnly. "Elizabeth, shall I tell you what I want? Shall I? I fear I would frighten you and you would indeed run from this room." He could not tell her he wanted to rip the gown from her body and bury himself in her heat. He could not say he wanted to kiss her nipples until they were wet and hard from his attention. He could not say he wanted to touch her between her legs, to feel if she was wet, to caress her there until her back arched, until she cried out. He could not tell her he wanted to taste her, dip his tongue inside, make her writhe beneath him. He could not tell her his arousal was so painful that he needed to put himself into her, to thrust again and again until he found release.

"Touch me," he said. He thought she might actually dart from the room, but she surprised him when her eyes drifted to his chest and she lifted her hand to touch him. He closed his eyes when he felt her hand on his chest, tentative and warm. He tried not to react, but God above, he was only a man and she was so incredibly desirable. The blankets tented and he prayed she wouldn't notice. Some day she would see that and smile. But not this time, not now.

"It's soft," she said, moving her hand, feeling his chest hair. He opened his eyes and found she was staring at her hand touching his chest.

"What do you want, Elizabeth?" She looked up at him and he saw no fear.

"I . . ." She looked down at her hand again. "I wouldn't mind kissing. I suppose."

He smiled. "Then kiss me."

She giggled, delighted. "You are serious, aren't you? You actually mean for me to lead the way. To take the reins, as you said."

"Yes." For some reason, that made her eyes well up. "What have I said to make you cry?"

"You are so kind, and I . . . I am not." She shook her head and looked away.

"I can be quite mean. If that's what you want," he said, completely confused and wondering if he were making a muck of things. She wasn't supposed to cry until after.

She let out a watery laugh. "That is not at all what I want." Then she leaned toward him and kissed him, her hands going to either side of his face, her soft breasts pressing against his forearm. It was a soft kiss, full of question and innocence, and it made his heart ache in a queer way he'd never before felt. He tasted her, and deepened the kiss, letting out a groan and bringing his hands up to pull her closer. She was soft and lush and so very feminine. Without her corset, she had a real woman's waist that curved gently to her hips, curves so exaggerated by her underclothes he decided he would ban her from wearing them. He could not wait to see what she truly looked like, how her breasts arched, how her waist dipped, how her thighs curved to her firm behind.

She let out a sound, a sigh of pleasure, and it was all he could do not to pull her virginal gown over her head and see what his wife looked like beneath the lace and cotton that flowed around her. Pulling back, he smiled, noting her lips, red and lush from their kisses, her eyes slightly dazed. He could see not even a hint of fear in them.

"What is next?" he asked.

"I truly don't know," she said, grinning. "Are you fully naked under the covers?" Her eyes darted quickly to the place where his skin ended and the blankets began.

"Would you like to find out?"

"No," she said quickly. Then she tilted her head a bit. "Well, perhaps just a quick peek."

And that's exactly what she did. She lifted the blanket, gave a look, squeaked a bit, then pulled them up even higher. "You *are* naked. Fully naked," she said, sounding more delighted than horrified.

"It's much nicer to do what we need to do without clothing," he said, watching as she fingered her cotton gown. "May I take off your gown?" he asked, holding his breath.

"You mean all the way?"

"That would be helpful."

"Can I get under the covers first? It's cold."

It wasn't cold at all, but he nodded, perfectly happy with how things were proceeding. She climbed over him, not caring a wit that she nearly kneed some very vital parts, and pulled the covers high before squiggling out of her gown. She held it up for him to see like a prize.

"Very well done," he said, turning and resting his head on one hand. She lay there with the covers pulled right up to her chin, looking at him uncertainly.

Elizabeth simply could not believe she was naked in bed with a man. With her husband, she amended. It was, by far, the strangest experience of her life. Even though she knew thousands of women had done this before her, to her it was a unique and utterly disconcerting experience. She had never seen a man's naked chest in the flesh until that evening. She looked to him expectantly, but he was staring at her as if waiting for her to do something. She decided then and there to hand the reins back to him. After all, she was certain he had done this at least one other time and this was her first time.

"I do believe it's time to let you take the lead," she said.

He nodded, his eyes searching. "I'm going to touch you and kiss you in places you never imagined," he said, his voice low. "I want you to close your eyes, love, and let me. I . . ." He let out a breath. "I'm no expert, but I'll try to please you. I will try."

"Should we lower the light?" she asked, looking toward the gaslight near the bed.

"No. I want to see you. But for now, close your eyes."

He let out a shaking breath and she realized for the first time that perhaps he was nearly as nervous about all this as she. She closed her eyes, her body tense as she waited for him to proceed.

Then he kissed her cheeks, a soft buss that was so comforting, so loving, she opened her eyes and smiled at him. He smiled back and kissed her jaw, another gentle kiss and she let out a sigh. And then, oh then he put his mouth near her ear and it was as if a jolt of electricity shot down her body to between her legs. Now, that was quite unexpected.

He said nothing, he barely touched her but with his mouth, on her neck, her shoulder, her clavicle. He moved back to her mouth, letting out a deep sound that made her smile. So far, this wedding night stuff was quite wonderful, she decided. He laid a hand beneath the blanket and she stiffened for an instant before deciding she liked that, as well. Oh, she could kiss him forever, she decided. He was quite good at these long, drugging kisses that made her want to squirm against him, that made her wish he would move his hand and touch her everywhere and everywhere and everywhere.

And then he did, his thumb brushing against one nipple, an exquisite sensation she'd never imagined. She grew hard beneath his caresses and the feeling intensified, shot heat between her legs. He kissed her neck, her chest, the mound of her breast above the blankets, and, finally, he pushed away the blanket and laid his mouth on the nipple he'd been torturing with his hand and she arched against him, letting out a cry. He didn't stop, simply moved to her other breast, suckling her. "Please," she said, not knowing what she was asking for. But the pressure, the exquisite pressure building between her legs, making her move her hips, making her want something she'd never guessed at before.

"Elizabeth."

She opened her eyes and saw such a look of raw desire on his face, she shivered. "What?"

"Please touch me."

"Oh." She blushed, feeling suddenly completely inept. There she'd been, lying like a statue, feeling wonderful, and not thinking for even an instant that he might want to be touched as well.

"Here," he said, bringing her hand down. Her fingers felt his arousal, the smooth skin, soft and taut at the same time. And so completely foreign. He lay still as he moved her hand over him letting out short, harsh gasps of pleasure. She smiled, liking to please him, happy that it was so simple. Feeling daring suddenly, she wrapped her hand around his hardness, watching his face, listening to his breathing, and was rewarded when he arched against her hand and stopped breathing altogether for a moment.

"Oh, God, that should do for now," he said, laughing a bit. "I'm afraid I can't manage more than that at the moment." He sounded so English, so proper, that Elizabeth had to smile.

"You are far, far more than I hoped for when I left England," he said, bending down and kissing one nipple. "Far more." He looked up at her and grinned, and for a moment he looked so boyishly endearing her heart gave a little wrench. "And now it's down to business."

She wrinkled her brow. "Business?"

"I want to give you pleasure. Make you come. Do you understand?"

"I don't think I do."

"Close your eyes." She gave him a suspicious look. "Keep them open then," he said good-naturedly. He kissed her, one of those drugging kisses that made her want to melt into the covers. And then his hand, his wonderful hand, touched her between her legs, and he let out a sound of pure male satisfaction.

"You are so wet," he said, sounding inordinately happy. Elizabeth was faintly embarrassed by that revelation, but she barely had time to process what he'd said when he touched her in a place that made her entire body sing. There, that was it. That feeling that had vaguely plagued her, that made her wish for something, some thing, and he was touching it, making her . . . oh, good Lord above, she hadn't imagined such a feeling in all her life. It was pressure and heat and the most beautiful feeling she'd ever experienced. Just from touching her in the right place. There and there and there. "There," she whispered, and he kissed her. She moved her hips slightly without thinking, without being aware of anything but his hand between her legs, moving, touching, making her want to scream. And she did. A pulsing heat spread through her suddenly, emanating from between her legs and shooting through her toes and the tips of her breasts. Slowly, luxuriously slowly, she came back to herself.

"Oh, goodness."

Rand looked down at her flushed face, her swollen lush lips, her tangled hair, and knew without a doubt that he loved her. He kissed her again, so happy he'd given her pleasure before he did what he'd been dreading and looking forward to for weeks.

"That was nice," she said.

"There is more, you know."

"I know." She said it bravely, like a soldier being sent into battle.

"After tonight, it will all be nice. Better than nice, I should think." She looked impossibly beautiful in the gaslight, her skin flushed from making love. He kissed her neck, moving a delicate chain there to gain access to her clavicle. He loved that spot on her, that feminine beautiful place. He traced his finger there and looked up to see her smiling at him. He kissed her, simply because he found he couldn't help himself. And then he moved over her, kissing her, pulling back to see her face when he entered her. She was wet and languid and completely trusting.

"Go on, then," she said, smiling up at him. Oh, God, he loved her. Loved her like he hadn't realized he could love. He closed his eyes against the rush of desire and love, hoping she wouldn't see what was so clearly written in his heart. He pushed inside her, stopping when he heard her gasp.

"I'm perfectly fine," she said.

He was shaking above her, his body bathed in a cold sweat as he pressed deeper. She was tight and wet and warm and so damned perfect. She lifted her hips and he lost what little control he had, thrusting deep, making her his. She let out a small cry as he broke through her hymen, and he let out a small cry of pure joy. And then he kissed her, loving her with his body, as well as his heart. He moved slowly, as slowly as a man who was dying of desire could move, but passion overcame him and he thrust again and again until he found his release.

He didn't know what came over him at the moment. It wasn't as if she was his first woman, but she was his wife and just then he truly had never been happier. His heart was nearly exploding with it. "I'm in love with you," he said, not thinking, not really even caring in that split second that she didn't love him.

She looked appropriately stunned, and then inappropriately horrified, though she tried desperately to mask it. The worst was, he couldn't take it back, even though he'd meant every syllable. What was he thinking to have confessed such a thing to a woman he knew did not love him.

"I know you don't love me," he said, though he desperately wished she would argue that point.

"Perhaps some day I shall. I feel I don't truly know you. You said yourself it's impossible to fall in love with someone so quickly."

"I know what I said." He was cursing himself for being so impulsive and just slightly angered that she would remind him, in their marriage bed, that she was—or at least had been—in love with another man.

She lay there silently for a time, fiddling with her rings, staring up at the ceiling, probably feeling as wretched as he did. "I need to clean up I think. And then I'll go to bed."

He had hoped she would stay with him, but perhaps that was too much to ask for. "Good night, then," he said, feeling like the greatest of fools. He should demand she stay with him, but he knew to do so would only make things worse. Few married couples he knew did share a room, but he'd hoped . . . oh to hell with what he hoped. He watched her pull on her nightgown, her back turned to him. She was probably thinking she was being modest, but her backside was so lovely, it was all he could do not to drag her back to bed beside him. He let her go, let her walk to her room. When she reached the door, she turned.

"Thank you." When he didn't respond, she explained. "For being kind. Good night."

Kind. He did not want to be kind at the moment, but he was, even so. "Good night."

Chapter 17

Elizabeth sat at her writing desk pouring out her heart to Maggie in a letter she was uncertain she'd ever send. *"He told me he loved me and I couldn't say it back. If I had, would he not have known I was lying?"* She stared at those words, feeling awful and mean. But she did not love him. She knew what love felt like, knew it made your heart sing. Love made you a bit crazy, it made you dream of the other person, long for them, and when you saw them, it was like all was right in the world. That was how Henry had made her feel. She put her hand to her throat and guiltily touched the chain, wondering if she would ever love the duke.

Wear this heart against you, keep it with you forever, as I will keep your heart with me.

"Oh, God, help me," she whispered. It was Christmas day and she was sinning already against her husband by longing for another man. She was a horrid, horrid person. It wasn't as if the duke were cruel or ugly or offensive in any way. He, quite simply, had been far kinder, far more considerate than she could have hoped for.

But she didn't love him.

Elizabeth stared at the letter knowing how hurt the duke would be if he saw those words she'd written. *"I am so unhappy because I am hurting someone who does not deserve to be hurt."* She stared at her words, knowing they were true. She did not want to hurt the duke. Squeezing her eyes shut, she realized she still thought of him as "the duke" not as Rand, not even as her husband. He had called her Elizabeth last night and she had been silent.

A knock sounded at the door and she quickly tucked the letter away. "Come in," she called.

"Merry Christmas." He stood there wearing only breeches and a white shirt. He really must find a valet, she thought fondly. He was quite disheveled, his pants a bit wrinkled and his shirt askew.

"Merry Christmas," she answered.

"I've got a fire going in the dining room and sitting room, but I don't know how to turn on the furnace." He shrugged. "I've never lived in a house with heat."

"Bellewood isn't heated?" she asked.

"It is in desperate need of modernizing. I'm afraid we've no plumbing or electricity, or even gaslight, either."

Elizabeth smiled slightly. "A bit like living in a medieval castle."

"A bit better than that, I should hope. It is cold in here. Would you happen to know how to turn the heat on?"

She shrugged helplessly. "I'm beginning to think I was a bit rash suggesting everyone take the day off. I do know there's a massive furnace in the basement. And a coal bin. But I think there's more to it than shoveling the coal in. We'd better not chance it. Fires should get us through one day, don't you think?"

He looked extremely uncertain standing in her doorway, as if he meant to talk about more than the cold but couldn't bring himself to do it. "I've a present for you," he said, finally. He backed out of the room and brought out a large box, very prettily wrapped.

"I've a present for you, as well," Elizabeth said, running to her wardrobe and pulling out the pen her mother had picked out. She knew she would think of Henry each time she saw her husband using it, so had been rather reluctant to give it to him. But as he was standing there presenting her with a gift, she felt she had to give it to him now.

He laid the box on the bed expectantly, and she hurried over to open it. "I do love presents," she said, smiling up at him and handing him her gift. She tore open the paper and opened the expensive-looking box to find clothing, made from rich brown velvet.

"It's a riding habit," he said. "You said you didn't ride, but I plan to teach you and you will need a habit."

Elizabeth pulled it from the box. "It's lovely," she said, meaning it.

"Your mother helped me with the sizing."

"I will look like the finest horsewoman in England even though I don't know a lick about riding. Thank you." She kissed his cheek. "Now, open yours."

He smiled and did as she requested, looking inordinately pleased with the pen. She felt another stab of guilt knowing she had absolutely nothing to do with selecting it. As he studied it, his smile faded slightly.

"You had it inscribed," he said, his voice sounding odd.

She had? "Oh, yes. I forgot to check it when I picked it up at Tiffany's. I hope everything is spelled properly."

"Quite," he said, handing it over to her for inspection.

The pen was beautiful, rosewood with gold inlay at the top and solid gold in the second half. It was there she saw the inscription, "To my husband, from your loving wife."

He must have seen the surprise in her eyes, though she did try to mask it.

"Everything's fine," she said with false cheer, handing the pen back to him. Oh, *what* had her mother been thinking? The woman didn't have a romantic bone in her body and *that* was the inscription she chose?

"Yes," he said thoughtfully, as if he knew she'd had nothing to do with the inscription but was too polite to come out and ask. She certainly wasn't going to set him straight.

"How many horses do you have?" she asked in a desperate attempt to change the subject.

"None," he said shortly, "but I hope to amend that some day."

It was an awkward reminder that he had been poor until their marriage.

"I should think one of your first expenditures would be a fine valet," she said, hoping to make him laugh. Instead, he actually turned slightly ruddy and looked down at his rather wrinkled clothes.

"I was teasing," she said, feeling simply awful.

A loud clanking noise startled them both. "The heat!"

Elizabeth said, rushing over to one of the steam radiators in her room. It was ice cold, but she knew that sound was the pipes expanding with hot steam. She went out the door and down the stairs to find a young man standing in the foyer, his cheeks and nose red from the cold.

"Dad sent me over, miss. In the excitement of last night, he forgot to fill the furnace. You should be right as rain until tonight. Then the duke here can fill it for the night. There's plenty of coal."

The duke came up behind her looking bemused. She would have bet her fortune that no one at Bellewood would ever have suggested the duke shovel coal.

"Why don't you show me where everything is, then?"

Elizabeth watched as the duke disappeared into the cellar with the young man. She'd met enough members of the peerage in her travels with her mother to know most dukes would not have lowered themselves to shovel even one bit of coal, never mind fill a furnace.

When he returned and the boy had left, they went to the only sitting room with a fire. Even though the heat was now on, it was still chilly in the house. They stood close to the fire, close to each other as they silently gazed into the fire.

"I don't understand you," she said.

"I'm afraid I don't understand myself, either."

Elizabeth let out a small laugh. "You are being so kind and—"

"Please don't tell me how kind I'm being," he interrupted.

"It is not a flaw," she said, wondering why a compliment would upset him.

"It is that I don't feel kind," he said harshly. "Do you know what I want to do at this moment? Right now? Let me tell you, kindness has nothing to do with it."

"What do you want to do?" she asked, even though she was slightly afraid of the answer.

He let out a harsh breath. "I want to wring your neck," he said. "You did not buy that pen and you did not put that inscription on, either, did you?"

She gave him a guilty smile. "No. But I was so busy and Mother would not let me out of the house."

"Why?"

"Why what?"

"Why wouldn't your mother let you out of the house?" he asked, his words succinct and far from kind. He asked even though Elizabeth was quite certain he knew the answer. Was he trying to torture her or himself?

Still, Elizabeth refused to tell him the truth, that her mother feared she would run away. "To protect me. Everyone was so excited about the wedding . . ."

"Everyone but you."

She glared at him. ". . . and she wanted to keep people away from me."

"People or person?"

"I am not discussing this. You sound like—" she stopped, searching for the right word. He supplied them.

"A jealous husband?"

"Yes, that exactly. And you should stop. Now. All this over a silly pen. I'll buy you another gift if that's what you want."

"And perhaps put a more honest inscription," he muttered.

Elizabeth closed her eyes briefly. She did not want to hurt him and that's exactly what had happened. Again.

"I apologize," he said, giving her a curt bow.

"You're being kind again," she said, praying he would truly smile. "You don't really want to wring my neck, do you?"

He gave her a lopsided smile. "No."

"Then what do you want?"

"I want to make love to you," he said, his voice rough. "I should want to wring your neck, but all I can imagine is something else entirely. You are driving me mad."

She walked up to him, already feeling some of what she felt the night before, and put a hand on his chest, two fingers touching bare skin. "Then why don't you?"

With a groan, he pulled her to him and she lost herself in his kiss. This was good. If all she ever had with him was this feeling, it was good enough. It was more than good enough.

She wore a gown that buttoned up the front and no corset at all, only a thin chemise. When he saw that, he gave a sound of satisfaction, putting his hands around her waist and pulling her even closer.

"You should never wear anything beneath your dresses," he said against her mouth. "You are beautiful just as you are."

They fell together onto the thick carpet, warmed by the fire and by each other. Within seconds, her dress and chemise were pulled down to her waist, her skirts were shoved up above her hips, and he looked down at her with such naked desire she could hardly bear it.

"I could look at you, touch you, all day," he said, moving his mouth to her breast and his hand between her legs. She let out a sigh, knowing that the amazing things he'd done to her the night before were going to happen again. He kneeled and pulled his shirt over his head in one quick movement, and she reached up to pull him down to her again. He hadn't shaved that morning, so his beard was rough against her skin. She liked it, the sense that he was so different from her, making her feel impossibly feminine.

He paused only long enough to remove the rest of his clothing and when his hand moved between her legs, she widened them, welcoming the sensation. And then she felt something entirely different, his mouth where his hand had been, his tongue there. Oh, his tongue moving and making her feeling something far beyond what she'd ever felt.

"Oh. Rand," she said. "Yes. There." Her body was racked with such an intense pleasure she cried out as if in pain, her heart pounding hard inside her as she arched against him. She was still pulsing when he entered her, moving in the rhythm he created, pushing her to another precipice as he kissed her and thrust inside her, as he suckled one nipple, as he told her he loved her. She came again, holding him against her, holding him until the sensation slowly ebbed away.

That afternoon they went for a walk holding hands. Rand couldn't stay morose for long. After all, he was in love with a beautiful woman who pleased him far more than any woman he'd ever known, and she was his for all time. She would come to love him, he knew she would. Certainly she was not pretending to enjoy their lovemaking or giving him false smiles. He was not so blinded by love not to see that. And she had held out her hand for him to take. That meant something, did it not?

They talked about their childhoods, argued about how many children they should have. She happily reminded him that she was only required to produce the heir and perhaps a spare, while he insisted they have ten children.

"A dozen," he said, pulling her to him for a quick kiss.

"I shouldn't know what to do with all those children," she argued.

"We could have a cricket team. The Bellewood Blackmores. That sounds rather nice, doesn't it."

"If we had two they could be tennis partners," she pointed out. "Girls don't play cricket."

"My girls would," he said.

"Why not baseball? Baseball is a far grander sport."

"Baseball is for heathens," he said, teasing her.

That was what they did all day. They discovered favorite colors and foods, they teased and kissed and held hands. When they came in from their walk, their cheeks rosy from the cold, they ran up the stairs to his room and made love again, falling asleep in each other's arms.

Elizabeth woke up and stretched, feeling slightly sore in places that had never been slightly sore before. She was completely naked and completely happy. It was amazing, really. Just that morning, she'd been miserable thinking she'd never fall in love with her husband, and here she was, smiling, drowsy, and completely satisfied.

And thinking that perhaps she might be falling in love. She looked over to him to find him watching her.

"Hello," she said, and kissed him.

"Hello."

"I think today was the best day of my life," she said, meaning every word. "I have never gone without a corset for so long and I feel wonderful." She was teasing him, of course, and he growled and pulled her to him.

"You shall never wear one again," he said, nuzzling her neck. "I must say I like the results."

"Rand, I am happy. I am," she said, feeling ridiculously close to tears.

"I'm glad," he said, and pulled her close, tucking her head beneath his chin.

It was so warm in bed beside him. She was quite surprised with herself, that she could feel completely comfortable in bed naked with a man.

"I'm also glad to hear you say my name."

"I've thought of you only as 'the duke' for so long, I have to admit it was difficult. But you don't seem much like a duke without any clothes on."

He chuckled and kissed the top of her head. It seemed he liked kissing her, and that was just fine, too. Elizabeth let out a long contented sigh. "Twelve children might do," she said sleepily.

"Don't you dare fall asleep. All we've eaten all day was cold chicken. You have to cook us something, wife, else I will lose all strength and be unable to do anything but sleep."

She turned in his arms. "That would be a tragedy,"

she said. "I just hate to get out of bed." She snuggled down further. "It's just so nice here with you."

With that, he tore off the covers and stood up.

"You are mean," she said, pouting.

"No. I'm hungry. Come on. I'll help." He held out his hand and dragged her from the bed. After they were dressed, they snuck down to the darkened kitchen like naughty children and prepared a simple meal of boiled potatoes and soup warmed up.

"I wish the servants weren't coming back tomorrow," she said, spooning some rich beef soup into her mouth. Once she smelled the food, she found herself absolutely famished.

"I shall send them away," he said, her knight in shining armor.

"Alas, this is the last of the food and I absolutely refuse to toil with my fair hands," she said, ending on a giggle.

"They are fair," he said, his gray eyes darkening as he lifted one up to his mouth.

"You, sir, think nothing except the bedroom." She pulled her hand away and crossed her arms over her chest. Rand went about clearing the large wooden worktable in the center of the room and said devilishly, "Who said anything about a bedroom."

The next three days were fairly magical. Elizabeth ripped up the first letter she'd written to Maggie, glad it had never been sent, and wrote another one filled with happiness.

"I wish we could stay here forever, make Rosebrier our home and never, ever have to go into society again," she wrote fervently. Indeed, Elizabeth thought she could happily live out her life there, raising a family, making love with her husband, taking long walks in the brisk air. Making love some more. It was one of the nicer surprises of her marriage and she could not believe she had been so dreading it. She vowed that when it was time for her daughter to marry, she would tell her to do what she wanted and make certain her husband did the same.

I'm falling in love, she realized. And that is how she ended her letter, smiling down at the words with a slight bit of disbelief. But how could she not fall in love with a man as handsome, as kind and thoughtful, as loving as Rand was? She found herself looking forward to seeing him, feeling her heart pick up a beat when he walked into a room, missing him when she did not see him for just a few hours. It was insane, she knew, but there it was. She would tell him soon, tell him when she felt he would believe her and when she believed it herself. She would tell him and watch him smile down at her. But for now, she wanted to hold the feeling to herself, to make sure it was real, for this was all so new and wonderful.

She finished writing her letter to Maggie just as Rand walked into the small study. She'd taken to writing there instead of her room, for the study was the warmest room in the house.

"Writing home?" he asked, coming over to her and kissing her.

"Writing to Maggie to tell her what a fine husband you turned out to be."

"And kind. Don't forget to mention that," he said, teasing her. "Shall we go for our walk now?"

Elizabeth glanced at her coat and nodded. "I'm ready when you are," she said, noting he already was in his overcoat and gloves. "Except for my gloves." She let out a sigh. "I'll have Trudie fetch them."

"Don't bother. I have forgotten my hat. I'll get your gloves at the same time." He kissed her nose. "You are very right, love, I do need a valet."

Rand left her, taking the stairs two at a time. God above, he was the luckiest man alive. He didn't even care if the world knew how much he loved his wife, because he had a very good suspicion she loved him, as well. At least she was coming 'round to that emotion. He went to his room and grabbed his hat, then strode into her room and scared a poor maid nearly to death. She'd been dusting Elizabeth's desk and screamed like a banshee, upsetting half the contents when he entered.

"I'm so sorry, sir. I didn't mean to startle you," the girl said rather comically.

"I fear I'm the one who startled you. It is I who should apologize." She was about to argue, but he interrupted. "I've just come to fetch my wife's gloves." He looked around the room, finally spying them on the ground with several other items. Bending down, he picked up her pair of fur-lined gloves. He was about to straighten, when a bit of pink paper peeking out from her overturned address book caught his eye.

"Would you go tell Her Grace I shall be down shortly," he said, his eyes never straying from that familiar pink paper.

"Yes, sir," Trudie said, bobbing a quick and inexpert curtsy.

Rand stared at that paper a good long time before he reached out for it, telling himself it was likely nothing, perhaps even that old note Ellsworth had given her all those months ago in Newport. She'd put it there and forgotten about it. That's all. He picked up the address book and slipped the paper out, unfolding it carefully.

And he read the words Ellsworth had written to her just a couple of weeks before their marriage. He knew, because the scoundrel had conveniently put the date—December 12. He read the words until his hand shook with rage and he was struck with a despair so deep he nearly collapsed from it.

Do what you must to deceive and be safe, pretend anything to get you through the months ahead and know that I will always know the truth: that you love me alone.

He neatly refolded the letter and placed it back in her address book, took up her gloves and walked down the stairs as if nothing untoward had happened.

"Are you ready?" he asked, handing her the gloves.

"Yes. I do hope it snows later today. It feels like snow, does it not?" she said happily, heading out the door.

"I wouldn't know," he said absently. *It isn't true. It can't be true. She loves me, she does.*

"Does it snow much at Bellewood? It's so pretty in the snow. Not Bellewood, but snow in general. Of course I've never seen Bellewood in the snow. Or the sunshine, come to think on it."

She was babbling on happily, as if the world had not just

tilted crazily, as if everything were wonderful, as if every word out of her lovely little mouth wasn't a horrible lie.

"I'm not feeling well," he said, suddenly unable to be with her, see her.

She put on a look of concern. "What is wrong?"

"Something," he said, before turning back to the house. He went directly to his room and shut his door and lay on his bed to stare at the ceiling. The shadows lengthened and the room went dark before he heaved himself out of bed again, and that was only because he had to relieve himself.

Later, he heard a knock, then a maid asked if she should send up a tray for him.

"No. I'm not hungry." He wasn't hungry. He wasn't anything at the moment, simply very, very numb. His dutiful wife checked up on him twice, but then left him alone. He couldn't bear to look at her.

It wasn't until nine o'clock, when he saw her light on through the crack in their adjoining door, that he got out of bed again. He walked into her room to find her sitting on her bed already in her nightclothes and brushing her hair. She smiled at him and his heart hurt, God it hurt so much to see that smile.

"Are you feeling better? I was growing worried."

"I'm fine," he said, sitting down next to her. He moved her hair from her neck and kissed her there, trying not to let his hand tremble as he touched her. It was there, the delicate chain, and he felt his heart tear a little bit more.

Elizabeth smiled, glad he was feeling better. She'd missed him terribly all afternoon and had done nothing but wander about the house. She felt his mouth on her neck and tilted her head over to accommodate him.

"This necklace," he said.

And she stopped breathing, just like that.

"You wore it on our wedding night. I remember it."

Elizabeth felt her stomach wrench painfully. She'd forgotten it, she had, she had. It was so light and she'd gotten used to it and, oh, God, she had forgotten she was still wearing it. And he knew. Somehow he knew.

"You're wearing it now," he said, his voice so strange, his eyes looking at her in such an odd way.

He knew. He knew. She touched the thin chain, watched as his eyes followed the gesture. "It's nothing," she said. *Please, please, God.* "Rand." Why hadn't she taken it off? Why, why, why? "It's nothing."

Suddenly he changed, as if her words had enraged him, as if had she said one more word all his control would completely snap. "It is not *nothing!*" he shouted, his voice ending on a crescendo of pain. She winced as if he'd struck her. He was breathing harshly, looking at her as if she were some sort of monster. He closed his eyes and jerked his head away as if the very sight of her was too painful for him to bear.

"Take it off," he said, low and harsh.

She immediately moved her hands to her neck, but she was shaking so badly she couldn't find the clasp, never mind undo it.

"Take it off!" he shouted, coming toward her.

She started to cry. "I can't," she sobbed. "My hands."

He pushed her hands roughly away and yanked the necklace from her neck in one sharp motion. Then he looked at it in his hand, as if he held something vile. "We are leaving within a week. As soon as I find a ship, we are going to England. So there will be no time for tearful good-byes with Ellsworth. So he cannot see you wearing this . . . this . . . thing."

"Rand. I forgot about it. I didn't know I was wearing it. I swear I didn't."

"I don't care," he roared. And then, softer. "And I don't believe you. You are a liar. You told me you had not seen him. But then how did you get this little gift, I wonder."

"I knew you'd be upset."

"Upset?" he asked, as if that word could not come close to what he was feeling. "My dear wife," he sneered, "you have not seen upset."

Chapter 18

Elizabeth knew what was coming. Already she was sweating and the nausea was starting and she could still see Manhattan Island on the horizon, like tiny dark teeth jutting above the Atlantic.

She could not believe that just three days before she had felt happier than she'd ever been, looking forward to long, luxurious days with a husband she was coming to love. All that was gone and she knew in her heart she could only blame herself. Certainly, she had forgotten she was wearing the necklace Henry had given to her, but she had worn it purposefully beneath her wedding gown and on her wedding night. It had offered some comfort then. But it had been so wrong of her to do, adultery in her heart, if not her body.

Rand, in the space of a day, became a completely different person. His easy smile was gone, his kisses, his caresses, his laughter. His love. And Elizabeth had no idea how to get it all back, or truly whether she wanted to. She was barely getting to know the pleasant kind man and now he was someone entirely unpleasant. Her tears, her pleading had been met with only stony stares or his back. His only kindness was in allowing her to say good-bye to her mother and father.

Elizabeth swallowed, trying to keep the sickness at bay as long as possible. The journey on this wretched boat would take more than a week, a week of pure misery. Her mother had been more than surprised when she'd arrived home after only four days of their honeymoon to announce they were leaving in two days. Her mother, who'd never coddled her as a child, had blanched.

"Is he aware of how sick you become at sea?" she'd asked, her lips pressed tight with anger. "It is the whole reason we planned a spring departure, to save you the sickness. In winter, my God, Elizabeth, it will be impossible."

Elizabeth had forced a smile. She could never let her mother know what had transpired; there was no need to anger her mother when she might not see her for many months or even years. She knew Alva would take the duke's side, would be livid that she had allowed Henry to interfere with her marriage. If she knew she had worn that necklace, Elizabeth feared her mother, like Rand, would never forgive her.

"He knows only that I am a poor sailor. He's terribly homesick and the journey won't be that long. I'll be fine."

"I hope the ship is a large one. And comfortable," she said.

"Very large and very comfortable."

The ship was neither of those things. It was an ancient cargo vessel with an antiquated engine that shook the ship so much, Elizabeth wondered that it did not shake apart simply from that. The captain had already told them it was unlikely they would reach England on the coal they had on board, and very likely would have to hoist sails for part of the journey. That meant, of course, it would take even longer, and her torture would be extended. The ship was rusted and wholly the sorriest vessel Elizabeth had ever laid eyes on. But it was the only ship in port that would accommodate them on such short notice. The finer passenger ships did not travel in the dead of winter when seas were roughest and the danger of icebergs so great.

The English captain did keep an impeccable ship. He was polite, his men deferential to them—after all, it wasn't every day a sorry vessel like theirs carried a peer of the realm. The captain's cabin, which he had willingly given up to them, while tiny, was well heated. He'd told them the food was fine, as well, though Elizabeth knew she wouldn't be putting a morsel into her mouth until they reached the Thames and London.

Outside was frigid. She knew from experience that the best place for her to be was outside and staring at the horizon. She'd tried this, but had gotten so numb she was forced back inside in a matter of minutes. The ship heaved and Elizabeth let out a groan, more sick about what was to come than actually ill. More than one captain had remarked that he had never seen anyone get quite as ill as Elizabeth had. On the way home from Europe the last time, her mother had promised Elizabeth that she would never force her to travel to Europe again. She'd actually feared her daughter would succumb to the illness, and to be honest, Elizabeth had as well. Her mother conveniently forgot her promise, however, when she was looking for a titled husband for her daughter.

Three hours into the trip, Elizabeth vomited for the first time. Her head throbbed unmercifully; her body was bathed in a cold sweat. Moments later while she was still heaving over a chamber pot, Rand stuck his head into the room, took one look at her, and said rather cheerfully, "I suppose you won't be joining the captain and I for dinner. It's scrod." She shook her head and he left, and she swore she could hear him whistling lightly as he walked toward the dining hall. Apparently, His Grace had a stomach made of steel, she thought miserably, wondering what she had ever seen in the man.

Later that night, Rand returned, then immediately called for one of the crew to empty the chamber pot and clean it out. It was not a kindness, Elizabeth realized, but simply a way to make his own stay more bearable, for the stench was rather potent.

"I shouldn't worry about the smell of vomit," she said glaring at him in the lamplight. "I shan't have anything in my stomach for at least a week."

He simply stared at her and looked almost delighted by her news. "That is too bad. The cook is wonderful. I'll sleep on the floor. Do try not to vomit too noisily as I'd like to get some sleep."

At that moment, Elizabeth wished the chamber pot were full, for she would have thrown it at his smug head. How could she ever have thought him kind? How could she think she'd been falling in love with such a complete ogre? What had she done, really, but wear a necklace that an old beau had given her. He was overreacting and she would have told him so had she the strength to do it. But at that moment, she was desperately trying to control her uncontrollable stomach and losing the battle.

"How is your wife?" the captain asked Rand the following night.

"Still sick. She cannot keep even the smallest thing down. Not even water." He did not want to care, but he did not like to see anyone suffer the way Elizabeth was suffering. Even if she deserved it.

"It should pass," the captain said jovially. "She'll get her sea legs, you mark my words. Though not tonight, I daresay. We're heading into a storm."

"Not too big, I hope," Rand said, thinking Elizabeth was barely holding on in relatively calm seas. He'd never seen anyone as violently ill as she was. Saying she was a bad sailor was a vast understatement.

"No way to tell, really. But I saw some nasty clouds to the north. Crossing this time of year is always exciting. And always profitable." The captain lifted his drink as if he hadn't a care in the world. "You seem to be holding up well enough, Your Grace."

"I have a stomach of iron, it seems. I only got a bit queasy on the way over, and those were in some big seas."

"Should have been a navy man, then, like Admiral Nelson. Now there was a fine seaman," he said, as if he'd known the man. Again, he raised his glass and Rand got the distinct notion that the captain would likely toast anything given the opportunity. With a storm bearing down on them, now was not the time to be making too many toasts. "Duke and duchess on my ship. Now there's a story to tell my grandchildren," the captain said. He'd said the same thing during dinner the previous evening.

"Yes, well, I'd better see to my wife. I imagine you'll be needed at the helm this evening," Rand said, pointedly looking at his glass.

The captain accepted the censor good-naturedly, although with a bit of obvious regret. "Yes, that I will be."

Rand was satisfied when the captain motioned his steward over and waved the brandy away. Just then the ship dipped dramatically, then flew upward. "Hell. We're in for a night," the captain said, sounding actually excited by the prospect of a violent storm. "Begging your pardon, Your Grace, I'd best get back to work."

The next four days were nightmarish in more ways than one. Rand, who certainly didn't have vast experience at sea, had become convinced in the midst of the two-day storm that the ship would certainly break apart. The ship slammed into the waves with such bone-jarring force, it felt as if the very steel would shatter beneath them. And Elizabeth, she had been nearly driven unconscious from a combination of fear, sickness, and simply being battered about the small cabin as the waves crashed again and again into the ship's hull. While he sat in the cabin's only chair, white knuckling it through the worst of the storm, she clutched the bed trying not to be thrown to the floor. On one occasion, beaten into a fitless sleep by hours of wakefulness, she was thrown to the floor, knocking her chin hard against his boots.

Rand helped her up, asking if she were all right, but she pushed him off her without uttering a word. In fact, she managed only three coherent words during the height of the storm: "I hate you."

Rand was fairly certain she meant every syllable. He would probably hate himself, too, had someone been responsible for the kind of suffering Elizabeth was going through. If he had known the extent of her predisposition to seasickness, he might have delayed their trip. He'd wanted her to suffer, yes, but he began to fear she might actually die. And that was not endurable.

On the fifth day of their journey, Elizabeth was finally able to sit up, though she looked like death. Her hair, usually lustrous and neatly piled atop her head, was a tangled, straggling mass that no doubt stank of bile and vomit. The circles beneath her hollow eyes were downright frightening, her lips were cracked, and her skin had taken on a greenish cast. Guilt gnawed at Rand when he entered their cabin, feeling hail and hearty after a fine breakfast of sausage and potatoes. Even at the worst, Rand had felt little more than slight dizziness and a touch of nausea. But today, the sun was shining brightly, the seas were calm and a rich blue, and even the temperature had risen above the freezing point.

"Good morning," he said, staring at her and trying to mask the horror in his face. The morning light was doing nothing to make Elizabeth look better. Indeed, the harsh light gave her an almost ghoulish appearance. She didn't acknowledge him, simply turned her head away. As he stood there, her stomach heaved and she bent over the empty chamber pot, her poor stomach heaving and heaving but expelling nothing.

"You must try to eat something, Elizabeth."

"Go away," she croaked.

"Then at least drink water." She remained silent, staring at the wall. He stood there looking at her helplessly, watching as she listlessly drooped to lay upon the bed. He immediately went to her side.

"Why the hell didn't you tell me this would happen?" he demanded, his fear and frustration coming out in anger. "You knew, didn't you?"

"I did tell you," she said softly.

"I knew only that you were a poor sailor, that you got a bit seasick. Everyone gets a bit seasick sometimes. This goes far beyond what anyone on this ship has experienced. If I had known you would be this sick . . ." He likely would have left anyway, he thought guiltily. As he looked at her helplessly, he saw a large spot of blood, wet and bright and red on the sheets, and he felt his entire body go so weak, he sunk to his knees beside the berth.

"My God, you're bleeding," he whispered.

"I am?" she asked, as if it were no matter.

"Yes, and quite a bit," he said, pulling the covers from her, searching her for a wound. Blood was everywhere. "Oh, my God," he said, his voice shaking. "I'm going to get the captain. Oh, my God."

"Rand," she whispered.

"Don't worry, my love. You'll be fine," he said rushing to the door.

"Rand," she shouted, though it came out more like a croak. He turned, torn between going to her and running for the captain.

"It's only my monthlies," she said.

At first it didn't register, and then he looked at the sheet again, at the blood between her legs. "Oh." He nearly collapsed in relief, and in fact felt his knees give out beneath him so he was kneeling by her bed again. "We should clean you up. It's quite a lot there," he said, looking at horror at the blood on the sheet. Women bled this amount every month? Good God.

"It's not so much as it looks," she said. "Women wear padding. But I forgot to. So sick."

"I'll need clean sheets and clothes. And pads you say?"

"In my trunk, on the right side, near the top. Folded cloths for my pads. And a nightgown, too." Every word was such an effort for her. No doubt losing blood when she was already weakened had further sickened her. He would feed her, make her drink if he had to force it down her throat. As if to mock his thoughts, her stomach heaved uselessly again and the sound of her retching painfully nearly unhinged him.

"I can't take much more," she said. "My head is going to explode. Boom."

Rand felt his eyes burn. She was making light when she was so very, very ill, trying to make him laugh.

"Your head is not going to explode," he said.

"I wish it would."

"No," he said fiercely. "I'm going to get you cleaned up and well dressed and I am going to take you out onto the deck and sit you in the sun and you will get well enough to at least drink some water. And toast. Toast is just the thing when you can't eat anything else." He had opened the trunk and already found the pads and a fresh nightgown. "I'll be right back. I'm going to get some warm water and fresh linens. I hope to hell the captain has some. Don't go anywhere." She somehow managed to give him a withering look before he rushed off.

Elizabeth lay listlessly waiting for Rand to return. Her head felt as if, indeed, it were about to explode. Every time the nausea hit, it pounded even more. If anyone for the rest of her life suggested she take a sea voyage she would shoot them on the spot. She couldn't help think that God was punishing her for her sins. She'd been seasick before, yes, but this was so far beyond what even she had experienced she could only think that God was particularly displeased with her. If she had even the smallest bit of energy, having Rand discover she was having her monthlies would have been agonizingly embarrassing. She supposed she should at least be grateful that at the moment she truly wouldn't care if the ship sank to the bottom of the ocean. She simply wanted the pain and sickness to go away.

Rand returned in minutes, carrying a pitcher of warm water and several clean rags. He helped her out of her gown, and stared at her body, saying only, "We've got to get some food into you." He cleaned her with the warm water, then removed the soiled sheets from the bed as she sat listlessly in the cabin's only chair watching. Eyeing the bloodstain on the mattress that remained even after his attempt at cleaning it off, he smiled a bit mischievously at her and turned it over. "Good as new," he said. Instead of leading her back to bed, Rand wrapped her up in several blankets, covering her from head to toe, then carried her out to the deck.

The cold air felt wonderful against her skin, and Elizabeth closed her eyes, only to open them immediately when she felt the ship's movement.

"Look at the horizon," he said, leaning against the bulkhead and holding her in his arms, much like a baby. She rested her head against his shoulder, tucking her forehead against his neck. "The captain insisted that no one has ever died of seasickness. But people have died for lack of water. You will drink, Elizabeth. Small amounts your stomach can tolerate. I don't care if you vomit it up, you'll drink again. And again, until we reach the Thames. And then you are going to eat every bit of food in sight until I fatten you up."

"My mother will be quite upset with you if I get too fat."

"I don't care. I want you plump," he said, pulling her closer to him.

They were silent for a long time, Elizabeth staring out to sea, feeling better than she had in days. For the first time in nearly a week, her head was not pounding unmercifully, but only contained a dull throbbing that was easily tolerated. She still felt a bit queasy, but the body-racking vomiting had abated. For the moment.

"Do you still hate me?" she asked softly.

"You know I do not," he said, his words clipped.

"I don't hate you. I think I said I do, but I don't."

"That is good to hear." She stared at his profile and thought she detected the hint of a smile. For now, it was enough.

* * *

Maggie stepped through the door to her home and let out a sigh of relief. She was so tired of smiling, her face actually hurt. No one must ever know how very un-happy she'd been since waving wildly at Elizabeth's de-parting carriage. She had a sickening feeling that she would never see her friend again, which was silly be-cause Elizabeth wouldn't be departing for England until at least March.

It was purely awful not being able to talk to her friend. Even though they'd often been separated for months at a time, thanks to Alva's penchant for travel-ing, Maggie never quite got over not having her around. After Elizabeth left, it might be years and years before they saw each other again. She'd received one happy letter from her and wondered if everything her friend had written were true or was she simply trying to put a happy face on a miserable situation. Her words certainly seemed sincere, and Maggie hoped they were. She liked the duke and she wanted them to be happy together.

Happy, she thought, as she would never be.

After that horrible scene at Elizabeth's wedding break-fast, she had not seen Lord Hollings and she assumed he was already gone to England. Without a proper good-bye, and certainly without promises to return. Or send for her.

Maggie drew her hands out of her fur muff and crushed it in her fists. She was the most foolish, ridicu-lous girl in New York if she hoped for even one minute that Lord Hollings would suddenly find it impossible to live without her. And yet . . . how she did hope for just that thing. For far longer than a minute, as well.

"I'll take that, Miss," her butler, Saunders said. He eyed the crushed muff thoughtfully. "Already dead, right, Miss?"

Maggie gave him a withering look, trying, and failing, to suppress a smile. "If it wasn't, it is now. I've had a purely awful day, Saunders. Where is Mother?"

"In her sitting room, I believe."

Maggie shrugged off her coat and handed him that as well. "I needed that smile. Thank you."

Saunders beamed at her and disappeared with her cloak and muff as Maggie headed toward the stairs and her mother.

"Oh, I nearly forgot. This came for you in the post today." Saunders held up a letter and Maggie rushed down to retrieve it, her silly heart beating fast. She didn't look at it until she reached the first landing, telling herself over and over that it could not be from Lord Hollings. Why ever in the world would he write to her? But he might have, she could be holding his letter right now and in it he would beg her to come to England to be with him. It could be from him.

But it wasn't, of course. It was another letter from Elizabeth, which made Maggie smile faintly. It seemed her friend missed her as much as she missed Elizabeth. Taking the stairs a bit more slowly, she broke the wax seal and opened it up, only to lean heavily against the banister.

"I've no time to come to say good-bye, but wanted you to know I am leaving for England Monday. I'll write more later when I have the chance. Your dearest friend, Elizabeth."

Maggie sank down to the step, the letter held limply in her hand. She hadn't said good-bye. Surely she had time to stop by for a quick, tearful hug. Surely she couldn't have been in that much of a rush. Maggie felt as if her battered heart could not take much more and wondered if she could remain cheerful when all she wanted to do was cry for about a week. Feeling as if the life had been sucked from her, she made her way up the stairs and to her mother's sitting room, pausing before entering to gather herself together. Her mother hated tears; not because she had no tolerance for them, but because she simply could not bear to see them.

Maggie knocked smartly, and entered when her mother called out. "Mother," she said, "I've had the most dreadful news." She said it in a tone that certainly did not express her sadness. Indeed, her mother smiled when she made the announcement, if a bit uncertainly.

"Then you know," she said. "My poor girl, your heart must be broken."

Maggie smiled. "Not broken. Not nearly so. But I am a bit upset Elizabeth didn't stop to say good-bye in person. We are best of friends, after all," she said, waving the letter in her hand.

"Elizabeth is gone?"

"Well, yes. She left two days ago. Isn't that what you were talking about?"

Her mother looked down at her needlepoint, worrying the fabric between her hands. "Lord Hollings stopped by this morning while you were out. He's gone,

Maggie. Left just hours ago." Her mother searched her daughter's face, likely hoping her daughter wouldn't dissolve into tears.

Maggie suddenly found it necessary to sit. "Gone?"

"Yes. He's such a nice man. He stopped by to tell you he's leaving for England. I'm so sorry dear. I had hoped . . ."

Maggie was able to smile at her mother, though she was not quite certain where she found the courage. "He stopped by today?"

"Yes. While you were with your cousins."

"Did he leave a note?" she asked, hating the hope she heard in her own voice.

"No, no. Just stopped by. Are you heartbroken, dear?"

"Goodness, no, Mother. I never held out hope that the earl would make an offer, though I know you did. I'm sorry. We did get on well enough, but, my goodness, neither of us had any strong feelings. But I can always say I danced with an earl. Not every girl can, you know." Maggie smiled so brightly she thought her mother must know it was simply an act.

But no. Her mother beamed back at her, visibly relieved that her daughter didn't have a broken heart. "The Wright brothers are still vying for your hand, particularly that Arthur. I think your flirtation with the earl made you much more desirable in his eyes. And his mother's. Did you have a fine time with your cousins?"

The subject of Lord Hollings was swiftly dropped and Maggie managed to talk about her cousins for five minutes before escaping from her mother. She loved her dearly, but Maggie simply could not bear another minute of pretending her heart had not been broken not once, but twice, in the space of ten minutes.

When she reached her room, Margaret Pierce did something she had not done since she was perhaps ten years old. She threw herself upon her bed and cried body-racking sobs until her face was swollen and her nose so clogged she couldn't breathe. At supper time, she pleaded a sudden cold, made believable by her stuffed-up nose.

Why hadn't she been home? What had he come to say? She tortured herself with thoughts that had she been home, he would have fallen at her feet and begged her to marry him. But she hadn't been home. For the first time since Elizabeth's wedding, she'd gone out of the house. And he'd come to see her. She couldn't bear to wonder what might have been, if only she'd been home. She had a wild idea to run out, to try to find him before he left. But she didn't know where he was, how he was traveling. It would be impossible, though part of her, the part that was so very desperately in love, told her she should try. In the end, her practical side won out, as it always did. He was gone and she would never see him again and it was much better if she simply fully realized it. She'd always known she would never marry and now she was more certain than ever. For how could she ever love someone as much as she loved Lord Hollings?

"It hurts. My God, it hurts," she whispered, hugging herself and rocking. She knew one thing, she never wanted to hurt like this again. Never.

Chapter 19

It was strange that when Elizabeth, the new Duchess of Bellingham, stepped from their carriage, she felt much like she imagined she would all those months ago when she'd agreed to marry the duke. She was completely overwhelmed and more than a little frightened by what lay ahead. Bellewood, from first appearances, was the most elaborate and beautiful private palace she had ever seen. It was almost ridiculously grand, making their Newport cottage look like an outbuilding in comparison. Nothing had prepared her for the grandeur, the immense size, of Bellewood. Her first reaction when she stepped out was to let out a small giggle. She turned to share her feelings with Rand, but he swept past her, staring at the palace with the oddest expression.

The center of the baroque building was dominated by a huge portico with six grand columns. Two wings stretched out from the main hall in an ominous embrace of granite and mullioned windows. It was a blustery, cold day, but Elizabeth, who was finally feeling more herself, did not care as she stared at the manse that would be her home. For all its massive grandeur, a closer look revealed that the palace was in disrepair, the grounds neglected. Even the long winding drive leading to the palace had been rutted and lined with rather sick-looking trees. It was obvious that not a penny had been spent on Bellewood in years.

"This is where you grew up?" Elizabeth asked, trying to picture a little boy running about.

"I used to get lost, all the time," he said, staring at the palace. "You can see, it needs repair. I'm afraid most of the servants have been let go. I've only a butler, cook, house-keeper, and a handful of servants. I know you're used to more." She watched as the muscle in his jaw bunched.

"This is plenty," she said, referring to the vastness of the building. Though she would never say so, she found the palace completely uninviting.

He turned to her. "My first priority, as I've said, is to help my tenants. I'm afraid conditions here are not what you are used to." The wind buffeted his hair and drove his collar up against his neck, making him look much as she'd pictured Heathcliff in Emily Bronte's *Wuthering Heights,* angry, masculine, and unapproachable.

"You've told me about the heat. A nice big fire will be fine," Elizabeth said, trying to be cheerful.

"There is almost no furniture. It's filthy. The grounds are in ruin."

"You've told me this," she said, getting impatient. She wanted to simply go in and have her things un-packed. Perhaps having a nice warm bath would be lovely and then she'd crawl into bed. She was feeling better after their ten-day sea trip, but she was still weak from what she'd gone through.

"If I had a choice, I would not bring a bride here," he said, his eyes still on the palace.

It was such a ridiculous statement, Elizabeth almost laughed. In front of her was perhaps the grandest palace in England, but for Buckingham Palace. If it needed a bit of sprucing up, well, a bit of dust wouldn't hurt her. "Where would you bring her?"

"Anywhere else."

Rand took one step toward the entry, and the massive door swung open to reveal perhaps ten servants waiting inside, lined up like a small troop of soldiers bundled against the cold. The damn place had always been difficult to keep warm, even when there had been funds to do so. The list of things facing him was overwhelming, and would have to start with such basic things as ordering coal and hiring servants. He certainly couldn't expect someone who had grown up in the luxury Elizabeth had to huddle by a fire for warmth. No doubt she'd never lived in a home without central heating or a toilet and bath for each bedroom. No doubt she was wishing she was anywhere else at the moment but standing in front of this broken-down mausoleum. But Rand had nowhere else to go and the great responsibility of bringing back the estate to its former grandeur weighed heavily. But all that would have to wait until the tenants' homes had been completely refurbished. It would likely be years before the palace was the way he wanted it. Again, he found himself humiliated with the knowledge that the woman standing next to him meant the difference between vast wealth and complete ruin. He'd thought he'd gotten used to the idea, but standing at his family's estate, he fiercely felt the shame of what had become of Bellewood.

"Your Graces," a man in a formal black suit said, bowing. Those servants in line bowed or curtsied, deep and low.

"Tisbury," he said in greeting, looking about the massive and quite empty entry hall. The private apartments on the southern wing were far more homey than this, which at one time had been opened for passing tourists. Now, the tourists would have nothing to see but a great amount of marble and dust. The contrast between Bellewood and Elizabeth's finely decorated homes was quite glaring, and he dared a look at her to gauge her reaction. She stood next to him, smiling at the servants, looking amazingly uncertain for a girl who had been drilled from birth for such a life.

"We have had a difficult journey, particularly Her Grace. I pray her room is ready and a fire lit."

"Yes, Your Grace. We've done what we could do to make your apartments comfortable."

"If you please, Your Grace," a maid said, dipping a curtsy in front of Elizabeth that would have looked far finer if she hadn't been wearing two thick sweaters over her uniform. "I will show you to your rooms."

Rand could feel Elizabeth looking at him, but he let her go without a word. The last time he had held her had been on the ship when she had been so very ill. He had told her he did not hate her, and that was true enough. But nor could he allow himself to love her, as he so foolishly had. Every time he thought of making love to her, every time he'd kissed her neck, he'd touched that necklace, and she had known it was there, giving her comfort so that she could bear his touch when she obviously longed for another.

Rand would be a good husband. He would make certain they had an heir. He would work himself into exhaustion to make Bellewood as beautiful as she ought to be and his tenants well off and happy. But he would never allow his heart to be willingly given to Elizabeth. At least he prayed to God he would not. Even now, as she walked away, bewildered and probably a bit frightened, a small part of him called out for him to go to her, to comfort her, to let her know everything would be all right.

"We have much to do in the next few days, Tisbury. Including hiring enough servants to take care of Bellewood as she deserves."

The servants cheered at that news. They'd likely worn themselves into a frazzle knowing the duke was arriving with his new duchess. "Mrs. Stevens, you have my permission to hire your staff as you see fit. Enough to care for the main public rooms and the south wing."

"Yes, Your Grace," the woman said happily. She'd been with the family for fifteen years, and had been heartbroken when she'd been forced to let go of most of her staff.

"If you could direct someone to bring in our luggage, I believe it has arrived behind us."

"Dinner at eight, Your Grace?"

Rand smiled. Even with such commotion, there were some things that had to remain constant, and one of those was dinner at eight. "Yes, Mrs. Stevens. I'm looking forward to some fine English cooking."

Elizabeth followed the maid, feeling a bone-deep chill in the long hallway that a dozen fires could not change. When she was a girl, her father had brought her to an ice barn in the middle of June, and she had marveled at how cold it was inside. That was how cold it was inside Bellewood. She still wore her long coat and muff and realized why no servant had come forward to take them.

"Should be a bit warmer in your room, Your Grace. We've had a fire blazing all day," the maid said in an accent that was difficult for Elizabeth to understand. Her footsteps echoed on the marble floor that was completely unadorned by carpets. Finally, the maid paused and opened a set of towering French doors. "This is the private dining hall," she said. She nodded to a door on the left. "His Grace's rooms are there." She moved to a door opposite and separated from Rand's by the large dining room. "These are your rooms, Your Grace," she said, opening the door to reveal a wonderful blast of warm air.

"Oh, it's so warm," Elizabeth gushed, immediately going to a large, ornate fireplace where a fire merrily danced. "I feel as though I haven't been warm in ages."

"Yes, Your Grace. The porters will be bringing you your things shortly. Dinner will be served at eight." With that, the maid curtsied and left.

Elizabeth stared at the fire a moment before turning

to survey her new rooms, letting out a small "oh" when she finally comprehended what her eyes were seeing. It was a perfectly lovely room, nicely lit by floor-to-ceiling windows that even now rattled a bit from the wind outside. But the room, as large and lovely as it was, contained only three pieces of furniture: a large wardrobe, a bed, and a washstand. Elizabeth eyed the washstand with a bit of amused disappointment. Her rooms back in Newport and New York had a private bath with a flushing toilet, a wonderful round tub with hot and cold running water, and a basin. Seeing a room off to the side, Elizabeth hurried over, struck by how cold the room got once she was away from the fire. It was a small, and quite empty, sitting room. No toilet, no bathtub. No hot and cold running water. Looking back to the room, she spotted a chamber pot, ornately decorated with nymphs running about, probably in search of a proper toilet, she thought. Obviously, installing indoor plumbing had not been a priority for the cash-poor Blackmores.

A sound at the door took her attention away from her thoughts of a warm bath. Rand stood at the entrance, staring at her as if it were her fault the home was inadequate. Then again, Rand seemed to look angry all the time of late. She missed the way he'd been at Rosebrier before, and knew she had no one to blame but herself. Which made her angry and surly and completely unhappy.

"At least it is warm in our rooms," he said, looking about her room.

"It's lovely," she said. When he raised a sardonic eyebrow, she smiled sheepishly. "Sparse, but lovely."

"Perhaps you should rest before dinner," he said.

"You are still recovering from our trip. I'll see you at eight, then."

"I am tired," Elizabeth said, realizing that she, indeed, was exhausted.

He looked as if he were about to depart without another word, but he stopped. "I shall be extremely busy in the next few weeks and rarely here. I will leave it to you to get the house in order. Servants must be hired, things ordered. I had forgotten how empty this place was. It's completely inadequate. I realize that."

"May I order plumbing first?" she asked, making what she thought was a joke.

"You may do whatever you wish with your father's money," he said.

He left then, leaving Elizabeth feeling quite horrid, and ridiculously guilty for something that was not her doing at all. She'd never once thrown in his face that every penny they would spend was from her family. She loathed the entire discussion of money and how it surrounded their entire wedding like some malevolent cloud. How dare he use that to make her feel even more awful than she already did.

"I didn't hear you ever complaining about the settlement before," she shouted to his retreating back. "I will not be made to feel badly about something I never wanted in the first place."

He was back in an instant, his face dark with anger. "You have made it entirely clear, many times in fact, that you did not want this marriage. Spend the goddamn money, Elizabeth, for it will be your only comfort in the months to come."

She shrank back from his anger, from the venom in his voice. "I meant only I never liked the idea of buying a title."

"Then we are in agreement about this entire marriage, for I never liked the idea of being bought. Yet here we are, my dear."

"Here we are," she said, feeling sadness overwhelm her.

"Our things have arrived," he said, backing from the door to allow two young porters into her room with one of her massive trunks. By the time she was done directing the men where to put it, Rand was gone.

Chapter 20

"Are you not yet breeding?"

Elizabeth stared at the dowager duchess with horror and not a little fear, for the woman was, without a doubt, the most intimidating person she had yet to meet. She made her mother seem a cozy, country lass who cooked apple pies for a brood of children. The dowager sat on a thronelike chair, her hair piled high and ornately upon her head, draped in jewels and squeezed into a gown so intricately made, Elizabeth imagined an army of seamstresses must have been employed. She gazed down at Elizabeth through a pair of quizzing glasses as if she were a new and inadequate servant. And she wanted to know if she were "breeding."

One must have sex in order to have children. How she longed to say those words, especially because Rand stood behind her, likely highly amused that his mother was treating her so abhorrently. "No, ma'am," she said, her cheeks burning with humiliation.

"You do know that is your most important duty." She looked back at Rand. "She does know this, does she not?"

"Yes, Mother."

Elizabeth could hear in his voice that he was trying not to laugh. She only wished she were sharing his great amusement instead of being put on display. Rand had warned her that his mother would be angered that he married an American, and that his mother knew almost nothing of his financial difficulties. It gave Elizabeth little comfort to know that her family's money would no doubt go a long way toward making this woman's life more comfortable. The dowager lived in a lovely town house that Rand had been on the verge of losing, for it was the only piece of property, other than Bellewood, that he had left to sell. His mother had been completely ignorant of this. How Elizabeth longed to tell this woman that she was completely dependent upon her money, to bring her down a bit. It was clear within minutes of their meeting that she thought Elizabeth specifically, and Americans in general, far beneath her consideration.

After her torturous interview, which lasted perhaps five minutes, the dowager dismissed her, forcing Elizabeth to wait in the hall like a wayward child while Rand spoke with his mother. She could not hear a word they said, only certain tones that told her Rand was placating and his mother enraged. Honestly, one might think she'd been a wharf rat the way the woman was carrying on. Elizabeth, who all her life had been treated with the utmost respect, found herself in the position of being made to feel inferior. She did not at all feel that way, however, which likely had the older woman in a snit. Elizabeth would no sooner apologize for being American as she would for her father's overly generous settlement that would benefit the old cow.

Inside the room, Rand was only mildly irritated by his mother's behavior. She was behaving precisely the way he imagined. If anything, she had deported herself with immense calm and restraint, compared to how Rand expected her to act.

"Mother, she comes from an excellent family."

"An American, really, Rand. When you wrote to me, I could not believe it. I simply could not fathom why you would choose an American when there are so many fine English ladies who would far better fill the role of duchess. Why her? By the way, I heard she was brought about by her mother last year and I must say at the time I thought it completely vulgar of the mother to think anyone would consider the girl. And then my own son . . ." Apparently, her rage made her unable to continue.

Rand let out a sigh of impatience. While he could not tell his mother the true reason for the marriage, he also would not lie and tell her he'd fallen madly in love with her. "She'll make a fine duchess. She is beautiful and extremely intelligent. I believe she will handle the duties with ease."

"She looks like a child. How old is she?"

"She is nineteen."

His mother pressed her lips together. "She *is* a child."

"You were seventeen when you married Father," Rand pointed out.

"But I did not become a duchess until I was well into my thirties."

Rand was so very tired and completely overwhelmed by everything that needed to be done with the estate, he had no energy left over to deal with his mother. He'd only arranged this meeting to get it over with. "I cannot argue with you, Mother. Time will tell if Elizabeth is up to the task. Right now, I would be more worried about me."

His mother waved away his concerns. "You will do fine. I do wish you'd spent more time with your brother and father, but it is in your blood to lead. I have no doubt, none at all, that you will fill those shoes and fill them well."

"Then please have confidence in my choice of duchess."

She pressed her lips together and forced a nod. "I shall visit you when you can present me with a grand-child," she announced, dismissing him. "See to it that it is done quickly."

With a nod and a barely hidden smile, Rand left, glad the interview was over. He'd been away from Bellewood for four necessary days, but with everything he had to do, it seemed far too long. Their days had been spent ordering massive amounts of goods, including basic furniture for their apartments and consulting with builders for the necessary upgrades to Bellewood. Nothing would be done until spring, but they could at least come and see what putting in central heating, a modern kitchen, and central plumbing would entail. For now, he was busy working on the tenants' homes, some of which were barely livable. He'd also hired a property manager, and a valet, though he hardly thought he needed one with their social life nearly nonexistent.

The visit with his mother was the last appointment on their long list of things to do while in London and he was more than glad to return home. He had been back in England for a month and was pleased with the progress being made on the cottages. Roofs were being repaired, walls whitewashed, doors and windows replaced, and every home under his domain would have central heating and plumbing. It was humbling how grateful the tenants had been for even the smallest repairs, and it made him even more ashamed that they had been neglected for so long. It was difficult for him to believe his father and brother had actually collected rent on some of the places, which had become little more than hovels. It was a modern age and there was no reason anyone should live in such poverty. At least not on Bellingham lands.

He found Elizabeth pacing outside his mother's sitting room, obviously upset about the interview with his mother. As soon as she saw him, she marched over to him, fists clenched. Perhaps she was more than upset.

"How could you allow your mother to speak to me in such a way?" she demanded in a harsh whisper.

"I have no control over what my mother says or thinks. She is old and set in her ways. I knew she would be disappointed with my choice in a bride and I believe I warned you."

She glared at him, which for some reason he found extremely funny, though he tried hard not to show it.

"You're laughing at me," she declared.

Apparently he was not at all good at hiding his mirth. "No. Well, yes. You look so very . . . fierce."

Elizabeth let out a puff of anger. "She asked me if I were breeding."

"Yes. I heard that." He looked decidedly amused.

"Don't laugh at me," she said, getting quite cross. "I should have told her the truth. That one cannot breed if one does not share a bed with one's husband."

Rand's apparent delight at her anger vanished immediately. "We should go now if we wish to get back to Bellewood by dark," he said, turning abruptly away.

"Yes. As soon as things get the slightest bit difficult, it is always best to turn away," she shot at his back. She was so sick of being punished for something she was beginning to believe wasn't that large a crime. Was he to treat her this way their entire marriage?

He continued walking out the door, his entire body stiff with anger, and Elizabeth walked after him, just as angry that he was angry. When they reached the outside, he turned on her.

"You made a fool of me. You broke my . . . trust." He swallowed and looked away, working his jaw. "That, my dear, is not a slight difficulty, as you say. Not to me."

Elizabeth felt her anger immediately deflate and her eyes prick with unshed tears. "We should go," she said, stepping down toward their waiting carriage. The footman immediately leaped down and assisted her in, and

Rand followed, sitting across from her and gazing out the window.

It was a long, silent journey home. They stopped once to eat at an inn, then continued on to Bellewood, reaching it after dark. Rand immediately went to the stables, as he had each night for weeks. She had no idea what he was doing inside, because there were no horses to tend to other than the two that pulled their carriage. It wasn't as if Bellewood wasn't large enough for him to disappear in so he wouldn't have to be near her.

Elizabeth let out a sigh and trudged up the small set of steps that led to the private apartments. She'd been in the massive home for weeks, and still hadn't seen an entire wing of the house where the formal state dining and meeting rooms were and honestly didn't much care to. They were no doubt another series of vast, empty and very dusty rooms.

"Good evening, Your Grace," Tisbury said, holding out his hand to take her cloak and muff.

"Good evening, Tisbury. It's nice and warm in here," she said. Tisbury had been one of the original servants, and no doubt remembered the chilly days spent inside the place. Elizabeth walked to her room, her footsteps echoing in the long, empty hall, feeling as if she were quite alone even though she knew the house was now filled with servants. When she reached her room, she sat upon her bed, feeling depressed and out of sorts. She didn't know how to fix things between her and Rand, and desperately wanted to. Simply put, she missed him. She missed the way he looked at her, as if she was the most beautiful woman on earth. She missed how he touched her, how he made her feel so incredibly wonderful. She missed feeling his warmth next to her in bed. And she didn't know how to get it back. That letter had been so damning. No matter what she said now, he would think her actions filled with ulterior motives. She was honest enough with herself to admit that when she was first married, Henry's words had filled her with a small amount of solace, and that only compounded the guilt she felt.

Worst of all, perhaps, was that she had absolutely no one to talk to. Her days were endless and tedious, filled with duty and very little joy. She longed for Maggie, her cousins, even her mother—anyone who would listen to her. She found herself alone most of the time with nothing but her thoughts to keep her company. She'd never thought of herself as a frivolous girl, but how she longed for a ball or dinner or the opera, for one single reason to get dressed each day.

If the days were endless, the nights were purely solitary. Rand never appeared at the dinner table, and never came to her, not even to say good night. Their rooms were so far apart, she hardly even heard him enter his own rooms. If it hadn't been so very cold everywhere in the house, Elizabeth might have sat in the mansion's only other furnished room to curl up with a book. But the long walk from her room to the sitting room made such a thought extremely distasteful, especially since the servants did not tend to fires in rooms that were not occupied.

Like every other night, Elizabeth found herself sitting

alone at the dining table, feeling slightly humiliated to be accompanied by only the footman, who stood so still at the door awaiting to serve her slightest need. She hadn't much appetite, and the large amount of food put in front of her could have fed five people. After forcing down a bit of each course, Elizabeth stood and thanked the footman and disappeared into her room. It wasn't even half-past eight and she was done for the evening. Back home, she would have been getting ready for a dinner or a ball or for a night at the opera. She would be chatting with Maggie or her mother about something. Anything.

She felt much as she had in Newport when she'd been confined to her room and not allowed to participate in any amusements. It wasn't, she realized, the amusements themselves that she missed, but the basic human interaction. Discussing the weather, the newest fashions, politics, something that would stir her brain a bit. She was surrounded by servants, who still looked at her curiously, and the one other person she could talk to hadn't mumbled more than a few words since their arrival in England. She looked at her embroidery and grimaced, refusing to take it up out of pure boredom. Elizabeth, along with the finer womanly arts such as pianoforte and needlepoint, had been educated much like a boy, she realized. She was used to being challenged mentally and found herself missing reading the many books her family's houses always contained. How wonderful it would have been if Bellewood had a large library, but the books, along with everything else, had been sold.

Rising from her bed, Elizabeth went out into the

dining room and toward the entrance, bracing herself against the cold. No matter how warm the rooms were kept, the halls were always chilly.

"Tisbury, do you know where I might find the duke?" she asked.

"His Grace is in the stables, Your Grace."

"Would you please fetch my cloak and muff," she said, peering out a window into the darkness. She couldn't see the stables from that vantage point. Indeed, she wasn't certain where they were.

"The stables," she said, after pulling on her cloak.

"Behind the west wing, Your Grace."

"Thank you, Tisbury."

He gave a little bow and opened the door for her, and Elizabeth was immediately buffeted by an icy cold blast.

"'Tis a bit raw out tonight. Might snow. Shall I accompany you, Your Grace?"

Elizabeth smiled. "I shouldn't think I'll get lost. Or buried in any snow should it start. Thank you."

She followed a gravel drive that swept around the massive home, huddling down into her cloak. It certainly was cold enough for snow, she thought, and found herself longing for the warm days of summer. She turned the corner and stopped, her eyes searching for something that could be the stable. About two hundred yards away she could seen a dim rectangular light and started walking that way, hoping she was going in the right direction. If her eyes hadn't told her, her nose would have, for the closer she got to the large building, the stronger the scent of hay and horse. As she drew

closer still, she could hear pounding, the distinctive
sound of a nail being driven into wood. Having grown
up with a mother who was constantly redecorating, it
was a familiar sound to Elizabeth.

The stable was a huge stone structure that resembled
more of an English country home than a place that housed
animals. The windows were dimly lit, as if only a single
lamp was illuminated within, and the door leading into
the stables was slightly ajar. She heard nothing but the
periodic hammering and the rustling of leaves pushed by
the wind into the stones. Elizabeth withdrew one hand
from her muff and pushed the door open just enough to
peek inside. There, at the far end of the stables, she saw a
lantern sitting near a sawhorse. She could see no soul in
the stable, but for the two carriage horses. She eased herself into the room, immediately struck by how warm it
was, far warmer than any room inside the house. A large
woodstove near the center of the long row of stalls was
likely the source of the wonderful heat.

Elizabeth padded toward the hammering, her slippers
nearly silent on the smooth stone floor, walking past one
empty stall after another. Here and there, fresh wood had
been nailed to the stalls in apparent repairs, and Elizabeth was aware of the smell of sawdust over the smell of
hay and horse. She was nearly even with the wonderfully
warm stove, when she reached the stall where Rand
worked, unaware she was in the building. She peeked
over the stop of the stall and gasped lightly, for he was
naked from the waist up, his back glistening with sweat,
and she stared with a painful longing at his beautiful

form. As he worked, one knee on the stone floor, a hand bracing against the wood where he hammered, the muscles on his back moved in an almost erotic rhythm. Desire hit her, swept through her body so unexpectedly, so brutally, she found herself clinging to a rough wooden post gasping for breath. The hammering stopped, and he stood and stretched, giving off an intoxicating groan that sounded, to Elizabeth's overheated ears, like a man in ecstasy, all those wonderful muscles on his back expanding and contracting. She watched silently hoping he wouldn't notice her standing there staring at him. He reached for another board and picked up a nail, putting it in his mouth as he adjusted the plank and all the time Elizabeth watched, her mouth going dry.

Elizabeth slowly turned, mortified by her thoughts and suddenly desperate to get away before he knew she'd been watching him. Rand jerked his head, cocking his ear, and Elizabeth had the ridiculous urge to throw herself down into the nearby stall to hide. And then he turned quickly, taking a combative stance, as if he were about to attack. When he saw her, he straightened and immediately reached for his shirt, which hung limply on the stall gate.

"Elizabeth," he said, sounding slightly irritated as he pulled his shirt on and began to button. "I beg your pardon, I didn't hear you come in."

Elizabeth swallowed, her eyes drifting down to his still-exposed chest. "You were hammering," she said stupidly.

"So I was. What do you want?"

What did she want? Not quite what she wanted when

she'd left the house to come in search of him. Then, all she'd wanted was a bit of companionship, a conversation about the weather, perhaps. She certainly could not tell him what she wanted now.

"I was lonely," she said, which was true enough.

"I have work to do." It was a dismissal, and one Elizabeth chose to ignore.

"May I watch?" she asked. She didn't care if she sounded pathetic. Certainly watching Rand hammer was far more fascinating than staring at the walls in her room, as lovely as they were.

He gave her a strange look, then shrugged, and turned back to his work, picking up the board and repositioning it.

Elizabeth frowned at his back where his shirt stuck to him uncomfortably. "You could take your shirt off again if you like. It is dreadfully warm in here," she said cheerfully.

He froze, then straightened slowly, his eyes burning into her. He took a step toward her, then stopped. "Perhaps you should return to the house, Elizabeth."

Elizabeth smiled to hide the sharp stab of disappointment. Feeling foolish for being so bold, she nodded, then shook her head in disgust for being so meek. He was her husband and she was going to talk to him whether he liked it or not. "I'll stay," she said, lifting her chin in a challenge. "I won't bother you. I promise." She smiled hopefully.

Tossing down the hammer in disgust, he muttered, "I'm done for the night, then."

"You are a coward," Elizabeth declared.

He was at her in two long strides, his hands wrapping around her upper arms. "Tell me, dear wife, what am I afraid of?"

"Me."

He stared down at her, pulling so close she had to bend her neck back to see him. She was done with being meek, done with sitting alone every night, done with wanting him and not having him.

"I am afraid of you," he admitted, rather nonchalantly, his voice deceivingly soft. "I'm afraid that if I touch you I won't be able to stop."

"You're touching me now," she pointed out blithely.

"Not the way I want to. Not nearly the way I want to," he said, then brought his head down as if he planned to kiss her. Instead he let out a groan of anger or frustration, Elizabeth didn't know which. He pushed her from him, his breath coming out harshly and he looked at her as if he hated her.

"Why are you here?" he demanded again, his eyes, almost unwillingly, dropped to her mouth. *He wants me,* she thought, feeling the slightest bit of hope.

"Because I miss you," she said, opting for complete honesty.

He closed his eyes briefly, and let out a short breath.

"I miss you touching me." She bit her lip, wondering if she'd said too much. He let out a small, tortured laugh, then shook his head as if to clear it.

"That's too damn bad for you," he said, walking

stiffly over to the sawhorse and grabbing a saw and a long plank.

"So this is how it's going to be? Forever? You're going to punish me forever?"

He looked at her as if she'd gone mad. "Punish *you*," he said incredulously. He shook his head, clearing his thoughts or shaking away the anger, she wasn't certain which. "Go back to the house," he said finally, as he began sawing brutally through the wood. The sharp smell of fresh sawdust stung her nostrils.

Elizabeth stared at him for a few minutes before turning with a little huff. Stubborn, ridiculous man, she thought as she marched to the stable door. As she passed the last stall, one of the carriage horses whickered at her, and she muttered, "To hell with you, too."

When Rand was certain she was gone, he knelt by the board he'd been sawing and pressed his forehead painfully against it, letting out a strangled sound that might have been laughter, but held far too much misery for that happy sound.

Why had she come out to the stable, his one sanctuary where all he had to think about was pounding and sawing and backbreaking work? Every night after a long day working with his tenants and the men repairing the multitude of houses on his land, he'd come to the stables and work. At first, it had been a way to escape her. If he was in the stables, he couldn't hear her moving quietly about her room, the way she hummed without even knowing it. Her heavy sighs. The sound of the bed creaking when she finally succumbed and went to bed

Now, he found he enjoyed the work. He missed the physical nature of soldiering, and realized his blue blood needed hard labor to be content. He didn't think of her; he didn't even want her. But she'd come to him and now whenever he worked in the stables, he knew he'd see her standing there in the lamplight looking so damned beautiful, her eyes filled with desire, her body soft and so inviting he'd nearly taken her there on the straw-covered floor. She'd wanted him. He'd seen it in her eyes like a stab to his heart. My God, she'd been fairly panting with desire and he'd sent her away. He was either the biggest fool or still half in love with her. Rand squeezed his eyes at that errant thought.

Perhaps it wasn't love, perhaps it was the physical release that she offered that had him so half crazed. He ached for her, a physical pain that was not going to go away until he had her—or any woman. He should travel to London and look up his old mistress from his days in the Guards. Mary had always been able to slake his needs, and was mighty pretty if a man wasn't too particular about straight teeth. Even as he thought of Mary's charms, he knew he would not be able to drive Elizabeth's face completely from his mind. He did not want any woman; he wanted his wife. He wanted to hear her sigh as he kissed her breasts, the way she whimpered lightly when she was about to come.

Rand tore a hand through his hair and squeezed until the pain of desire simply became pain. He was aroused and sweating and if he didn't have sex this night he'd kill someone for merely looking at him strangely. He was damned to live this hell because he knew he didn't simply want sex, he wanted to make love with his wife.

And she wanted him.

Hell, he might as well give them both what they wanted, he thought, throwing down the saw for the last time that night. He'd simply have to find a way to guard his heart.

Chapter 21

Elizabeth had been gone for less than two months and already Maggie's life had changed to such a degree that it was mind-boggling. She realized quite quickly that nearly every invitation that came her way from the coveted New York Four Hundred, had come via Elizabeth. It was a rare event indeed when she was included on the list of guests at one of the most prestigious balls of the season, and it was likely more of an oversight by the hostess rather than a pointed invitation.

Lately, she'd been attending less grand affairs within the social fringes of the Four Hundred, or else been staying home entirely. Attending anything wasn't the same without Elizabeth at any rate. It seemed everything had dulled, and she knew it wasn't only her friend's absence that was to blame, but memories of someone else entirely. She simply found everyone lacking after Lord Hollings. They weren't as witty or handsome or tall. And she couldn't imagine losing herself in a kiss with any of the men whom she met.

She walked into the Von Platt's home on the arm of

her brother and saw the same faces she'd been seeing for years. The Four Hundred was a rather exclusive club with only a limited number of eligible bachelors, most of whom seemed to end with the name Wright.

Arthur Wright, it seemed, was courting her in earnest, and other than telling him outright to go away, she wasn't certain what to do. If she were completely honest, which she always tried to be, she had to admit that she liked Arthur for there was nothing really to dislike. She supposed he was good-looking. He was intelligent enough and was now heading a vast portion of his father's interests. But, my goodness, he was boring. They could stand side by side for nearly an hour and not say a word unless Maggie brought up a topic she knew he could talk about—Egyptology. Unless they were touring a museum that held the remains of mummified kings and queens, the man had nothing to talk about. He would stand by her rocking heel to toe, heel to toe, looking about the room as if everyone in it was remarkably fascinating.

She stood by him at the moment, watching New York's elite waltz by, wistfully thinking back on another ball when she stood by another man chatting happily about everything and nothing. Lord Hollings had been a man she could completely relax with—as long as they were in public. If ever she was alone with him, she had been anything but comfortable, she'd been wonderfully terrified. And hopeful. And desperately in love.

"Hello, Miss Grayson," Arthur said next to her. Charlotte Grayson had been in Elizabeth's wedding party, much to her best friend's objections. Charlotte was a nasty girl, inside and out. Some people found her attractive, but to Maggie there was something about her face that was as mean and spiteful as her insides. Her hair was blond, her eyes blue, but set too close together for her to be a true beauty. And her mouth was so thin, it would have been nearly invisible but for the rouge she put on it.

"Mr. Wright. Oh, Margaret. How are you? I do have the most wonderful news." She looked at Arthur, who didn't get the hint that he should leave until Maggie gave him a bit of a nudge. When Arthur was gone, she held up her hand, and Maggie couldn't help but smile.

"You're engaged! Congratulations, Charlotte. Another grand wedding already. Imagine." Other than Elizabeth, Charlotte was known as one of the wealthiest heiresses in New York. Thus far, her money hadn't attracted a husband, no doubt even all that cash couldn't overcome Charlotte's personality, Maggie thought rather uncharitably. To be fair, she didn't really know Charlotte all that well and was basing her opinion on tales Elizabeth and others had told her. With this in mind, she decided to be pleasant. Being pleasant when she did not want to be had become quite a necessary talent of late.

"You were at Elizabeth's wedding, weren't you?" she asked, and Maggie couldn't help think she was only asking to remind her she had not been included in the wedding party.

"Yes, I was."

"Mother is beside herself with joy. She had given up hope, but I found the perfect man. Henry Ellsworth."

Maggie could not stop her shock from showing. "Henry Ellsworth?"

"He's perfect." She let out a laugh. "Oh, stop looking

at me like that. I know perfectly well he's marrying me for my money and I don't care," she said, making a gesture as if it was inconsequential. "We understand each other and get along famously."

"I'm certain it must be more than that," Maggie said graciously.

Charlotte shrugged. "I'm twenty-four," she said, as if indulging a great secret. Maggie looked suitably shocked, although she'd actually thought her a bit older. "I know for a fact that he secretly courted Elizabeth. He told me himself. He held up hope 'til the end that she'd jilt the duke. Do you know what he did?" As a footman passed with a tray of champagne, Charlotte took one and Maggie realized it wasn't her first drink of the night. By far.

"He told me on the eve of her wedding he actually gave her a note, begging her to remember him." She laughed. "Oh, God, he is such a nasty man, but I do adore him. Truly." She took a sip. "Sad thing is, I think he actually loved her. Idiot," she said rather fondly.

Charlotte laid a hand on her arm, nearly overcome with mirth. "But he loved her money far better. Oh, can you imagine sending her such a note? Oh, goodness, he can make me laugh. I think he actually thought she'd jilt a *duke* for him. I told him he was going to have to work on his charms. He was so insulted." She took a sip of her champagne. "And then he found me." She smiled, but there was something tragic about that smile.

"I think you'll make a wonderful couple," Maggie said, feeling slightly sick to her stomach. She hadn't known about the note, Elizabeth hadn't said a thing. Oh, poor Elizabeth. She'd been so upset about marrying Bellingham. It was bad enough to run into Henry right before the wedding, but for him to have given her that note was unforgivable. "Is he here tonight?" she asked sweetly.

"Oh, somewhere," Charlotte said, waving one hand negligently. "Probably in the billiard room. It's where I always find him."

"You know, Charlotte, some people might think what Henry did was unforgivable. Especially members of this set. You know how powerful the Cummings are. I hope you haven't told too many people about this," Maggie said, praying for her friend's sake that such a humiliating tale had not been spread.

Charlotte seemed to sober up before her eyes. "No. No you're right. Of course." She gave Maggie a sharp look as if realizing for the first time what she had said and who she was talking to. "I can count on your discretion."

"You can. I see no need to hurt anyone unnecessarily," she said, thinking only of Elizabeth.

Charlotte smiled at her, which served only to make her appear as if she'd eaten something nasty. Her own words, perhaps.

"Oh," Charlotte said, craning her neck a bit. "I think I see . . . someone. Nice chatting with you, Margaret."

Maggie watched Charlotte walk away and said a quick prayer that she'd gotten through to her how awful it would be if such a story about Henry and Elizabeth spread. She could not remember feeling so angry her entire life. Her temples pounded, and she could actually feel the anger roiling in her stomach. Spying her brother, she waved him over.

"Sam, I think we'll be leaving the ball early tonight. Do you mind too much?"

Her brother grinned. "I mind about as much as missing the opera," said her brother, who loathed the opera.

"Good. I'll meet you at the front door. Could you please fetch my wrap, as well?"

Sam rolled his eyes but gave her a little bow. "At your service, Madam. And I get two scones for breakfast tomorrow morning."

She gave him a look of sisterly exasperation. "Fine."

As soon as her brother was gone, Maggie headed for the billiard room on the second floor of the large home. Having fetched her brothers from said room on many occasions, Maggie knew exactly where to go. She didn't know what she was going to say, but she knew she was going to let Henry Ellsworth know she thought him the most despicable man on earth. She smelled the thick cigar smoke long before she reached the room, making a mental note to ban those things should she ever be mistress of her own home. It took her only a few moments before she was noticed and able to wave Henry to the door. The cad gave her a wide smile, and she had to admit he was a handsome devil, in an overly polished way.

"Why, Miss Pierce, how nice to see you," he said as Maggie stepped back from the door.

And then, not even knowing what was coming, Maggie punched Henry right in the stomach, making him double over with a muffled woof. "That's for Elizabeth you miserable son of a bitch."

Maggie walked away, her body thrumming with adrenaline, her wrist aching from the impact to his

stomach. All those years tussling with her brothers—
and hearing their colorful language—had paid off apparently. Had anyone asked Maggie just moments ago
if she was capable of such violence or such language,
she would have denied it heatedly. But at the moment,
she felt as if she were floating toward the front door.
Keeping a straight face, she accepted her brother's help
with the cloak and didn't dissolve into a bit of hysterical laughter until they were out the door.

"My goodness, Meg, what's this all about," Sam
asked, smiling at his sister's laughter even though he
hadn't a clue what was going on.

Maggie could hardly stand, she was laughing so hard.
"I just laid out Henry Ellsworth."

"You what?"

"Punched him," she said. "Hard. I don't think I killed
him, though," she added rather darkly.

"Good God, Maggie, why would you do such a
thing?" Then his face changed, tightened, and he pushed
up the sleeves of his coat as if ready to spar.

"Oh, don't be silly, Samuel," Maggie said, putting a
restraining arm on her brother's shoulder. "He didn't do
anything to me. I punched him for something he did to
Elizabeth."

"Oh," her brother said, relaxing. "Laid him out good,
did you?" Clearly her brother was impressed.

"Hmmm. I hurt my wrist a bit. Perhaps I hit him too
hard."

"Your wrist's about as thick as a twig. You're lucky
you didn't break it. Show me how you punched him," he
said with brotherly concern.

Maggie demonstrated, without making contact with her brother's stomach.

"Well, you held your fist right anyway." Her brother chuckled. "What did he do to Elizabeth, anyway?"

Maggie told him the story and swore him to secrecy.

"I knew there was a good reason I didn't like that man. Too slick."

"He's Charlotte Grayson's concern now. They're engaged."

Sam threw back his head and laughed. As they stepped up into the carriage, Maggie looked back at the house and realized she had never had so much fun at a ball.

Chapter 22

Rand stood outside her door and stared for several long minutes at the small slice of light showing through the bottom, willing his body to relax. He should get drunk, as he'd done on the other nights when his desire nearly made him mad. He would have, too, if she hadn't strolled into the stable and looked at him as if she wanted to eat him alive.

Rand took a deep breath. *I just need a good fuck. That is all and I'll be fine.*

He wiped his forehead where a fine sheen of sweat had formed, and then knocked on his wife's bedroom door.

"Yes?" came the muffled response.

He opened the door to find her sitting on her bed in her nightgown, her bare feet not quite touching the floor, looking quite shocked to find her husband standing there. She was not looking at him with desire at the moment, but with a certain amount of wariness, which only increased the farther he walked into her room.

"I need to discuss something with you." When she nodded, he continued. "Do you remember when we first met we discussed how our marriage would be?" he asked, keeping his voice even.

Elizabeth nodded again, her blue eyes suddenly holding a spark of something he couldn't identify.

"I think it best that we proceed based on that conception of marriage. It will be best for all, I think, that we don't get all muddled up in emotions. Then you will have a child, something to keep you occupied. And I will have done my duty. My mother will be quite happy," he added as an afterthought.

"And then?"

"And then we shall go about our lives. I have been giving a great deal of thought to this marriage of ours over the past few days and I realize that I have been unfair to you. I changed the rules, so to speak, without even letting you know. You, on the other hand, have never swayed from that original conversation. Your expectations remained the same."

"You need an heir," she said.

Ah, she understood. Good. "Precisely. We don't have to make each other miserable, do we? We can go about our business, live our lives. Many couples do. *Most* couples, in fact. It's what we planned."

"Yes. That sounds . . ."

Horrid.

"Fair." She even smiled a bit, a smile that tore into his heart, for she looked so damned relieved. Ah, hell. He realized at that moment he'd secretly been hoping she'd argue with him, get affronted. Anything but sit there calmly and accept what seemed now to be a completely dismal proposition.

"That's exactly what I was thinking," he said. He forced a smile, just to show her he was in agreement, as if glad to have finally gotten this tedious conversation over with. "I shall visit you in your room perhaps two or three times a week, if that is fine for you. Until you conceive."

Elizabeth stared blankly at him, her stomach knotting uncomfortably. She simply could not believe what he was saying to her.

"We could start this evening, if that is convenient with you."

"I have no other plans," she said, feeling much like she was making an appointment with her seamstress.

"Well, then." He shut her door and walked toward her bed, unbuttoning his trousers as he did so, and Elizabeth cringed involuntarily. This is not what she wanted. She wanted what they'd had before the discovery of that wretched note. She wanted him to love her again, to make love with her. Seeing her cringe, he hesitated for a moment, before shucking off his shoes and taking off his pants completely, a look of determination on his face.

Dismayed, she lay down on the bed, uncertain what she should do. Instinctively, she knew not to embrace him or kiss him or say even a single word. It was dreadful, and much like she'd imagined the marriage bed would be, with her lying stiffly, uncertain and nervous. He climbed onto the bed and she looked at him, afraid what she would see in his eyes—or not see, perhaps. But at that moment, he looked at her, his eyes tender, his touch when he brushed the hair from her face almost loving.

Then, he moved between her legs, spreading them with his body as he lifted the hem of her nightgown up.

And without touching her but with his large body, he entered her, finding her humiliatingly ready for him. Silently he plunged in and out, the only sound his harsh breath, the movement of the bed. Just as she was beginning to feel the slightest bit of a pleasant tingle between her thighs, he groaned and stiffened, his face pushed against the pillow next to her head.

Almost immediately he withdrew and pulled up his drawers, which he hadn't even bothered to remove completely.

"Good night, then," he said, tumbling off the bed and grabbing up his pants. As almost an afterthought, he looked back at her, then leaned in and kissed her forehead. "This is better, Elizabeth. You'll see."

She stared at him, her nightgown still shucked up about her waist, feeling his seed seep from her body.

"Better than what?" she asked, feeling angry and hurt.

"You misunderstood," he said, his voice unusually clipped. "This is better for me. I really don't give a damn about you."

With that, he left.

Elizabeth sat there stunned for perhaps three seconds before she rose and picked up the first thing her hands found—one of her slippers—and flung it at the door. "You son of a bitch," she screamed. She could almost swear she heard him chuckle on the other side of the door. "You'll not have me again. Do you hear? Do you?" She glared at the door hoping he'd come crashing in so she could truly yell at him the way she wanted to. "You son of a bitch," she said more softly, but with just as much venom. "Treat me like a broodmare, will you?

I hate you Rand Blackmore." And then, feeling as if she might explode, she screamed, "I hate you." Then, just like that, the anger was gone, replaced by a terrible despair and she found herself sobbing into her pillow and praying he wouldn't hear just how much he'd hurt her.

"Your Grace, if you've a minute."

The housekeeper, Mrs. Stevens, hovered at the parlor door as if she were interrupting some great and important meeting. Elizabeth sat alone, as always, staring out a window. As always. "Yes, Mrs. Stevens. Come in."

"Now that you're all settled in, I thought it was time for you to take over the rounds," she said, her cheeks flushing a bit, as if she were stepping out of bounds for saying such a thing to a duchess.

"Rounds?"

"Yes, Your Grace. You see, it's a Bellingham tradition that the duchess takes food and the like to the poorest of the villagers. I've been doing it these past years with the old duchess in London. But for years and years before that when she was in residence, the Duchess would bring a basket 'round to the poor, as her mother did before her. There's many more now that need the food, and since it truly is something Your Grace should be doing . . ." Her voice trailed off and she seemed to tense for some wild reaction.

"All that food," Elizabeth said thoughtfully. "I wondered what became of it. I'm so glad it went to help someone. Of course I'll take over the rounds if you just tell me where to go. Perhaps the first time you could accompany me." Elizabeth couldn't have been more excited than if she were a child on Christmas morning. Finally, something to do except sit around this house moping and feeling sorry for herself.

"The baskets are all prepared. I've put the names of the tenants on each one. The old Duchess used to just scrape all the leavings, desserts and all, into one large pile, but since she's been gone we started arranging it a bit more nicely."

"How wonderful," Elizabeth said, meaning it. Something to do. Some meaningful thing to do to keep her mind off her hateful husband and his awful visits. She'd bar the door if she thought it would keep him out. He continued coming to her even though he knew she hated him, hated the way he released himself with a grunt and then left her lying on her bed wishing for her own release. She lay there like a statue, refusing to look at him, refusing to touch him, refusing to let him do anything but empty his seed into her. She prayed to become pregnant, but just that morning her monthlies had begun again and she was beginning to despair that she'd ever become pregnant. She'd been married for two months already. Surely that was enough time to have become pregnant.

"Let me get my wrap and muff," Elizabeth gushed, rushing off to her room to fetch a suitable hat. Tisbury apparently had been alerted to Mrs. Stevens's mission, for he stood at the door holding her coat and muff.

"Thank you, Tisbury," Elizabeth said happily. Oh, she was so glad to be out of this mausoleum even if it was only for a few hours.

As they headed out of the long drive, Mrs. Stevens

filled Elizabeth in on who they would be visiting. Most
were widows, with or without children, who were left to
fend for themselves with little income coming in. But
more than a few were families who could hardly afford
the little food they needed, never mind the rents they
owed the duke.

"The new duke has been a savior, as I'm sure you know.
I think they're planning to write to the Pope to nominate
him for sainthood and they're not even Catholic," Mrs.
Stevens said, giving off a hearty laugh.

Elizabeth didn't know what she was talking about,
but sat back enjoying the sound of a voice that wasn't
her own. She didn't even care that a fine drizzle fell
from the gray, heavy sky. To her it was the most glorious day.

"We'll stop at the Gibbons' house first. It was a sight
before His Grace came back, but now it's the coziest
little cottage in all of Bellingham."

Elizabeth smiled at the small cottage, thinking it
looked like the perfect little English cottage. In the
spring it would be covered with roses, no doubt, if the
multitude of dormant rosebushes were any indication.
The roof looked new, the outside walls freshly whitewashed, and the multipaned windows sparkled as if
they'd just been polished.

"It's lovely," Elizabeth said, smiling as Mrs. Stevens
handed her down a basket heavy with food.

"There's Mrs. Gibbons now," the housekeeper said
with a nod toward a woman who was hurriedly smooth-
ing down her skirts and patting her hair to make certain
it was neat.

"Mrs. Gibbons," Elizabeth said. "You are the first of my husband's tenants that I've met. It's such a pleasure to meet you. Your home is lovely." Elizabeth didn't care if she wasn't acting like a duchess might, and from the shocked face Mrs. Gibbons was giving her, she probably wasn't. Or perhaps it was simply her American accent that was so enthralling the woman.

Mrs. Gibbons gave a quick curtsy. She was wearing a stained apron over her blue flower-print dress, which she hastily removed, throwing it somewhere behind her. "So glad to meet you, Yer Grace," she said, smiling widely. "Please come in."

Elizabeth followed the older woman into the house, expecting it to be as cold as her own house when she noted the empty fireplace, but was pleasantly surprised when she was greeted by warmth.

"Don't need a fire 'cepting on the coldest nights now," she said, seeing where Elizabeth looked. "His Grace put in heating. And indoor plumbing."

"You have a toilet?" Elizabeth asked, purely surprised given that she had been using a chamber pot since she'd come to England.

"A *flush* toilet," Mrs. Gibbons said, beaming. "Come an' see." Elizabeth followed Mrs. Gibbons into a room that had obviously been recently added to the house to accommodate a sink, toilet, and, heaven above, a bathtub. Mrs. Gibbons proudly flushed her toilet, then turned on the hot water. "It's like a little bit of heaven right here in my own house," she said.

"It certainly is."

Mrs. Gibbons flushed, as if suddenly aware how she

was going on about indoor plumbing. "I'm certain you're used to such luxuries."

"No, indeed, Mrs. Gibbons. In fact, you have far more indoor plumbing than Bellewood. I'm quite jealous," she said, laughing a bit. "His Grace wanted to make certain his tenants' homes were brought up to date first, you see."

"His Grace is a saint," the woman said, meaning every syllable. "Why, I see him at a different house every day, making sure the workers are doing their jobs, inspectin' the goods that come in. He even helps out some, and no duke I've ever known would do that. It's a miracle."

Elizabeth let the woman gush on, feeling none of the charity toward her husband that everyone else did. She had to stop herself from telling the woman that the money her "sainted" husband was using was her own. No doubt, the woman knew that. She felt rather catty just thinking such a thing, but he had been so wretched to her lately she couldn't stop herself, even if such a thought made her immediately feel guilty.

They made their way from the new bathroom to the kitchen, where again a new sink and faucets had been installed. "Makes me feel like a queen," Mrs. Gibbons said.

Elizabeth looked around the small cottage, smiling at its quaintness. It was obvious they were poor, but the cottage was neat, the floor spotless, even if the furniture was a bit worn or covered with blankets, no doubt to hide something unsightly. Above the mantel, Elizabeth spied a lovely collection of carved figures that seemed out of place in such a humble home. They appeared to be costly works of art that would look far more appropriate in an expensive home than in this tiny English cottage.

"These are lovely," Elizabeth said, picking up one figure of a woman sitting on a chair knitting, a small cat at her feet playfully batting a bit of yarn. She realized, with a start, that the woman look remarkably like Mrs. Gibbons. The detail, given the piece was carved from wood, was nothing short of remarkable.

"Thank you, Your Grace," a man said from behind her. Elizabeth whirled about to see a man sitting in the shadows in a corner. He was covered from head to toe with a blanket, and only his head with its three tufts of hair—on top and on each side—were showing. He hadn't gotten up or said a word when she'd entered before, so Elizabeth hadn't realized anyone else was in the house.

"Oh, my manners," Mrs. Gibbons said apologetically. "This is my husband, Nathaniel. Those help him pass the time." She said it rather dismissively, or apologetically, which completely baffled Elizabeth.

Pass the time? They belonged in a museum, Elizabeth thought. It took her only a few moments to realize why Mr. Gibbons hadn't gotten up. The poor man had lost his legs from the knee down.

Seeing her notice, he said gruffly, "Boer War."

Elizabeth nodded her understanding and turned back to the carvings. "Mr. Gibbons, these are the finest carvings I've ever seen," Elizabeth said.

"They're just to pass time," Mr. Gibbons said, repeating his wife's words, but Elizabeth could tell he was pleased.

Elizabeth looked back at the carvings. There were perhaps twenty of them, all different subjects, all completely charming. She knew people who would pay dearly for carvings as lovely as these.

"Mr. Gibbons, could I have one of these?"

The man looked completely startled, as if puzzled why she could ask such a thing.

"I'd like to send one to my mother in New York City."

"To America?" The idea had completely flummoxed him.

"Yes. I think she would love it," she said. And, Elizabeth was certain a great many of her mother's friends would also love such a carving. If she was right, Mr. Gibbons would be able to make some sort of living from his art.

"Of course. Take two, if you like." The man was beaming now.

"Imagine," Mrs. Gibbons breathed, "all the way to America." She looked at the carvings as if she hadn't seen them before.

"I'll just need the one for now," Elizabeth assured him.

Soon after, Elizabeth and Mrs. Stevens left the Gibbons to themselves and headed for the other cottages.

"That was very kind of you, if I'm not being too forward, Your Grace."

"It wasn't kindness at all," she said. "Those carvings are truly remarkable." Elizabeth felt a fission of excitement for she had discovered her first project as duchess. It was a wonderful feeling to know she had the power to change someone's life. If she got even a small order of carvings from one of New York's finer shops, the Gibbons' lives would be made so much better. Now she knew the power of money as she never did before. Of course she'd always been aware of her mother's philanthropy, but to meet the person who would be helped made such a thing more tangible. Begrudgingly, she realized that Rand likely already knew that. He didn't have to spend money on those houses the way he had. The tenants would have been satisfied with a new roof and small repairs. Instead, he was making them houses they could be proud of, houses with modern conveniences he didn't even have yet in his own home.

"There's His Grace now," Mrs. Stevens said, pointing toward another little cottage in the midst of repairs. He stood amongst several men, looking over a large piece of paper and pointing to the house. Even from a distance there was something about him that drew the eye, an intangible quality that made her want to look away because it hurt so much to see him. The noise from the carriage drew his attention away from the house and when he looked toward them, their gazes connected. Elizabeth immediately turned away and pushed back into her seat, not even lifting a hand to acknowledge that she had seen him.

"Just four more houses," said Mrs. Stevens, who rattled off names Elizabeth almost immediately forgot. She couldn't think of anything at the moment, her joy of the day sucked away by one chance sighting of her husband. Why did he have to be so handsome? Why did every single person she met have to gush on and on about how wonderful, how charitable, how lovely the new duke was? She should tell them all that he was a horrid, horrid man who didn't deserve their admiration.

Even as she thought such a thing she knew she was lying to herself.

Her heart was still beating madly simply from seeing him. He'd have a good chuckle if he knew how his wife was pining after him. He wouldn't come to her tonight, thank God, because she had her monthlies. She wouldn't see him or touch him, or smell him. Not that she wanted to. What they'd been doing in her bed, it was not something she enjoyed. Nothing had changed since that first time. No tender words were exchanged, no caresses that made her burn. She would look into his eyes hoping to see something, but was disappointed each night. She dreaded it and yet . . . it did give her the ridiculous hope that one night he'd come to her and drag her into his arms and tell her he loved her. Or maybe some night she'd get the courage to tell him she wanted more, she didn't want a baby. She wanted him. She wanted him to love her.

God, how she missed him.

Chapter 23

Elizabeth went on rounds twice a week on Mondays and Thursdays and spent the rest of the week wishing it was Monday or Thursday. Just as she was about to go mad from boredom, their furniture began to arrive. She hadn't realized they'd ordered so much until wagon after wagon began pulling up to Bellewood. Decorating, apparently, was an inborn talent, she realized, gotten from a mother who had been incessantly changing their houses and furnishings to match the latest styles. While Elizabeth wasn't as obsessed as her mother, she found her choices were perfect for the massive house. For the next week, when she wasn't going on rounds, she was directing men where to put various pieces she'd picked out weeks ago. Huge carpets were rolled out, covering the cold marble floors and making the rooms instantly more welcoming. Massive tables were placed in the grand entry hall, towering gilded mirrors were placed on either side of the hall, making it appear even larger.

Once in a while Rand would walk into his house and look around, his expression inscrutable. She never knew what he was thinking, whether he was pleased or disappointed in her choices, and she told herself she didn't care. His visits had continued after her monthlies were over, but they had little contact other than that. When he did come to her, it was almost as if he didn't want to, as if his visitations had become a chore—and an unwanted one at that.

Nearly all the public rooms were filled with furniture, paintings, rugs, and expensive vases stuffed with flowers that arrived weekly, brought in from London. Elizabeth didn't know why Rand had bothered allowing such a thing, for no one saw them but for her and the servants. She had mentioned casually that the house should have fresh flowers, and they'd begun arriving almost as soon as they had vases to put them in. She was quite sure the constant stream of workers hardly noticed the pretty blooms.

Then, as the days grew a bit warmer with March, renovations on the main house began. It was a constant nightmare of dust, banging, crashes, and men shouting orders. Amidst this, the first post from America arrived.

Elizabeth joyfully grabbed the letters addressed to her and ran to her room, where it was blessedly quiet—or at least more quiet than any other place in the house. Even though Elizabeth knew all the noise meant eventually central heating and plumbing, she was getting rather weary of the constant disruption of the workers.

The first letter she read was from her mother, detailing a new house she was building in the city, down to the type of Italian marble she was using for the mantel in her sitting room. Her letter was also filled with news about people she'd known all her life, little tidbits such as who was having baby, who was getting married, and even a rather risqué bit about a woman who was being shunned because she'd had the audacity to get caught with her lover by her husband. Elizabeth wondered blithely if that last story was true or simply a reminder from her mother for her to remain faithful to her husband. Elizabeth wondered if she should set her mother at ease by telling her the only men she'd seen since leaving New York were rough workers and a married man without legs.

Maggie's letters were simply wonderful. It was almost like talking to her old friend. She'd written three, which Elizabeth immediately put in order according to date. The first letter was written shortly after Elizabeth had left, for she could tell her friend had been truly hurt by her abrupt departure. The second was written after Maggie had received Elizabeth's first letter home, detailing her horrendous crossing, which apparently Maggie found rather amusing. She laughed aloud several times, as Maggie talked about the Wright brothers and how Arthur in particular was making overtures that were getting more and more difficult to ignore. Elizabeth almost sensed that Maggie was actually coming round to the idea that Arthur might perhaps make a good husband. Her friend mentioned Lord Hollings only once, asking whether she had seen him since coming to England. Elizabeth had wondered if Maggie had developed strong feelings for Lord Hollings, but apparently she had not.

She lay the second letter aside with a sigh. How wonderful it would have been if Maggie and Lord Hollings

had married. Then she'd have a friend here in England
and wouldn't be quite so lonely.

Maggie's third letter had been written only days after
the second, and was the briefest of the three.

> *Dearest Elizabeth,*
> *I pray this letter finds you well and happy. I had to*
> *tell you some news lest you hear it from someone else*
> *in passing. Henry has married Charlotte Grayson.*

Elizabeth lowered the letter and stared at the new
carpet at her feet. Charlotte Grayson? Henry had married *Charlotte Grayson*? Charlotte was perhaps the most
noxious person she knew both in looks and temperament,
and she was also one of the wealthiest heiresses
in New York. In fact, she was the *second* wealthiest,
other than herself. Her eyes went back to the letter, willing herself to finish it.

> *Please brace yourself for the next and remember I*
> *am your dearest, dearest friend. I am not trying to*
> *hurt you but to give you a chance at a good life with*
> *a man who I believe may love you. Charlotte does not*
> *know I am your closest friend and she confided it to*
> *me, the hateful girl. She knows fully well that Henry*
> *married her for her fortune and doesn't seem to care*
> *a bit (which doesn't say much for her character). She*
> *is the most horrid girl I know. Oh, Elizabeth, Henry*
> *has joked about you with her, about your meeting in*
> *Tiffany's, about how he was certain you could not go*
> *through with your wedding. Perhaps those feelings*

*he professed to have for you were sincere, but I find
it unforgivable that he made light of such a thing with
Charlotte. I had to tell you, even at the risk of losing
you as a friend, for you cannot hold out any hope that
you can ever be together. I'm so very sorry.*

> *I pray I am still your very good friend,*
> *Margaret*

Elizabeth let out a short sob. "Oh, God," she whispered.
It had all been a lie, every word out of his charming
mouth. She felt beyond foolish to have loved him, to have
believed he loved her. All those hours yearning for him,
all those heartfelt stolen moments, those ridiculous tender
words. She'd worn that necklace, read those words and felt
a bit of sick hope that some day they'd be together . . . And
he'd been laughing at her the whole time. How Charlotte
and he must enjoy talking about her, the silly little rich
girl. All those hours crying and begging her mother to let
them be together. All the wasted tears. What a ridiculous,
naive girl she had been. Never before in her life had she
been so filled with self-loathing.

Perhaps the most unforgivable thing was that she'd
hurt a good man because of her foolishness, thrown real
love away because of some pretend emotion. Tears
coursed down her face unchecked as she realized for the
first time exactly what she had done to Rand. She did
not warrant his love, was only getting what a silly, foolish girl deserved.

"Have you received upsetting news?"

Rand stood in the doorway, his eyes hard, taking in
her tears as if they were highly offensive.

"I was just reading a letter from Maggie," she said, her voice thick with tears.

He walked casually into the room. "May I?" he asked, holding out his hand for the letter.

"It's private," she said, clutching the letter tighter. If he read the letter, he would surely think she was crying because Henry had married, and that was not at all what her tears were about.

"It's of no consequence," he said blandly. "I believe I already know what news it contains. Your father wrote me, you see. I like your father. He's an honest man."

Elizabeth looked at him and knew exactly what her father had written. She lowered her eyes, so filled with shame and remorse, she could not look at him.

He tilted his head, a mocking gesture of commiseration. "You'll get over him."

She swallowed and shook her head. "You don't understand."

She watched his fists clench, and then, as if realizing what he was doing, he slowly unfurled them. "Are you saying, my dear, that I don't understand what it is like to be betrayed?" His voice was so calm, but Elizabeth could hear the fury beneath it.

She shook her head and looked up at him. "You don't understand why I am crying. I'm so s-s-sorry," she said.

He looked sharply away and let out a short, humorless laugh. "Finally, something we have in common. I'll not be bothering you tonight. I'm sure you don't mind."

"No. I don't mind," she whispered, looking dully at the carpet and waiting for him to leave.

Chapter 24

Rand was away in London when Elizabeth began to suspect she was pregnant. Her monthlies had always been exceedingly regular, even on that terrible Atlantic crossing. And now she was a week late, her breasts felt decidedly odd, and she was more afraid than she ever had been in her life.

She did not want to be pregnant. She wanted her husband back.

Unfortunately, he disappeared to London the night he'd received her father's letter, the night he discovered her crying in her room. She never got the chance to explain to him why she'd been crying, how terrible she felt about what she'd done. And part of her knew he would not have believed her anyway. He'd caught her in a lie; if there was one lesson she'd remembered from childhood it was that no one believed a liar.

She'd been five years old and had broken a priceless vase. Horrified, she hid the pieces in a cabinet only to have them discovered by a maid. When her mother asked if she knew who broke the vase, she'd made a very convincing wide-eyed denial. "What vase?" she'd asked.

Everyone in the house was interviewed; her mother had been in a rage. Someone broke the vase, someone was lying about it. Elizabeth could still remember huddling on the stairs peering through the banister at the poor servants being chastised, at the fear on their faces that they would get dismissed, for that is exactly what her mother threatened. That night, with the threat of dismissal hanging over everyone's heads, Elizabeth had not been able to sleep. She knew what she had to do. Feeling slightly ill, and more afraid than she'd ever been, she'd padded barefoot to her mother's room and confessed. And her mother had said, "You lied to me, Elizabeth. I will never believe you again. No one believes a liar."

And now, Rand had caught her in a lie, a terribly damning one, and she knew he would never believe her. She'd told him she had not seen Henry when she had, when she'd taken his gift and worn it around her neck. He had not believed her when she'd told him she'd forgotten about the necklace, and he certainly would not believe her when she tried to explain her tears over the letter. Frankly, she could not blame him for his skepticism.

For two excruciatingly long weeks, Rand had been absent from Bellewood without a single word as to where he was. He could have sailed back to America for all she knew.

Swallowing her pride, she turned to Mrs. Stevens, who seemed to know everything that went on in the house. The thought of going to a servant to find the whereabouts of her own husband was beyond humiliating, but she didn't care. She wanted him back and she was going to get him.

"Why he's with Lord Hollings, of course. At his house in Hanover Square."

"Oh, of course," Elizabeth said, laughing lightly. "He mentioned that but I quite forgot. Would you happen to know the precise address? I need to go to London to order some draperies for the library."

Mrs. Stevens looked a bit confused. "But they just put them up two days ago. Lovely forest green ones."

"I don't like them," Elizabeth said, trying to sound like her mother. "Now that they're up, I do believe a deep burgundy would look so much better. But I'm not certain of the precise shade. I have to select them personally. I cannot depend on His Grace to pick the proper color."

"Of course not. Mr. Tisbury should have that information, Your Grace," she said.

"Good. I shall leave today, in fact. Sally has my bags packed already. If you could tell Mr. Tisbury I need a porter to bring them out to the carriage."

"Of course, Your Grace."

Elizabeth smiled serenely, even though her insides were roiling with nervousness. What on earth was she doing? she thought in a panic. Surely Rand would not be pleased to see her, especially when he was visiting a friend. But she didn't know what else to do. What could be keeping him away from home for so long? Other than the fact he loathed his wife, she thought sardonically.

Elizabeth arrived in London that evening, having the driver bring her directly to Lord Hollings's lovely home on Hanover Square. It was well lit and surrounded by traffic, fine carriages, well-dressed men and women, almost as if . . .

Her carriage got in a queue with the other carriages and Elizabeth peeked out to see a woman disembarking from a carriage wearing a formal gown of red silk.

"Looks like a bit of a fete," the driver called down.

"Yes, it does," she said loud enough for him to hear over the din of traffic. She drew her head in, using curses she'd only heard from the workmen when they'd errantly beat their thumb with a hammer. There was nothing for her to do but join the party, she realized. It was far too late to return to Bellewood. The horses, not to mention the driver and footman, were likely exhausted. She was feeling especially weary herself. She didn't know where to go, a woman alone in London, a city she'd visited only with her mother briefly and with Rand when she'd met his mother. They'd stayed at a fine hotel, but for the life of her she couldn't remember its name or where it was. Sitting in her carriage in the queue for a ball, Elizabeth felt the sting of unshed tears.

"No," she said to herself. "I am not a child any longer and I refuse to act like one." She took a fortifying breath and resolved to enter the building alone with some excuse she'd likely come up with as soon as someone asked who she was. Oh, Lord.

Elizabeth looked down at her wrinkled dress and grimaced. She'd known she was traveling all day and hadn't worn her best day gown, but her most comfortable— a simple navy blue gown with lace embellishment at the sleeves and modest neckline. She looked more like a well-dressed governess than the new Duchess of Bellingham.

There was nothing to do now but lift her chin and act like the duchess she was. Perhaps the London elite would forgive her; after all, she was an American.

When the carriage reached the head of the queue, her footman leaped down, lowered the steps, and swung open the door. He seemed to know this was an unexpected development, for he gave her a shy smile of commiseration as he helped her from the carriage. Taking a deep bracing breath, Elizabeth stepped into a short line of well-dressed, well-heeled men and women and pretended she belonged among them When it was her turn to cross the threshold, the footman took a step toward her. It was not quite menacing, but rather a polite, "Who the hell do you think you are?" sort of movement. She just adored English servants.

"Please inform Lord Hollings that the Duchess of Bellingham is here," she said, softly enough so no one would hear. Then she added unnecessarily, "He is not expecting me."

To his credit, the footman didn't bat an eye, but escorted her to a small private room not far from the large foyer, no doubt hoping he'd done the right thing and she was, indeed, the Duchess of Bellingham. Minutes later, Elizabeth almost collapsed with relief when she saw Lord Hollings's smiling face.

"My goodness, Your Grace. How unexpected."

Elizabeth gave him a sick smile. "I didn't know you were having a ball. I didn't write ahead because, because . . ."

"You didn't want to give Rand the chance to escape?" he guessed with pinpoint precision.

"Is he here?"

Edward scowled. "Unfortunately, yes. And if you've come to take him home, I'll go find him now, truss him up and deliver him to your carriage."

Elizabeth found herself laughing for the first time in days. "That's not necessary. The truth is, I don't know London very well and I wasn't certain of my reception here. But I made no other accommodations."

Edward took pity on her. "Not to worry, Madam. I'll find Rand directly and the two of you can hash out what happens next. In the meantime, can I get something for you to eat? Or drink? A sherry perhaps?"

Elizabeth hadn't realized how hungry she was until just that moment. She'd taken a bit of food with her on the carriage, but hadn't eaten for hours. "That would be wonderful."

"I shall return shortly to escort you to my private study where you might eat something while I find Rand."

Given that the house was not overly large, Elizabeth couldn't imagine that finding Rand would take that much effort, but she said nothing as Lord Hollings disappeared. As she sat, she could hear an orchestra playing and the general mumbling of a large crowd of people. Rising, she peeked out into the foyer, and finding it empty, thought she'd take a quick look into the ballroom. Double doors were flung open wide and from the hall she saw a few couples dance past, women's skirts twirling and men's tails flying out during the lively polka. How she missed balls and dancing and wearing her finest ball gowns. She hadn't thought she would miss such frivolities, but she did. The music and gaiety drew her closer and to her lonely eyes it looked like everyone was having a grand time. She knew better, of course, and couldn't count the number of times she wished to be removed from just such a ball. But at this moment, it seemed like this was the most wonderful fete.

And then she saw Rand and stiffened. Everyone, it seemed, *was* having a grand time. Particularly Rand.

He was dancing with a beautiful blond girl, laughing at something witty she'd no doubt just uttered. He was dancing and having a good old time while she'd been pining away in his cold mansion in the middle of nowhere being miserable and downright lonely. And pregnant. Don't forget she was carrying his child, which he'd deposited in her with about as much emotion as a man delivering milk to her door. The music stopped and the floozy curtsied, dimpling up at him, while he bowed then held out his arm to escort her off the floor. They stopped to chat with another couple, all smiling, all without a worry in the world while Elizabeth watched, hungry, wearing a downright ugly and wrinkled dress, with her hair all frizzy from the damp weather and her stomach so empty she thought she might faint. She actually thought about it, how awful he would feel if she fainted right at that moment. Everyone would turn and gasp and run to her and he would exclaim that she was his wife and they would look at him as if he was the ogre he truly was. He would be found out finally. No Saint Rand, but a mean and cruel husband who would leave his poor pregnant wife in her ugly dress to go out dancing.

But no. Even pregnant and hungry, she wouldn't faint. She would, however, leave. Imagine, her coming to London to find him, to throw herself at his feet and beg forgiveness for having the audacity to fall in love with someone, then feel slightly put out when she was forced to marry a stranger. Put that way, it was all quite Rand's fault, she decided.

Certainly she could find the carriage and find her way to a hotel. She was the Duchess of Bellingham. No hotel would turn her away. At least, she didn't think they would. Right now, she didn't care. She wanted only to get away from this lovely scene filled with lovely happy people and her husband who was having far too much fun without her.

Minutes later, Lord Hollings returned to the small room having arranged for the duchess to have a light meal in his private study while he calmed his friend down. He knew Rand would be extremely agitated when he told him his wife had arrived unexpectedly and he wanted to give Rand a chance to recover his wits before showing him where he'd put her. It wouldn't do to have a scene in the middle of his ball.

He entered the room and looked about, baffled. It was a small room, so it took only a moment for him to realize the duchess was gone. "Bloody hell."

Rand saw Edward coming toward him, his face grim, and decided to turn around and hope his friend would go away and leave him alone. No doubt he had another woman he would insist he dance with as a way to get his mind off his new wife. He'd danced with Edward's little sister, it was the least he could do, but he'd be damned if he danced with anyone else. If anything, attending this ball was making him more miserable than he already was. Every waltz reminded him of Elizabeth. Every woman with brown hair, every one with blue eyes. With breasts, even. They all reminded him that he wished he was with her instead of here. Until he reminded himself that he'd been even more miserable with her around.

"Rand. Damn it, man, stop," he heard Edward say close to his ear. "Elizabeth is here."

Rand stopped as if he'd hit a rock wall, and spun around, nearly bumping into his friend. "Here?"

"Well, she was here. But I can't find her."

"Here in this house? And you can't find her?"

Edward nodded. "I told her to wait in the front room while I prepared my sitting room and ordered a small meal for her but when I returned she was gone," he said quietly, obviously aware than a missing duchess would be quite a story for the gossips.

"Why was she here?" Rand said, completely confused.

"I don't know. She didn't say. And I didn't ask. Perhaps she is here for the same reason you are here."

"I am here to get away from her," Rand said pointedly.

"Perhaps she has taken exception to that."

Rand looked wildly around the room as if he might find her standing on the sides watching the dancers. "Why would she come all this way only to leave?" he wondered aloud. Then it dawned on him. Elizabeth would not be content to sit still. A woman who had traveled four hours to get to him would not wait for him to come to her. She would get up, look about . . . and find him dancing with a beautiful blonde.

"This is your fault," he said accusingly to Edward.

"Of course it is," he said dryly.

"She must have seen me dancing with your damned sister, beg pardon. No offense meant."

"None taken."

Rand strode from the ballroom ignoring the curious stares of onlookers, knowing Edward would follow him. He walked to the last place they knew Elizabeth had been, the small front room. Rand stood looking dumbly about the room as if she might suddenly appear. "Who knows she's here?" he asked.

"No one. I haven't begun a search as yet. We'll have to be discreet, of course."

Rand sighed. Elizabeth's position in the peerage was tentative at best, even that she was a duchess. She was an American, so it would take very little scandal for this group to cast aspersions on her character. A duchess wandering about alone in London would be just such a thing.

"I'll go out and see if your carriage is still about," Edward said. "She can't have gone far, Rand."

Four hours later, with the house now empty of guests, Rand was frantic. Elizabeth had, indeed, disappeared. The carriage and driver had been found quickly behind the mansion in the mews, where the grooms were still rubbing down the tired horses. Edward's footman had not been asked to call for a hack and he didn't recall seeing the duchess, but that did not mean she hadn't slipped by with other guests. Rand couldn't imagine her walking the streets alone. Surely Elizabeth knew better than that.

"She doesn't know this city. It's far more dangerous to her than New York. She's a stranger here," Rand said, feeling desperation seep into his veins. "Where could she be?" he shouted.

Edward could only shake his head, as upset and bewildered as his friend.

Rand had never in his life been more frustrated. And more frightened. The more time that passed, the greater his fear. It was completely out of character for Elizabeth to have come all the way to London alone, and then to disappear so quickly made it all seem like a horrible dream.

"Where could she be?" he said on a note of pure despair. He wanted to scream, to rip something apart, to shake Edward until he somehow got an answer.

"It may be time to call Scotland Yard," Edward said, his tone measured. "I'll have my man send over a message. Once they're involved . . ."

Rand roughly tunneled his fingers through his hair, as if trying to purge what was happening from his mind. "Yes. You're right." He squeezed his eyes shut.

"I'll be right back. You're all right?"

Rand looked up at his friend, not even attempting a reassuring smile.

"Right, then. We'll find her, Rand. We will."

Rand sat, his arms dangling from his knees limply, his head down, completely exhausted. He'd been all over London in the past four hours, visiting innumerable hotels, even ones he knew Elizabeth would never consider. He'd had to pretend as if nothing was untoward, that he was simply confused about which hotel his wife said she'd be staying at. He'd had to smile when his gut felt like it was being twisted in two when he'd been told time after time that, no, the duchess had not been seen. "Where are you, Elizabeth?" he whispered raggedly.

Hearing footsteps, he made an attempt to compose himself.

"I've found her," Edward said, smiling widely. "And if we are not the greatest fools, then I don't know who is."

Rand jumped to his feet. "Where, where is she?"

"Sound asleep in my private study," he said dryly. The two walked hurriedly up the stairs and down a short hall before stopping at an opened doorway. "I was on my way to my room to change when one of my maids inquired about 'the lady in my room.' And there she was."

From the door, Rand could plainly see her, laying half on and half off a small couch, a lamp still lit illuminating her prone figure. Rand pushed the heels of his palms hard against his eyes and leaned against the wall, suddenly feeling his strength drain away, the relief of seeing her safe was so overwhelming. "Bloody hell," he whispered, his voice breaking. He felt a strong hand give one shoulder a shake.

"I don't know about you, but I need a drink. Let's let her sleep, shall we?"

"Yes, she should be well rested when I kill her," Rand said, staring at his wife with such fierce longing Edward had to look away.

Edward was the first to speak after they'd both had a long drink of a fine Armagnac brandy. "Would you please tell me what the bloody hell is going on with you?"

Rand looked up at his friend rather startled, for Edward rarely raised his voice and at the moment looked downright angry. "It's a private affair," he said.

"Private?" Edward shouted. "I was one minute away from contacting Scotland Yard to find your errant wife, and you were about a second away from needing to be put into Bedlam because we could not find her and you have the audacity to tell me this is a *private affair*?"

Rand stared at Edward for a long moment. As he'd never seen him quite this upset, he wasn't certain how to proceed with him. Besides, it *was* a private affair. He couldn't very well admit that he was madly in love with his wife and crushed beyond measure that she held no feelings for him, was, in fact, so opposed to this marriage that she'd actually worn a gift from another man on their wedding night to remind her of their love for each other. It was personal and humiliating and . . .

"She doesn't love me," he blurted out, then instantly regretted spouting such a personal thing.

"And obviously you love her," Edward said, far more gently than the last time he'd spoken.

"She wore a necklace," Rand ground out, "from Ellsworth. She wore it during our honeymoon, every night. It was meant for her to remind her that he still loved her. Even though she was married to me." He drained his glass and stared into the fire dancing merrily in contrast to the room's dark mood.

"That was not well done, was it," Edward said finally.

"No. It was not." He let out a long breath. "Right before I came here I found her crying over a letter from Miss Pierce. Apparently, Ellsworth had gotten married. And I"—he let out a small laugh—"I suppose I was rather enraged to find her so. I came here."

"Thank you."

Rand chuckled. "I hate this, Ed. I truly do. It's damned unmanning. Promise me you'll never do anything so foolish as to fall in love with a woman."

Something flickered briefly in Edward's eyes before he smiled. "I promise."

Elizabeth opened her eyes, momentarily startled to find herself in a strange room before remembering the events of the previous evening. She put a hand to her forehead, brushing a mass of hair away, and squinting at the brightly lit room. It was morning, and far into it by the brightness outside.

"Good morning."

Elizabeth sat up, warily eyeing Rand who sat across from her, his elbows on his knees. He was disheveled from his hair to his stockinged feet. If she hadn't realized she loved him before, she did at that moment, for her heart nearly swelled out of her breast at the sight of him sitting there. In the instant before he schooled his features she thought she saw something in his face, something of the time when they were first married and he'd told her he loved her. But the look was gone before she could even be certain it was nothing more than her hopeful imagination. His eyes looked simply red-rimmed and tired, as if he hadn't slept in a long time. No doubt he'd been too busy dancing, she thought morosely.

"Good morning," she said almost as a question, because, really, she did not know yet whether this morning would be good or not.

"It appears you slept well," he said, his voice even, his face expressionless.

"Yes. I must have been very tired. The trip here was exhausting."

Rand straightened, bracing his hands against his thighs. "About that. What are you doing here, Elizabeth?"

She frowned, not knowing quite what to say. "I didn't know where you were," she said, aware even as she said the words how daft she must sound. One eyebrow quirked up on his otherwise expressionless face. "You didn't tell me where you were going and you've been gone more than two weeks, you know. No note, no message. And so I had to ask Mrs. Stevens where you were and, of course, a servant knew where you were, not your wife."

"I was angry. I still am."

Elizabeth blew out her own huff of anger. "That's no excuse for leaving without telling me you were going or where. You cannot do that even if you are angry. It is inconsiderate and wrong." For some reason, Elizabeth felt as if she were on the verge of tears, so she swallowed and squeezed one hand into the other to stop herself from a further emotional display. She needed her wits about her at the moment.

"You must promise me not to do this again," she said, lifting her head.

"Very well. I promise. Now. Why are you here? Certainly not to simply chastise me. A note would have sufficed for that."

She gave him a dark scowl. "I needed to tell you something that I felt was inappropriate for a note." She jabbed her thumbnail against her other hand to fortify herself.

"Go on."

"I'm going to have a baby." Elizabeth held her breath and waited for some sort of reaction from him. There was none. "I'm not fully certain as I have not been to a physician. However, as my monthlies are—"

"No need to go into female details," he said, raising one hand to stop her. "You should see a doctor while you are here in London, of course. I'll arrange that."

"All right."

He hadn't even smiled, not even a hint of it. She had imagined his face alighting with joy, of him coming to her and holding her against him, of telling her how wonderful it was that she'd conceived so quickly. Her throat ached and her eyes stung, but she managed to ask where the nearest toilet was without him detecting that anything was amiss. She suddenly not only felt like crying, but like being sick, as well.

Elizabeth vomited up the contents of her nearly empty stomach and sat down on the floor of the bathroom to stare blankly at the pretty tiles on the walls, her eyes almost painfully dry and she wondered if it were possible to be too sad to cry.

"Are you all right?"

Her heart picked up a beat at the sound of his voice on the other side of the door. "I was sick," she said, struggling to stand.

He opened the door cautiously. "Have you been sick before?"

She shook her head. "I think it's because I haven't

eaten in a while," she said, then turned to the small basin and rinsed her mouth.

"I'll have the cook prepare something for you. Elizabeth, I am glad about the baby."

She could only nod and waited tensely until he left without uttering another word.

"How is she?" Edward asked.

"Pregnant," Rand said, falling into the nearest chair.

"You seem overjoyed."

Rand gave his friend a withering look. "I am actually. Thrilled." He was not. The overwhelming emotion he felt was guilt from the way the baby had been conceived. Coming to his wife's bed all those nights had become surprisingly distasteful, something that had nothing to do with Elizabeth and everything to do with him. He realized, to his great shame, that he'd been not only trying to punish her for not loving him, but himself for that same emotion. Love was truly driving him insane.

"Do you have a doctor you could recommend?" he asked.

"Doctor Randall. Good man. Not too old, not too young. I'll have a message sent over to him if you'd like."

Rand nodded, too weary to speak. He was going to have his heir. And then they could get on with their lives.

He'd never felt quite so depressed in all his life.

Chapter 25

When the duke and duchess returned from London, life at Bellewood held a certain sameness that Elizabeth could not decide was wonderful or excruciating. She had to admit there was a comfort in knowing what each day would bring, and what it would not bring. She continued on her rounds to the poorest tenants, taking over once again for Mrs. Stevens, and those twice-a-week excursions were a pure delight. It seemed the tenants had taken a liking to her, enjoying her lack of pretension, her so-called candid "Americaness."

They enjoyed her accent, her turn of phrase, her ignorance of English history and basic way of life. They were shocked when she wrinkled her nose at Yorkshire pudding, a rather bland concoction that Elizabeth felt either needed a load of salt or a heavy dose of sugar. She ate what was offered anyway, but was unable to hide her dislike of it, which only caused more gales of laughter when she politely, but firmly, declined more. And, of course, there was Black Pudding, not pudding at all but a large frightening looking tube of pig's blood and other ingredients Elizabeth didn't want to know about. She was grateful they were not insulted by her delicate palate, but simply intrigued by her. She had been brought up on rich and well-flavored French foods, her mother having decided when she was an infant that their household must contain a French chef.

She did enjoy the scones and other pastries, and so found herself inundated with the things upon her next visit. The mood around Bellewood had improved markedly since the new duke began making improvements, and some of the tenants whose children had left for the factories, were actually talking about coming back home.

Elizabeth would have been completely content had her life with Rand improved as much as her relationship with the tenants. Once wary of her, they ran up to greet her, always telling her tales of the things her husband had planned for their homes and the land they'd worked for generations. She learned more about what her husband was doing from them than from the man himself. Each night Rand would join her for their supper, a pleasant meal with pleasant conversation. How was your day? Very well, thank you, and yours? Very well. How are the improvements going? Well, enough. And here at Bellewood? Quite nice. Sometimes into the mix Rand would ask after her health, which she would reply was wonderful.

It was enough to drive a person mad.

On their second week back from London, Elizabeth had retired to her room to knit little baby things, as she supposed she was ought to do, when the sameness of everything became a bit overwhelming. She was lonely, simply put. She could not possibly count dinners together with Rand as anything more than obligation. Every night, Rand would disappear and Elizabeth was quite sure he was going out to the stable. She pictured him there, working in the lamplight, sweating, muscles straining, and she squirmed in her chair. He no longer came to her at night. Even though he'd ceased being the loving, caring man she'd first married, she found herself missing even those passionless couplings, and resenting the fact he'd only come to her to impregnate her. His visits had been somewhat tolerable when she'd imagined it was because he desired her. Now she realized he'd simply been using her as a depository. To make matters worse, pregnancy had made her even more . . . uncomfortable in her skin.

Laying down her crocheting with a smile, for the little bonnet she was working on was so darling, she determined to spend some time with her husband. She wished she had the courage to tell him she wanted him in her bed, but she could not; it would have been completely mortifying. But perhaps if they spent a bit more time together, things would take their natural course, so to speak. She wanted her husband in her bed, simply put, and she wanted him there now. Well, if not now, then in the near future. Her body, having once experienced pleasure, was craving more. Not for the first time did she wish she had someone to talk to, for she had no idea whether what she was feeling was entirely normal.

When she entered the stable, Rand looked up immediately then just as quickly went back to work.

"Do you mind if I keep you company?"

He grunted, a sound that could have been "yes, I mind" or "suit yourself" so Elizabeth found a hay bale and sat down, tucking her legs upon it and resting her chin on her knees. It wasn't a very duchesslike pose but she didn't care and obviously Rand didn't either, for he didn't say a word even though he gave her a long dispassionate look.

"Why was Lord Hollings holding a ball?" she asked. It was something she'd been curious about, a single man holding a ball. It seemed highly unusual.

"For his sister."

"Oh. I didn't know he had a sister. I can't picture him as a big brother."

She watched him silently as he banged four nails into a stall. "Are you going to replace each plank?"

"Only the ones that need it."

She drummed her fingers against her shins. "Why not have one of the men do this?"

"I enjoy the work. Being out of doors."

Elizabeth looked about. "But you are indoors," she pointed out, and watched as he stopped banging in mid swing, sighed, then continued working. Elizabeth waited for a break in the banging before asking another question.

"I overheard one of the guests refer to Lord Hollings as Holly."

"A nickname," Rand said, his voice muffled by the nails he held in his mouth.

"Has anyone ever called you Belly?" Elizabeth said, grinning widely at the idea of such a silly name.

"Not more than once," he said darkly.

Elizabeth lifted her head off her knees and leaned back a bit. "I think I shall call you Belly. Just to annoy you. Belly. It is rather adorable, if you ask me."

He lifted his head sharply and Elizabeth thought one side of his mouth quirked up, just a bit.

"Good night, Your Grace," she said, using his title just to annoy him further. "I think I'll come each night to supervise your work, if you don't mind."

He gave another strange grunt, then pulled out a plank to cut, dismissing her without another word.

Every night for a week, Elizabeth trudged out to the stables and watched Rand work. She'd tell him about her day, about the tenants she visited, about the new flowers popping through the soil with the coming spring. She told him about Mr. Gibbons's remarkable carvings, how she hoped to attract a fine shop where he could sell them and make a nice living from his artwork. She'd talk mostly to herself, but sometimes he'd say something or smile. While she sat there watching mostly in silence, she began to notice things about him that she'd never seen before. His forearms, for example, were lightly sprinkled with hair that shone blond in the lamplight. And he had muscles there, clearly defined, that worked when he was banging and sawing. His hands were not at all aristocratic, but strong and broad, like those of a soldier more than a peer of the realm. His dark hair would curl as he worked, a sheen of sweat forming on his brow even on the coolest evenings. It was now warm enough to forgo lighting the woodstove as he worked, but at night the temperatures dipped. Sometimes she'd sit, wrapped up in a blanket, and watch with amazement as steam rose from his body. And she'd have a flash of what it had been like when he was over her, his body hard and hot and naked, his mouth on her breasts, his hand between her legs. It was almost a dream now, it was so long ago. She'd watch him, remember his body, remember how he tasted, how it felt when he slid into her, and want to scream. And sometimes the urge to scoot off the hay bale and touch him was so overwhelming, she'd find herself hugging herself tightly, a rather poor substitute for having Rand hold her.

She wondered if he knew what she was thinking, and she wondered if had he known, would he even care. For now, she had to be content to simply be with him, to talk to him and watch him work. It was rather delicious, she decided, secretly desiring him and him not knowing.

"Did I tell you I got a letter from my mother?"

He shook his head.

"Of course she is so happy to hear the news about the baby. She wants to be here for the birth," she said cautiously.

"She is welcome to come," Rand said. "And by that time, the house should be in much better shape for visitors."

"I do wish Maggie could be here as well," Elizabeth said, thinking aloud. It would be too much to ask of her friend, though, to travel all the way over to England simply on a friend's whim. Besides, Maggie's letter had been filled lately with news of Arthur Wright and her hope that Arthur planned to propose at any time. She hadn't even known Maggie liked Arthur, but apparently she did a great deal. If that was true, she probably would not want to travel anywhere.

"She'd be welcome, as well," Rand said, then cursed under his breath as the board he was trying to hold up kept falling.

"I'll get it," Elizabeth said, hopping off the hay bale. She held up one end of the board while Rand banged away at the other end. "I imagine the New York papers would love printing this little detail of our lives. I can honestly say that when I agreed to marry you, I never imagined spending each evening in a stable," she said, laughing.

Rand let out a chuckle, and looked over at her, making her breath stop, her heart beat a bit harder. He stood, wiping his hands on his rough worker's pants. "I'm actually nearly done," he said, looking down the stable at the fresh planks that had been laid in nearly every stall.

"I shall miss being out here." *With you.*

Then he smiled down at her. "The enclosure needs work. What do you say we tackle that next?"

Elizabeth clapped her hands together as if he'd just offered her the largest of diamonds. They were standing quite close, and Elizabeth could feel the heat coming from him. He seemed oblivious to her, to the desire that swept through her, that made her feel suddenly a bit light-headed. Oh, Lord, what was wrong with her? She stood next to him, fairly drinking him in, breathing in the sweat and wonderful scent of him, wanting to touch him, wanting to strip him naked so she could push herself against him and . . .

"I'm tired," she said, her voice sounding strange to her own ears. "I'm going inside."

He looked down at her and she realized he was completely unaware of her, as if she were no more important to her than one of the planks of wood piled up beside them.

"Are you quite all right?" he asked, finally noticing something was a bit off with her.

"Fine. Fine. I'm just simply . . ." Without meaning it, her eyes drifted to his mouth, the same mouth that had made her scream when it was between her legs, the same mouth that suckled her. She could feel a mortifying flood of desire between her legs, and she brushed a trembling hand against her forehead. ". . . tired."

"Elizabeth." One word and she knew. She knew that he knew. And then she found herself brought hard against him, hard against the solid heat of him, hard against his mouth. And she pulled tighter, pushing herself against him, letting out sounds that she hadn't realized she could make.

He kissed her, moving her against the stall, where the rough wood dug into her back, and even that was glorious. He was aroused, pushing against her as if he wanted to take her through her dress, as if he was being driven by the same demons that made her hands go to his trousers and begin unbuttoning them as her knuckles brushed against the hard length of him. He let out a harsh cry and wrenched her dress down her shoulders, exposing her breasts to the cool night hair and his hot mouth. He pushed her breasts up, moving his mouth from one nipple to the other as if he could not get enough quickly enough.

And then his pants and drawers were down at his booted feet and he was in her hand, hard and warm.

He grew still, as if her touch were almost more than he could bear.

"Elizabeth," he said on a groan. "Oh, God, please."

She bent down and took him in her mouth, not caring that she was possessed, only knowing that something had taken over her. His large hand pressed against her head and he pushed gently against her, all the time his harsh breath sounded above the strange roaring in her ears.

"You must stop," he said, then laid her down on the clean hay and lifted her skirts. "I can't wait, love. I can't. Please."

She lifted her hips, welcoming him, and drew his head down to her for a kiss that was more erotic than anything she'd experienced in her life. She simply could not get enough of him, of his body moving into hers, of his mouth, his tongue, his hard buttocks. She wrapped her legs around him, pulling him close, moving with him, grinding against him in desperation for release. When it came, she held him, letting wave after wave of pleasure course through her, unaware that he, too, had found his release.

Finally, still panting, still feeling her heart beating wildly in her chest, she kissed his cheek. "Thank you," she said, and he chuckled.

Rand leaned on one elbow and looked down at her, picking bits of straw from her hair. God, he felt so much better. He hadn't been certain how long he was going to be able to hold out with her coming each night to watch him work, chatting away, looking so incredibly lovely in the lamplight he wanted to beg her to stop coming out to the stables.

And, apparently, she'd been going through the same agony.

"I'm afraid your hair's a bit of a mess," he said, smiling down at her.

"It'll come out," she said, suddenly shy. He'd not known his proper wife had had it in her. She'd been amazing, just the thought of her hands struggling with the buttons on his pants was enough to send desire coursing through him again. And then she really shocked him.

"I'm sorry for making you do that, Rand."

"You're sorry?" he sputtered.

"I know you didn't want to do that. That it's only for making a baby and we don't need to worry about that any more, but I . . . I couldn't help myself, I suppose."

"You're sorry," he stated. And then he started to laugh, real body-shaking laughs that made his eyes water. When he finally recovered enough to look at his lovely wife, she was scowling at him.

"You don't have to laugh at me," she said with a small pout.

"My dear, I would love for you to be sorry every day of our lives together," he said, and watched as she realized what he was saying. "I should apologize to you."

"Yes, you should," she said with a nod. Then, "For what?"

He looked down at her still-flat stomach. "For the way I treated you before," he said quietly. "It was not well done of me. I didn't even really like it."

She gave him a look of skepticism.

"Well, not overmuch," he said with a grin. He sat up and pulled up his drawers and pants, handing her a clean monogrammed handkerchief. "You know," he said, turning away so she could wipe herself, "I've never actually had a roll in the hay. Quite nice, really, don't you think?"

"I do prefer a soft bed," she said, grimacing when a bit of hay stuck into her soft behind. He helped her to stand, then kissed her mouth softly. The flood of feeling that came with that simple kiss nearly unmanned him, and he cursed inwardly. A roll in the hay was one thing, falling back in love with her quite another. He tried to remind himself that not long ago she was crying because her former love had married another, but looking down at her, all disheveled, her lips slightly swollen from their lovemaking, her dress still askew, he found the only thing he could think of was making love to his wife again. God, he was cursed.

"I suppose I should go inside," she said, hugging her arms to herself as if she were suddenly cold.

Rand blew out the lamp. "I'll walk with you." They walked silently to the house, not touching, just a couple out for an evening stroll with nothing to say. He wanted to invite her to his bed or invite him to hers, but that seemed far too intimate even given what they'd just done. Their lovemaking was a rather animalistic slaking of desires and had more to do with base needs than love. At least, he felt certain, on his wife's part. He would not make the mistake of handing her his heart when he was not at all convinced she wouldn't crush it with her heel. And so, when they reached their private dining room,

Rand gave a small formal bow and bid his wife good night. He turned to the left and she to the right, their doors closing almost in unison.

The next day, Elizabeth discovered blood in her drawers. She looked at it in dismay, that small spot of red on her pristine white underclothes. She'd heard stories, all girls had, of women "losing" babies, of blood and doctors and pain. The doctor had told her the pregnancy was early, that some pregnancies did not end with a baby, but with blood and a small amount of pain.

She was bleeding.

"Oh, God," she said, praying fervently. "Please let me keep my baby." Her eye caught the little yellow bundle of wool, the tiny cap she'd just finished, and she let out a sob of despair. Then, she took a deep breath and hunted out her pads, and smoothed her skirts before inquiring of the staff where the duke was supposed to be this day. Rand always left long before she woke up, especially lately as she'd been so exhausted.

"Mr. Tisbury, would you please have the buggy sent 'round. I need to speak to His Grace."

"Certainly, Your Grace."

"Would you happen to know where he is today?"

"At the Foresters' place. That'd be at the end of Coggshell Lane, Your Grace."

Elizabeth rode in the buggy, keeping her face completely void of emotion, her back straight, her chin up. She was nearly to the Foresters when she realized she'd forgotten her hat and gloves and worn her winter coat.

That alone was nearly her undoing, but she swallowed and pretended it didn't matter, that nothing mattered but that she find Rand.

The buggy stopped at a rather large home with chickens pecking about the yard and the distinct smell of pig wafting up from an enclosure not far from the house itself. Nothing, she'd always thought, stunk quite like a pig. Somewhere she heard hammering, and followed the sound until she saw her husband, hands on hips, looking up at the roof of the back side of the house, where several men worked.

"Your Grace," she called out, clutching her hands together at her waist, as if she were holding herself together. She'd thought she was hiding every emotion she was feeling, but he took one look at her and rushed to her side.

"What's wrong?"

She couldn't speak, she could hardly stand, she simply stared at him until she couldn't bear the weight of everything another second. With a small cry, she launched herself into his arms. He pulled her to him without a word, somehow knowing instinctively that she could not tell him anything at the moment.

He drew her away from the workers, and when they had relative privacy, he stopped. "Tell me what has happened, love."

"Oh, Rand, I'm bleeding," she said, and began sobbing in earnest.

He went pale. "The baby you mean?"

She could only nod.

"How much blood?"

Elizabeth clutched his shirt with her fists, using the

cloth to hold herself up. "I don't know," she said. "It's blood. I'm not supposed to bleed. The doctor said I wasn't supposed to." She'd never been so frightened in her life, hadn't known how much she wanted this baby until she saw that spot of blood.

He held her and led her to the buggy, helping her on board.

"Jake, is Dr. Walton still in these parts?" he asked their driver.

"Yes, sir. But it's young Dr. Walton now. His son." The young man gave a quick look to Elizabeth. "Shall I bring you there, sir?"

"No," Rand said. "Take Brownstar and make haste to the doctor and bring him to Bellewood. I'll take Her Grace home." He put a hand gently on either side of her head, forcing her to look at him, his eyes intent on hers. "It will be all right," he said, firmly. "No matter what, Elizabeth. Do you understand?"

She nodded, desperately hoping he was right.

Rand drove slowly to Bellewood, knowing there was no reason to rush, that there was nothing he could do until the doctor arrived. And he was so afraid jarring her would cause more harm. With agony, he remembered how rough he'd been with her the previous night. My God, he had taken her in a horse stall, come into her without a thought of anything but satisfying his body. If something happened to this baby, to Elizabeth, he would never forgive himself. And if everything were fine, he wouldn't touch her again, at least not until the baby was born. Torturing himself, he remembered the near brutality of what they'd done, turning what had been a mutual expression of desire to a near rape in his tormented mind.

When they reached Bellewood, he lifted her from the carriage, stricken by the fact she didn't protest. She buried her head against his neck and he could feel the wet of tears. Where the hell was the doctor, he thought savagely, even though he knew logically there was no physical way the doctor could have beaten him to Bellewood. To Elizabeth he said, "Dr. Walton should be here any minute. How are you feeling?"

"Nothing hurts," she said, sounding so unlike her usual self Rand's heart gave another wrench.

He brought her to her room and laid her down upon her bed. "Shall I get you something? A glass of water perhaps. A whiskey," he added, joking because he wanted to see her smile.

"Whiskey would be fine," she said with a straight face, then broke into a grin. "I'm certain it's nothing." She did not sound certain at all, for her voice held the tiniest quaver that he'd never before heard.

Tisbury appeared at the door, knocking lightly to gain their attention. "Dr. Walton has arrived," he said, then bowed out of the room, but not before giving Elizabeth a worried look.

The man who walked in appeared too young to be a doctor, but he strode briskly into the room, setting a large black bag at the end of the bed. Rand quickly explained what was happening, then Dr. Walton ushered him from the room so he could conduct his examination. For ten long minutes Rand paced outside, making bargains with God to make everything well again. When her door opened, he stood still and waited for the doctor to come to him, because he found suddenly he was unable to do anything more.

"Your wife and the baby are fine," Dr. Walton said without preamble. "At this point, the amount of blood is small and does not indicate a loss of the pregnancy. However, I would like her to remain in bed for at least another day. If the bleeding should continue or become heavy, you will need to call on me again."

Rand wanted only to hear that all was well. "Is there nothing you can do?"

Dr. Walton shook his head regretfully. "In most cases such as this, the bleeding is not an indication of a serious complication, especially so early in her pregnancy. Unfortunately, if she is losing the child, there is nothing we can do to stop it."

Rand did not find the doctor's words comforting in the least. He wanted her well; he wanted the baby safe. He wanted the doctor to goddamn do something.

"I do wish I could be of more comfort. But it is truly a matter of waiting."

Rand tunneled his fingers roughly through his hair. "Why did she bleed?"

"She is six weeks into her pregnancy, correct?"

"I don't know."

"As I said, it is early, and it is not unusual for some women to pass a bit of blood. My own wife did when she was carrying our children. I know it can be disconcerting to say the least," he said with a smile, as if remembering his own panic. "In most cases when the flow is so light, it is not an indication for alarm. Your wife has no cramps, no other signs that something has gone wrong."

Rand let out a long sigh, his mind only slightly put at ease. "Is it possible that I could have caused the bleeding?" he said, dropping his voice low.

The doctor gave him a sharp look. "How do you mean?" he asked cautiously.

Rand could feel his face heating. "We . . . I . . . That is to say we . . ."

"You had relations with your wife."

Rand let out a small laugh, feeling ridiculous. "Yes. Could that have caused it?"

"Actually, yes." At the look of horror on Rand's face, Dr. Walton quickly added, "But no baby was ever lost because a man made love to his wife. A woman's body changes, becomes more sensitive, more delicate, so to speak." The doctor cleared his throat. "Was this by any chance yesterday?"

"Yes."

Dr. Walton smiled. "It is probably that."

"Oh, God," Rand said, horrified to learn it was, indeed, all his fault. He'd been too rough, too urgent with her. He'd lost his mind when she'd looked at him with such desire.

"Your Grace," Dr. Walton said, placing a reassuring hand on his shoulder. "If that is the cause of the blood, then you should be vastly relieved. You cannot harm your wife or your baby in such a manner."

"But I did," Rand said harshly.

"Sir," the doctor said firmly, "you did not. If you must, be gentle. But I see no reason to abstain. None at all."

"Of course," Rand said.

Unconvinced, the doctor said, with a laugh, "Nine months can be an awfully long time. For both of you. Go see your wife, Your Grace. She's probably worried that I was not forthright with her and is waiting for you to give her bad news. I'll return tomorrow, sooner if anything changes."

Rand nodded and went into his wife's room, his emotions so raw he had to swallow heavily before speaking. She looked so vulnerable, sitting in bed in the daytime, covered up to her chin in bedcovers, her hair loose and spilling down her shoulders. "The doctor says you and the baby should be fine."

Elizabeth gave him a tentative smile, but squeezed the coverlet until her knuckles shone white. "That's what he told me as well. You believe him, don't you?"

Rand sat on the edge of her bed and took up one of her hands. "I see no reason for him to hedge the truth. In fact, he was rather forthright about the entire thing."

"I'm sorry to have given you such a scare. I just wasn't certain what to do. Seeing blood . . . I nearly fainted."

"I nearly fainted when you told me," he said, laughing.

Elizabeth looked to her window and watched as rain streamed down, making the outside world blurry and soft. "I didn't know it was raining," she said softly. She closed her eyes briefly. "When I thought I might lose the baby . . ." She couldn't end her sentence, for her throat closed up. She felt him squeeze her hand and gave him a rather tremulous smile.

"The other day with the letter," she began. "When I

was crying, I wasn't crying because Henry was getting married. I was crying because I hurt you so. I was crying because I had been such a fool. And when I thought I was losing the baby, I was devastated because I knew how much you wanted this child. An heir."

He started to interrupt her, but she stopped him with a gentle hand to his mouth.

"My whole life, I've only thought about myself. I never realized how much until recently. And now I find myself thinking only of you, of doing this or that because I hope something will please you. Of not doing things I know will make you sad. And I realized it's because . . ." Her throat ached so much from unshed tears, but she had to say this to him. She had to let him know, because even if the doctor said all was well, it might not be.

"I love you, Randall Blackmore. And I wouldn't blame you if you didn't love me anymore. I was horrid and awful and, and . . ."

He drew her into his arms, letting out a strangled sound, before she could say another word, pressing her against him. She pushed him away because she had to tell him everything.

"I did wear the necklace on my wedding day. I did and I did it because part of me thought I was still in love with Henry. And I did it because I resented being forced to marry you. Not you, but anyone. Do you understand?" She didn't wait for him to answer, but forged ahead. "And then you were so wonderful at Rosebrier. I think I started to fall in love with you then. I admit I was a bit horrified at first to find you loved me. I didn't know why. I still don't. You must believe me, Rand. I forgot about the necklace. I did. And when you found that letter . . ." She began crying in earnest now, letting tears flow freely down her face. "I hurt you," she whispered. "And I'm sorry." Elizabeth searched his face for some sign he loved her still. "Can you forgive me?"

He stared at her blankly for several moments, then shook his head as if coming to himself, a daydreamer being brought back to reality. "Beg pardon, what were you saying? I stopped listening at the part where you said you loved me."

She looked at him in mock anger and gave him a swat on the arm before launching herself into his arms with a small cry. "You brute," she muttered against his shirt.

"I daresay you deserve a bit of torture," he said, kissing her gently on her mouth.

"Oh, Rand, I do love you," Elizabeth said, feeling so full she just might burst from it. And then, in a mercurial change, she got suddenly fierce. "Don't you dare think for even a single instant that our original plan for this marriage is still valid. There will be no 'going about our lives.' You are my life. *You* are and no one else. I love *you*."

A look of bemusement passed over his features as he looked down at her scowling countenance. "I promised myself I would never say those words to you again. But not saying them did not make it go away. I did try, you know."

"I know."

Rand let out a sigh. "I suppose you want me to say it, then, do you?"

"It would be lovely to hear."

"I do love you so."

Elizabeth smiled, then took up one of his hands, holding it against her. "The doctor told me something else, Rand. Something quite nice, if everything turns out all right."

"What is that?"

"The baby," she said, her eyes watering ridiculously. "It should be born around Christmastime. Maybe a Christmas baby."

"He said that, did he?"

Elizabeth nodded.

Rand climbed into bed with her and held his wife against him, thinking how much his life had changed in such a brief time. Just a few days ago he had been miserable, thinking he would have to endure a life of loving someone who would never love him. His eyes drifted to the bit of knitting that sat on the bedside table, a soft fluff of yellow, and he said a quick prayer that all would be well, that they would have their little Christmas miracle.

Because lately, he'd begun to believe in little miracles. He was holding one in his arms, his wife, who'd just told him she loved him.

Epilogue

Each time Maggie got a post from England, her day brightened a bit. In all the things she worried about, and there were nearly too many to count, she needn't worry about Elizabeth anymore. Her latest letters were filled with happy news about her new home, her loving husband, and the baby that was making her stomach expand daily. Maggie had never felt jealous of Elizabeth, even though she'd had more dresses and richer things. Maggie had always thought she was the lucky one. How many times had she told her mother that she thanked God every night for giving her a family like hers and not like Elizabeth's. She wouldn't have traded the world for her life.

Except now, her life wasn't nearly as happy as it had once been and Elizabeth's had never been filled with so much joy. Not for a minute did she think the gushing letters she received periodically were filled with anything but the truth. Elizabeth had never been one to pretend feelings she didn't experience. When Elizabeth wrote Maggie she was madly in love with her duke, she believed her. And she was happy for her. She was.

But that didn't mean at night, when she was huddled beneath her covers in a world that was falling apart, she couldn't admit that she was also a bit jealous of her friend's good fortune.

So when she received a letter from England, she happily ripped it open, pausing only when she didn't recognize the handwriting on the expensive stationary.

> *June 3, 1893*
>
> *Dear Miss Pierce,*
> *As you know, my wife and your friend is expecting to deliver a baby on or around Christmas. It would be my fondest wish to give my wife the gift of her closest friend during this time. Elizabeth's mother will be unable to journey here for the birth, and I feel it is necessary for her to have some sort of female companionship at this time. I pray it will not be a large inconvenience to you. Elizabeth speaks of you often and with great fondness. Please let me know whether you can come, and address any correspondence to me. If, indeed, you can travel to Bellewood, as is my fondest wish, I would like this to be a surprise for my wife.*
>
> *Sincerely,*
> *Randall Blackmore, Duke of Bellingham*

Maggie looked down at the letter, her eyes watering, the finely scrawled letters mere blurs before her. The duke would never know what he had done, how those few words he'd so casually written would completely change her life. She had thought so many, many times in the past few months that she needed something good to happen. How often had she wished for just one thing good among all the bad and horrid things that had happened to her since Elizabeth had gone away. Maggie Pierce, whose life had taken a decidedly desperate turn, knew she held in her hand her only salvation.

Dear Reader,

I have long been captivated by the story of Consuelo Vanderbilt, who at the age of eighteen was forced to marry the Duke of Marlborough even though she was in love with another man. According to Consuelo's autobiography, *The Glitter and the Gold,* her mother threatened to murder her beloved unless she agreed to the match. Consuelo's marriage to the duke was not a happy one; they disliked each other almost immediately. After producing the required heir and spare, they divorced, a difficult and shocking thing to do at that time in England. Consuelo eventually married a Frenchman, whom she loved dearly. Her story inspired this one. I have borrowed some of her life and created a much different ending for my own American girl. Consuelo was, perhaps, the first American celebrity. Accounts of her wedding, down to what she was wearing beneath her wedding gown, were included in detailed accounts of the day. The *New York Times* ran several articles about the wedding, which had New Yorkers enthralled.

For the purposes of my book, I have borrowed many details of Consuelo's life, changing them to suit my fictional story. I have opened the Waldorf Astoria one year early so that my duke would have a pleasant stay in the city. I do hope the Astors don't mind too much.

Also, as shocking as it may seem, the new Duke and Duchess of Marlborough did, indeed, return to England after their wedding in a cargo ship, which I thought would be delightful for my heroine to experience, as well.

Sincerely,
Jane Goodger